T0299635

This Immaculate Body

This Immaculate Body
EMMA VAN STRAATEN

FLEET

FLEET

First published in Great Britain in 2025 by Fleet

1 3 5 7 9 10 8 6 4 2

Copyright © 2025 by Emma van Straaten

The moral right of the author has been asserted.

A CIP catalogue record for this book
is available from the British Library.

Hardback ISBN 978-0-349-12730-9
Trade paperback ISBN 978-0-349-12731-6

Typeset in Arno by M Rules
Printed and bound in Great Britain by
Clays Ltd, Elcograf S.p.A

Papers used by Fleet are from well-managed forests
and other responsible sources.

MIX
Paper | Supporting
responsible forestry
FSC
www.fsc.org   FSC® C104740

Fleet
An imprint of
Little, Brown Book Group
Carmelite House
50 Victoria Embankment
London EC4Y 0DZ

The authorised representative
in the EEA is
Hachette Ireland
8 Castlecourt Centre
Dublin 15, D15 XTP3, Ireland
(email: info@hbgi.ie)

An Hachette UK Company
www.hachette.co.uk

www.littlebrown.co.uk

For Patrick and our girls. O my soul's joy!

1.

THE KEY CATCHES IN THE LOCK, BUT I KNOW THE trick; a swift twist and I open the door, inwards, shoulder finding the worn spot His shoulder must do, and I am struck by the warm, rich scent of Him, salty as blood, and I am afraid, as I am each week, that something has changed, more than the seasonal shiftings of cotton to wool, canvas shoes to suede, glossy leather, doormat thick with envelopes bearing cheques from aunts and festive greetings. I set my bucket down, just inside, filled in technicolour haphazardness with bottles and two-textured sponges and, like a bloodhound, no, a spaniel, melting-eyed and caramel, I seek sugary florals in the air; check that no second toothbrush, pink, lolls in the marble tooth mug; no twin wine glasses on the kitchen counter or on the low table, jammy residue thickening acidly, or, even worse, prim matching mugs silty with morning coffee and shared murmurings. He is alone, and my heart squeezes crushingly tight with love as I hold my breath with leaden air and dispose of it. You think you know what love is, I imagine, but you don't. It's not holding hands, and feeling safe, fond smiles and tender kisses, bringing home silk-petalled flowers on a Friday, picking up that green and bone-dry wine you know He likes. I spit on that. Love is this: when it is your greatest desire to slice open His chest and crawl inside Him to rest. A compulsion to drink His blood, great copper gulps of it, to press yourself to Him, limb to limb, palm to palm, so that you might be absorbed. Burrowing inside His bones, becoming His very marrow. It is disappearing entirely into Him. This is the way I love Him, and the way He must surely love me.

Surely, surely I say, because we have not met – face to face, that is, although our correspondence is lengthy and a meeting of true, true minds. I clean His small one-bedroom flat once a week and I know every inch of it and so every inch of Him, that hard body that I have studied so diligently in photographs. He likes Radio 4, set to a volume where the white male voices whisper conspiratorially. He watches *The Wire* again and again, looping through season after season, spring to summer, sub-titles on to hear over the foamy brushing of His teeth, the buzz of His razor, carelessly showering apostrophes, semicolons. His eyelashes, discarded wishes, fit so dearly to the curve of my fingertip that I cannot bear to blow them away. I touch them to my tongue and press them to my eyelids, rather than watch them shiver into the air. He cycles to work when it isn't raining, and His shampoo smells like heady rosemary and lavender: like Provence, I imagine, in late summer, drowsy bees and His hair, tousled, just stirring in a breeze. His finger-prints are universes. The flat shimmers with them, and those of others, sometimes. Some must belong to friends, family, but His touch I recognise, a firm fingertip to a switch, a dimple in a pot of hair product, assertive. I see in the smeared hallway mirror and skirting board the uncertain, clumsy marks of His insufferable older sister and a doughy baby niece with raisin eyes and very little hair, the lack thereof often accentuated by a desperate bowed headband and pink knickerbockers: look, she's a girl. He is myself, cast into a different mould. And so it is each time I roll my hair into a knot, pierce it into place with a pin, push up my sleeves and work carefully, lovingly: smooth-ing, wiping, plumping, sweeping. I lick the floor clean. I run my hands over the fabric of the place, the bones of Him, and they sting and suffer from the cleaning products I use. I will never wear gloves; each little pain I feel is in service to Him, an act of devotion. I bury my face into His pillow and sometimes I am moved to tears by the hollow that His body has left under the duvet that still exhales the smell of Him. I carefully fit myself into it, seeking the last vestiges (do I imagine them?) of sleep-warmth and close my eyes. I am a cat, curled. The morning sun, already hot, strokes my eyelids with a rosy luminescence and I imagine John Donne, dark-eyed and neatly bearded, limbs tangled with his lady love, chastising that great star for gazing through the curtains at them, ending their ardent night.

I rise. *Busy old fool. Unruly sun.* I have spoken aloud; my voice is quiet, deeper than I'd like, so I practise breathy whispers at home, coaxing my voice up into a register that registers with men – it's primitive, I read – will register with Him, although His voice, rich and cool, ganache, will make my own sound light, clear, like a bird's, and He will run a finger along the line of my throat and say how beautiful it is to hear me speak, how thrilling, how He loves me desperately. I find myself speaking

3

every time I am here, or singing, or humming, or laughing, trying out sounds so the walls know me, so my breath mixes with His the way it will – soon. I smooth the duvet flat over our twin bodies. Moving through to the bathroom I slide His toothbrush into my mouth and absently suck. *Why dost thou thus, through windows and through curtains, call on us?* I wipe the mirror of its toothpaste constellations, His Virgo with my Capricorn, and wish His face were reflected with mine, on top of mine. How our noses and mouths might align, skin on skin, lips tracing the other's, His straight brows striking through my curved ones, His stubbled jaw blueing my own. I am prac-tised at removing the metal pin that gleams at the nape of my neck – I have done it a hundred times – so that my hair tumbles weightily down my back. My ear is cocked: should I ever hear His key grate in the lock, accompanied by an idle hum, a *tsk* of annoyance at a forgotten jacket, furled umbrella, perhaps, at leaving His mobile phone charging by His bed – I shall shake my hair loose and turn and glow at Him, and glow.

I methodically dust the tops of the few frames on the wall in front of me: a retro Wimbledon poster, holiday snaps – Greece, Barbados – and a degree certificate revealing a 2:1 from Warwick. My own graduation I did not attend; it seems relegated to the distant past now, bringing with it a move to London, after a restless six or seven months tucked back into village life at my mother's. It was laundry snapping seagull-bright, tiptoeing upstairs at 11.30, lonely and thirsty and drunk, in torn tights. I cohabited uneasily with my mother, sulking under her blue-eyed stare as I watched daytime TV in the sitting room (ideally drawing room, not living room, *never* lounge, scolded my mother in my youth), making toast in the kitchen, lying prone in the garden, reading and rereading books, plays, poems, until particular lines and paragraphs revolved in my head as if on a carousel. She did not, does not, know what to say to me, or how to talk to me, now, and any of her half-hearted attempts – *sweetheart* … coupled with an outstretched hand – I met with glib incomprehension, and she never pushed harder, relenting and moving on to a comfortable topic: my sister, now a lawyer, now earning this much, now attending this event, now living here, now holidaying there. (Unsaid: you are nothing, doing nothing, going nowhere.)

Once I had wrestled my life into two suitcases and left for London, I decided to become a cleaner, reckoning it would be a menial but short-term job where I could choose my hours and horrify my mother while applying for something respectable in my spare time. Respectable, or impressive, soaring, perhaps, a new life, where my mother would soon mention my exploits and adventures with embarrassing pride in her emails to close cousins, not just as a little postscript to my sister. Cleaning would be temporary, working when I wanted, my own boss – a freelancer – practically an entrepreneur, coolly swiping through the cartoonish app at my leisure, choosing, deliberating, o the choices. It was that or become a Deliveroo driver, whisking myself narrowly through traffic, squashy burgers gently steaming in a silvery nest, sagging falafel wraps, dully aromatic curries forced under cardboard lids, prawn toast – but after watching with my stomach twisting, eyes burning, the almost slow-motion spinning of a cyclist under the wheels of a lorry on the South Circular, I could not bring myself to do it.

In my search for a room, I had a humiliating failed interview with a house of three neat women with pale, clean hair and very white teeth, clad in lululemon leggings, yoga mats rolled up in a line by the front door, scented candles and Booker Prize novels written by BIPOC authors or northerners scattered about the place, Hendrick's and Fever-Tree bought by the crate, where they made forced, stupid conversation about the weather – *o the sun is giving me life* – university – *o my cousin Phoebe went there, and did Eng Lit too* – and job – *o you're still looking?* (accompanied by a scribble in a notebook on lap, circled, punctuated). One was hiding a regional accent of some sort, placing her consonants more carefully than her drawling companions whose voices purred with vocal fry. I wondered if she was from Kent. She asked if I liked 'hanging out' or whether I kept myself to myself. Unsure of the right answer, trying to work out if they would want me hidden away, a coarse Bertha Mason, when their little friends popped over for girl dinners, or if they envisioned me participating; perhaps topping up their rosé or clearing plates, allowed to perch appreciatively at their feet like a child, I pulled my knees together, where gravity and the great rolling of my thighs on their duck-egg sofa had coaxed them apart, looked at the white, bright space and said I would probably stay in my room most of the time. They paused meaningfully and I, impassive, marked the swift, flickering glances they shot each other. *Or not*, I said, too late: *I can hang out. I make a great* (hazarding a guess) *vegetarian lasagne, with butternut squash and puy lentils.* Getting desperate: *it's easily made*

6

vegan. The thinnest one was taking notes; she looked up. *We'll get back to you, Alex.* (It's Alice.) *Thanks so much. So nice to meet you* – a phrase, I noted coldly, always condemned as common by my mother. As I quitted the house, I imagined one turning to the others, drooping her willowy arms balletically to mime a substantial stomach, mine, blowing sweet air into her smooth cheeks, rounding her eyes to depict my heft. I imagined her friends laughing merrily together, voices like bells, tickled by my audacity at daring to envision a life in this house, then their smiles fading as I was forgotten, the Zara Home cushions I had disfigured replumped, the next interviewee expected and selected, a congenial evening ordering in celebratory sashimi enjoyed.

I ended up in one of those bay-windowed Edwardian monstrosities, with too much corridor and landing, and cramped little bedrooms, each featuring a sash window that welcomed in a waterfall of condensation on cold days, with dogged weeds thrusting through the cracked paving of the front garden, slightly too far from the station for comfort, but, you know, fine. I have two housemates, although I hate the phrase, which is too chummy and jovial and does not accurately reflect our relationship: some PhD student in his thirties with a beard, Canadian, whom I hear pouring cereal for himself in the early hours, and pacing in his room, I wonder every so often about appearing, spectre-like, in his bed; and a simpering charity worker, Sasha, round-cheeked, with teeth that go off in different directions like fireworks, who has polycystic ovary syndrome and lets us all know it. I have come to loathe their cosy sofa-sittings, heads turning in unison under the blue gaze of the television to peer and wonder and smirk at the front door as I come in.

After several months I found work in a small meaningless office nearby – the bargain version of my sister's sleek workplace – as a paralegal. My London life, once quivering with promise – acceptance, friendships, love – was reduced to a miserable high street, vastly more Levantine restaurants than necessary, Pret, a mobile-unlocking stall, New Look, the Shard a distant glitter on the horizon, needling the sky. By this time, I had accrued a despicable but regular cleaning schedule, only accepting the job requests of those who lived a walk or short bus journey away, and seemed like they might be unencumbered by children or responsibility (zooming in on their app profile pictures, finding them on LinkedIn), initially to avoid the toddler-scrawlings and repellent nappy bins of family homes, then so as better to examine their carefree young lives, detesting them all, and their bedraggled spirals of hair on shower floors and walls, toast crumbs sharply underfoot, hardening clementine Christmas-peelings on patchy sofa arms, endless ragged tissues and open-mouth lipstick blottings, the mildew stench of drying laundry, the sour unmade beds, the wispy scraps of underwear and tissue-paper bras, kicked off heels, half-drunk and undrunk cups of tea on every single surface, stacked *Evening Standards*, the cheerfully tinkling and convivial recycling bin, and bedside drawers of rolling sex toys, the occasional notes – *hi, can you look at bathroom today?* – the odd £5 tip for a job well done, a red wine stain scrubbed. I would pocket the money and any loose change I might find, then ladder the tights in their wicker laundry baskets, spit in their oat milk. I would examine used condoms with fascination and disgust. I would take underwear at random. I liked to imagine their tuts, their furrowed brows as they held a limp sock in one hand while searching for the other, or looking with increased panic for those lucky leopard-print briefs that I had washed and worn, the cruel waistband leaving red welts on my flesh, although they looked worse than they felt.

Tom was different. I still reread the first message He sent me after I idly accepted the job one unremarkable Friday morning. I had more or less decided to stop cleaning by this point, and was summoning the energy to reluctantly text my mother to see if she still spoke to her school friend who was a solicitor or something, sickened by and jealous of these blithe and slovenly creatures and their little lives I scrubbed weekly, but fate sent Him my way – just in time. How boredly I tapped 'accept', without even glancing at His profile picture, how little I knew how my life would change. I ran an eye over the message, then, stunned, read it again, cheeks warming, blood rushing: *Good morning! :) Thanks for agreeing to clean for me – bins are bottom of main stairs turn left. Tom. PS Sorry my flat so messy!*

Tom. The tentative smiley face, the nervous exclamation marks, no sense of self-importance, His simple kindness in thanking me. That full stop after His name, the solidity of it. But most of all, it was the sudden convulsion, shocking, painful, in my heart, as I read those words, that felt like a chaotic, agonising bursting – no – a blossoming in my breast, something taking deep root, searing into the dark muscle, snaking through the aorta, the vena cava, reaching frail green shoots to Him. I gasped, cried out, bent double, clutching my phone to my chest, His words, good morning good morning good morning pulsing in my heart, my bloodstream, until the ebb and flow of pain died, and I got my breath back and stood, euphoric and sweating. *Un coup de coeur*, the French say, for falling in love – a blow to the heart. Familiar yet strange – I felt it; this, this was real. I smiled for the first time that day, and love followed: setting foot in His flat for the first time felt like coming home, an enveloping. I could see the lacklustre trajectory of my career ahead of me, once I contacted my mother, the informal interview, the smile and wink as I left, understanding that the role was mine regardless of my talent. Safe in this knowledge, I stopped cleaning for others, deleting appointments without warning, smiling at the subsequent one-star and no-star reviews: I could now devote myself to Him, be His apostle. Week after week, as I dusted sconces, lint-rolled curtains, thudded clouds from rugs at His window, my heart beat and my love thickened, the way fine and insubstantial sheets of filo stacked on top of each other and steeped in honey, spices, become dense and yielding, cracklingly soft, so sweet, nourishing: pure pleasure.

I become aware I have been standing by the sofa (always sofa, not couch or settee, which are common, my mother whispers), gazing at its hue for several minutes. This small sofa is the exact shade of Tom's eyes, which I have studied in photographs, holding them to the light or zooming in to pixelated abstraction. I imagine His mother buying it for Him, perhaps, thinking of Him as soon as she saw it in a showroom or a catalogue – or it could have been a coincidence, realised only when the delivery men, unboxing the sofa after heaving it up a flight of narrow stairs, pointed it out – *matches your eyes, doesn't it, guv?* This is unlikely. I know I am the only one to see this, to see His eyes in the velvet cushions carrying the shape of His relaxed evening body. I rest my hand on each fabric indentation before pummelling it into voluptuous shape. I could make such beautiful casts from all these sleep-lined hollows, the crook of His elbow, the nape of His neck, the dip of a heel. I would pour gold and bronze into each one, prise the cool metal loose and hold them in my hands, rub them, wishing. If displayed, they could fill a gallery, draw an uneasy hush over an audience, but I would keep them only for myself, ungenerously, just looking and holding, burnishing, stroking, and then shutting them away.

I drink from a cup of water left on the kitchen counter, aligning my lips to where His have been, that Vaseline smudge, then wash it up with scalding water and upend it on the draining board, where it nestles by a solitary knife and fork, a lone plate, my hands steaming. That He eats alone both wounds and buoys me. I would not let Him busy about, stir-frying waterlogged vegetables for one, splashing soy sauce, sriracha, and eating alone, vacantly scrolling through His phone. I know well the food He likes from old Instagram posts back when we still did that: photograph laden tables at supper clubs, pub lunches, the chubby stacks of maple-drenched pancakes and sharp Benedicts of a bottomless brunch, Prosecco nipping the taste buds, the blackened bavette of a date night, lemony rocket showered in Parmesan, a soft shared pudding puddled with ice cream. I would cook Him a feast, drippingly fragrant rosemary lamb, grease-soft and pink, with dense knots of garlic pushed into the flesh, shards of salty and steaming potatoes slurping up gravy, a spitting gratin, spindly carrots rolled and gleaming with oil. I'd wrench off golden chicken legs from a plump roast, carve a bone-white wet breast; grill bright asparagus while crisping pancetta, tenderly tear wild mushrooms to fry in yellow Cornish butter, grinding pepper and adding a thick kiss of cream. I'd bake towering cakes airy with love, steam portly syrup puddings punctuated with raisins, prepare gravelly crumbles crunchy with sugar, sweet rhubarb and sour apples from my mother's garden. Cocoa-dust truffles, tooth-scrapings in ganache. Rough oatcakes, bitter Stilton, sharp chutney to spring saliva to the back of the mouth. A winking thimble of port. I would prepare a feast. I would drown Him in it.

I wipe the surfaces to brightness and trace my name, sinuously, with a finger upon the damp laminated wood: so He knows I've been here, that my heart is here. I pop off the lid of His multivitamins with a thumb; I am glad He cares for His health – o His fragile lean body – but He forgets to take these every day; last week there were forty-two of the stale-smelling tablets, and today, as I upend the pot and count, I see there are thirty-nine. Soon I shall remind Him each day, smilingly handing Him a glass and a terracotta pill before He rushes out of the door, throwing a kiss my way. He will call me a wonder, so easily, and my eggshell heart will burst. My heart aches now, with longing, with love, and I press my hand to my chest to numb it, as I take a vitamin, letting its dusty coating dissolve thickly on my tongue before swallowing it without water. I can feel my throat's resistance to this dry interloper and welcome the bitter taste that He must taste, in my mouth.

I dust His laptop, run a cloth over its smooth form, then open it. As always, it is unlocked: typically Tom, trusting and pure of heart. I scroll through His Facebook page – no important messages, as no one really uses it now, do they, only a few birthday notifications: Imogen is twenty-five. I roll my eyes and unfriend her for Him. Out of habit – He wouldn't mind, I know – I read His emails, inconsequential, really, a Eurostar promotion, a parkrun update, T.M.Lewin's mid-season sale, and one from His sister, which I barely bother to skim. I'd be doing Him a favour if I just deleted every inane missive; I feel sure that it is not normal to email one's brother so often. I expect she has some tiresome anxiety around abandonment; their parents divorced when they were children; I haven't been able to put my finger on exactly when, how old Tom was. I can't wait to ask Him, to comfort Him as He talks about it, perhaps even cries. I will kiss away each tear, and He will cling to me. There is only one photograph I can find of His family as a unit of four: an open-mouthed admonishing mother, a grinning stupid sister. He is beshorted and squinting at the camera, one thin arm hooked around the neck of His lithe father, who is crouching alongside Him unsmilingly. He is five or seven, I suppose. I go back through each message, clicking each one back to unread. As I do so Tom receives His daily gym newsletter, exercises demonstrated by a thick-necked man in a vest, arms vascular and dark. I imagine the plates of my skull shivering under the pressure of those hands, the click and give. He rarely emails others from His personal address – the odd line to His sister, and I imagine His phone messages are similarly infrequent, as no one understands Him like I do and He must long for such connection. Our correspondence has so far been simple, sweet nothings, a message here and there about cleaning, each dash an embrace, each comma a swift kiss, ellipses hiding His true thoughts, understood only by me – but I know that soon He will open His heart to me, pouring words upon words. Love letters, dreamy valentines, streams of texts when we are at work (I miss you, let's meet for lunch), I love you, scrawled in shower-steam, notes tied to gift-wrapped bundles: saw this and thought of you.

It is almost ten o'clock and I must go soon. My heart weighs heavy in my stomach as the one thing I look forward to, this time with Tom, draws to a close. I imagine our bodies moving about this flat together; Him walking from the window to the sofa, me from the kettle to the sink, opening a drawer, two, then, drawn to each other, meeting by the window, merging into one. I scan the flat with a shrewd and practised eye. The floor gleams glass and mirrors. The duvet shows no trace of our mingled bodies, the kitchen no hint of a visitor. The air is fresh and fragrant – mountain air and cedar trees. I rummage in the worn backpack I shrugged off earlier, and remove a small glass bottle of perfume, one that promises its wearer irresistibility, and spray some onto the hand towel in the bathroom. I walk carefully backwards out of the door, looking and looking at Tom's things, wishing I could slip behind the curtains, stretch out under the bed, dissolve into the walls.

Last rites: I haul the taut black bag into the communal bins with a whoosh of foul air. It is noisome, and I am unkissed.

2.

IT IS 11 O'CLOCK WHEN I ARRIVE AT THE OFFICE. I AM
sweating, as usual, armpits prickling and top lip slick, having
waited an unacceptable eight minutes for the nineteen-minute
bus home to leave the cleaning bucket in my room, and to sit
in silence for a while, pressing my chemical hands to my eyes
before walking to work, which is thankfully only twenty dull
suburban minutes away. I work with a handful of basic young
women who talk about Lizzo like she's Simone de Beauvoir
and about climate anxiety as though it's a common cold, who
smile at me over their computer monitors, although all I can
see is their eyes, wide.

How was the hot therapist? one asks me coquettishly, I don't
care which, as I push my backpack under my desk and blot
my hairline with my hands. When I started here, I knew that
Tom, above all other things, was my priority and I would not
(could not) forsake my time with Him, so I told them I was
seeing a therapist on Wednesday mornings, to shut them up.
My manager, Marta, couldn't have granted me the hours off
quickly enough when I asked on my first day in the office,

last year; I willed some tears into my eyes, held a damp tissue and mentioned – uncertain, wavering – my mental health and, you know, wellbeing – the blood rushed hotly to her face and she leaned forwards, panting (green bra, unusual), and emphatically said how of course I must do whatever I needed, of course, of course, of course. For some reason my esteemed colleagues have decided that the care I take over my appearance on Wednesdays, although I wouldn't say I do anything special, or different, means that my therapist must be male and attractive. I think of Tom, those eyes, and my stomach pitches, heart pines. Even in the future, when we are together, those hours, each Wednesday, 9 until 10, will remain sacred to me.

Fine thanks, I say. I hear them smile at each other through the dry unsticking of lips from teeth, but most of all the swinging of earrings: all geometric and looking like they cost about a tenner, apart from some heirloom or other that Anna's always wearing. A beat and they look at each other and raise their ridiculous bold brows; Rebecca's thick and black, powdered stern, diminishing to nothing, the haughty blonde half-moons of Anna, and Natasha's uneven and thin, a regrettable hangover from the nineties. I hope they all die.

My job uses about 20 per cent of my brain and I can feel my eyesight failing by the month – the longer I stare at my screen, its earnest numbers and tables, lines of wishes (best), regards (kind) and thanks (many), meetings blocked out in pastel colours, flagged emails, Word documents frighteningly white, cursor winking – the more the grey marl wash of daylight draws my attention like a dullard schoolchild longing for playtime. My view as I gaze out of the window is unlovely: a glimpse into an office kitchen across the narrow street, fringed by a row of orchids, behind which shadowy figures make cups and cups of tea, and microwave carrot and coriander soup and wax-pale baked potatoes. Into my line of sight stretch the tops of two bending branches from below, that change from black bone to tender green to yellow, and these signs of life, together with the thin rectangle of sky interrupted by darting birds and sketched in above the low building animate me, bring freshness to my weary eyes. Vacantly, I pump hand cream into my palms – chemical vetiver, bitter grass – and slickly caress them, drawing my fingers through those of the other hand rough-knuckled from Dettol, and look dispassionately at my neighbour. Nina, the colleague who sits between me and the window: the only reason I turn my head her way. Her hair is perennially in a ponytail, seeking to be neat and serious but betrayed by the thick yet wispy frizz of the English rose, over-brushed and under-conditioned. Despite her careful smoothing, the sting of the tightest hairband, Nina's head is forever ringed with an aureola of broken golden hair, backlit and unkempt. I bet her mother calls her hair her crowning glory and used to tell her to brush it one hundred times a night. I curl my lip. Nina smiles kindly or smugly at me and surreptitiously opens a desk drawer, removes a can of Red Bull and levers it open, releasing its syrupy Calpol smell. She's one of those who declare they hate hot drinks, tea and coffee, although I note that sort always love the childish cosiness of hot chocolate, the more toothy bobbing mallows the better, who look at me superciliously when others slump at desks, wilting and jelly-like only to perk up when someone else (never them) rustles the pre-measured ground coffee sachets, fills the per-colator and the curiously sweet, earnest dribble click of the machine starts, soon followed by the round aroma of coffee. I smile at Nina when she does this, we smile at each other, the small, plump shared mouth-closed smiles of the superior. I have let Nina think we're friends, or work friends – there's a difference. Despite spurning the desperate camaraderie of the filter coffee machine, I do keep a cafetière in my bottom desk drawer, and every few days when I find myself looking at Manager Marta during our catch-ups when she examines my to-do list with exaggerated care, asking about timescales and frowning slightly at my responses, hating her, wanting to crack her face off her skull in one satisfying piece like peeling an egg, I make myself a black and bitter coffee for one, slowly, eking out each task, counting my steps: walking the kettle to the sink, trickling in cold water, returning the kettle to its base, taking coffee from the cupboard to the cafetière and back again. To the drawer for a spoon, scooping, then back to the sink to rinse, discard. Waiting until the kettle is just about to boil, pouring. Waiting some more. Filling the cleanest mug I can find, washing up the cafetière and drying it. Walking slowly back to my desk, mug aloft. I have calculated that I earn roughly £4.46 (before tax) each time I make coffee in this way, which gives me grim pleasure. No one can begrudge me making myself a drink. I'd grind my own beans if I thought I could get away with it. I'm indifferent to the taste of coffee and I know milk and sugar would improve it, but I don't want to dilute its dark clarity and sleekness. Sugar is demeaning. I watch Dawn, one of the pink-cheeked secretaries, spoon it into her tea first thing and my teeth sing and I loathe and envy and pity her.

Are you OK? Nina whispers to me and I know now I have been staring out of the window, above her head, for too long, her ridiculous hair fronds fluttering at me. *Yes, thanks,* I say and smile. I hope I did not have the look of the disdain I am currently feeling on my face. My mother always said I wore my heart on my sleeve, one of her many sayings, not shared with pride or love, but with warning: hide it away. Unsaid: you must conceal, disguise, obscure, or no one will ever, ever love you. I have worked hard to conceal my heart, lapsing here and there; but now, now I have Tom, Tom who makes me strong, my good-little-girl obedience has slipped and I can break free of her petty rules. After spending time with Him, even imagined, Tom brings my shadowy secret self to light and it is just for Him, as it should be: beautiful.

I smile once more at Nina, and resolutely put in my earphones, settling down to work, in the loosest sense of the word, clicking through emails and calmly deleting them one by one. I listen to white noise; it rushes in my ears like a furious, distant river, bone-thrillingly cold, full of thrashing salmon, mouths opening and closing and gaping pink and red – and look, the flash of a kingfisher's wing. I spend the next hour or so lost in a pleasant deadness, surveying spreadsheets and tapping out the odd email, cold but polite. Best wishes. I burn for next Wednesday.

3.

I FEAR OLD AGE, AND DEATH, THE SLIPPING AWAY OF youth, but don't we all, I suppose. In the supermarket and on the bus I take sideways looks at the skin of children's cheeks, awed by its smoothness and vitality. In the same glance I catch the eyes of octo- and nonagenarians, trembling and frail, their pale scalps shining through neatly set hair, their glistening, rheumy eyes and horrifying drawn gums, lipstick smiles. It seems unlikely that I'd volunteer in a care home, albeit quite a good one, or as good as they get, but in a way, surrounding myself with decaying flesh, absent-minded gentleness, the odour of gravy splashed on laps, down chins, the air sweet with bleach, makes the firm, manila fat of my body seem almost obscenely young and beautiful. They listen to me, and sometimes pat my hand. It passes the drip and seep of time.

On the odd Saturday at Roseacres I make basic chit-chat, ask how their chair-bound exercises went, whether they're looking forward to film night (*The Sound of Music*). As a 'befriender' I'm more or less allowed to do what I want, to drift from the television room, the semicircle of wipe-clean padded chairs, to the dining room, along the corridors, past corkboards plastered with childlike, garish art, a printed photograph of Betty at 100, defeatedly holding her telegram. It was supposed to be a weekly thing, but I missed one or two, and no one seems to notice whether I'm there or not. When I feel like it, turn up, sign in, pop in and out of rooms, avoiding the sort-of-racist ones, who flinch when anyone non-white ministers to their pain, or sometimes scream hatefully. I pass, so I'm mostly OK, although sometimes I am eyed suspiciously or fearfully, but whether it's the colour of my skin or the look in my eye, or just paranoia, delusions, dementia, perhaps envy at my thrilling youth, I don't know or particularly care. To the chosen ones I read out loud, my voice hoarsening and straining, undignified large-print texts of their choosing, Danielle Steele, etc., which I reluctantly enjoy. To those who no longer talk, behind whose eyes wavering memories take shape and dissolve, I read a little of whatever it is I'm reading myself. Sometimes, shyly, poetry I have written for Tom, checking their faces for that loosening, the unlocking, that art facilitates. I always sit facing the door, and watch the depressing ebb of fine-knit-jumpered relatives wafting by, usually anxious, sad-mouthed daughters fitting their duty in between dropping the children off at ballet/football/their father's and the weekly shop – occasionally a bluff, suited son in a hurry, holding a tin of M&S shortbread with an embarrassed air.

I spend much of today's two-hour visit talking to Dorothy, who sits in her room looking determinedly at the birds pecking at a bird table bearing the marmalade-, margarine- and saliva-saturated remains of the residents' morning toast. Every so often she'll nod, exclaim: *and another one!* (at the birds) or call me Elsie, which I'm OK with. I think we're both just pleased to have someone to talk to.

Do you ever think about killing yourself, Dot? I ask, after a moment of companionable silence. We both watch the birds clap their wings and squabble. She says nothing. I lean forwards. *Don't you feel bored?* (Unsaid: lonely? unloved?) Dorothy turns to me and says: *what's that, dear?* Her face clears. *O, it's you, Elsie! You are kind for visiting.* I nod, and decide I'm not going to get anything interesting from her today. I consider touching her thin, Delft blue-and-white hand, but she turns back to the bird table, now empty, save for a magpie that must have frightened everything else away. It contemptuously spears a crust and flaps heavily off. I tell Dorothy about Tom and our love, how we fit so dearly together, and she nods obediently. Just as I'm talking about the way His hair is so dark as to be almost black but decidedly not, a grey squirrel scampers down from the fence and up the bird feeder, skilfully avoiding the spiked panels that have been affixed to prevent this very occurrence. I read once that grey squirrels eat baby birds. Dorothy closes one wet eye and with surprising deftness holds an imaginary rifle aloft.

Before I leave, I wander down the ground-floor corridor where I find who I'm looking for, butterflies thrashing in my gut. An elderly man sits reading a hardback book. He marks his place and looks up at my approach. *Good morning, Alice,* he says. His voice rumbles pleasingly. *Is it the weekend already?* It's a stupid question that would rightly deserve an eye roll if anyone else had asked it, but I find myself nodding and smiling.

And what have you been up to this week, he asks, twinkling knowingly. Over my visits in the past months, we have somehow started a little game: *o, nothing much,* I say airily. *Went to Thailand, attended a Full Moon Party, drank snake blood and swam in the black and silver sea.* He chuckles, an insult, I suppose, that he knows this is a falsehood when theoretically it could be true: I'm young, fun, with relatively decent independent means. I make a mental note to check the price of flights to Thailand, calculate my remaining annual leave.

And what about you? He taps his chin, thoughtful: *stole sherry from the kitchens,* he offers. I laugh, even though it's not a great attempt – my answers rove the earth, its possibilities, and his echo in the confines of his little life, his room, Roseacres, London at a push. I know he once sailed seas and lived in South Africa, drove the length of the Americas. I humour him, I pity him, although I am ashamed I feel these things for him. I feel he somehow deserves more from me. I wave my book at him – *read to you today?* He shakes his head, smiling. *I'm quite all right, thank you. Got to keep my brain going.* He gestures at his head with a square hand, which shakes, minutely. I linger at his doorway a little longer, morosely, trying to prolong our encounter. It's impossible to see what he looked like as a younger man, so old is he, colourless hair that might once have been unruly, sparse, his wine-dark eyes pressing back into his skull, thin skin forcing his nose to prominence, ever-growing ears stretching and stretching still larger, knobbly temples and cheekbones gauntening the face, aping the corpse it will soon become. With the elderly, I find I can converse with an ease that is lacking among my peers, perhaps because, unequivocally, my body is better, stronger, finer than theirs and any shame is lost, or lessened.

He's gone back to reading but when I step into his bedroom – strange that he has no control over this, really – he lowers his book and smiles at me again. *Are these your grandchildren?* I ask, not for the first time, pointing at one of the photographs in a frame on the wall, then allowing my finger to rest on it, lightly. In it crowd five young people in their late teens or early twenties, all angles, strong noses and bared teeth. He nods with benevolence or impatience. *Yes, although I have one more, who lives in Hong Kong, and a great-grandchild too.* I smile. *O, lovely. Do they visit often?* He nods contemplatively, deeply: *yes, I'm lucky – several live in London so I do see them from time to time. They lead very busy lives so I am lucky. Yes, very lucky,* I say. *Looks fun.* I imagine being cradled by jostling relatives, crooking my elbow round a neck. *Yes, it was rather,* he says. *My late wife's eighty-fifth birthday celebration, five years ago. We put a marquee up in the garden.* He is silent. I stare at the figures in the photo so hard, the bare limbs, that when I turn my eyes back to this gentleman, the bright, tangled silhouette dances in my vision. I blink and we smile at each other and I sense his gaze drifting, longing to return to his book. A worker bustles in through the open door, backwards, squeaking a little trolley with her, on which sits a cafetière, some sort of silver tea urn and a plate of custard creams and bourbons. What a choice. *Tea and biccies Mr M?* she asks, and I smirk and turn to leave wordlessly. *Ooh, lovely. Yes, please,* I hear him say, and the jolly meekness of it all makes me want to scream. I take a surreptitious photo of this medico-domestic scene, a smiling trolley-lady, a smiling pensioner, and send it to the WhatsApp group nauseatingly entitled 'famalam' and think of the photo popping up in my sister's phone, then my mother's with perhaps a slight delay due to the shockingly bad countryside signal. *Saturday volunteering*, I type, with a smiling emoji.

It should be obvious that I have an ulterior motive; good deeds don't come naturally. Once, when I was dusting Tom's laptop keyboard particularly assiduously, wiping the screen of finger marks, buffing scuffs, an email came in from Tom's mother and I couldn't help but read: they were thinking of popping Grandfather in a home now Granny is dead: Roseacres. I pass Roseacres on my walk to Big Tesco, funnily enough – although what is so funny about this great collision of our lives, bright and dark enough to spark galaxies? – and had often seen residents at thickly glazed windows, care staff clicking on a lamp, drawing curtains closed against the twilight, and the twilight years. It is a large building with an optimistically spacious car park, hemmed in with flowerbeds packed with immature and forlorn rose bushes. I can now confirm the garden at the back, with a few apple trees, four benches, a stone sundial and a bird table, is large but not large enough to qualify the acreage in the name, but there is business in promoting sanitised, depressing nursing homes as bucolic idylls: Seven Pines, Green Willow, The Vale, Oak Lodge. Liars.

They were pleased to have me volunteer; I just spouted some nonsense about possibly wanting to become a carer (I would rather die), and I located Mr M after a couple of methodical visits. I saw the photo on the wall first, that aspirational, familial gang, each body touching another body with a casually slung arm, shoulder to shoulder, cheek to cheek, then in his old face I detected the same determined, straight nose, the wave in the hair belonging to Tom. I hope to bump into Him one of these days; I am sure He will visit soon. He will walk into the room holding a book of poetry, and will be surprised by the beautiful figure sitting, holding His grandfather's hand as they talk. He will think me kind, and gracious.

As I pass reception, nodding at Jess, I pluck a chocolate from the tub of Quality Street that has miraculously survived since Christmas and secrete it in my pocket. I wonder how many Jess has eaten, idling away behind the desk, book in hand, if it's as hard for her as it would be for me. My mouth waters, anticipating the slow burn of sugar as I suck it, to make it last. Cass sends an angel emoji in response to my text, and I lock my phone irritably. I drag my feet on the way home, stopping off at a newly opened salon nearby, taking advantage of a 20 per cent discount to get a wax. I pretend I have to listen to a lecture for work and put my earphones in the whole time so the beautician doesn't talk to me, although I listen to nothing other than my own ragged breathing, the ripping of flesh and hair, and the slow tread of her feet moving from the wax pot, to the bin, to the table where I lie.

4.

IT'S TIME. I AM SITTING ON TOM'S LOO, IDLY WATCHING between my parted thighs the spools of blood unravelling, syrup-like, somewhere between golden and maple, from my stretched-feeling, aching womb, falling into the clear water and spiralling like inkblots (butterfly or skull, creation or destruction) before settling in a sluggish pool in the porcelain depths. A surge and a black clot slips free, sinks. This is women's way of feeling time pass, that sinister clockwork inching round the roundness of the body; the slow gathering of endometrial cells, a nesting, a fluffing of pillows ready to receive guests, the ripeness of the womb, fleshy and welcoming, all neat and tidy and, yes, ready to receive guests, even one, just a casual visitor, anything. And then realisation that the arrival time has been and gone, and no one is coming; the tearing of the wallpaper, great swathes of it, and tears of disappointment, of ageing, of loneliness. The womb revolts and shudders. The painters are in.

I'd never wanted children until Tom: babies are little puddings with soft skulls barely set, all smiles and glistening thick chins. Toddlers and children disgust me; their sour earth smell, thin curls, bones that bend like sticky green branches, milk teeth like grains of rice, crusty pink noses, wet hands and plastered knees. They always want something from you, but when you crouch and smile, hide your face, peep out from behind your hands, perhaps poking your tongue, you receive a sullen look and a turned head. Tom and I, well, our children would be better. His beauty and brilliance would temper my faults – I can see them now: the round cheeks and fat wrists of babyhood, feet like marshmallows puffed under the grill, with just the right amount of firmness and give. A slight, serious boy with hands in his pockets. A charming, clever girl with Tom's dimples, Tom's thick hair, Tom's anything. And more than two: three, four. Just let them be like Him. And me, a glowing coal in a hearth, the centre. At holiday parties: how does she do it? So poised, clever, knowledgeable, thin, funny, such lovely polite children, such a handsome husband. They have a house in the South of France, and a cottage in the Cotswolds. We've never seen Tom so happy. I can be that person with Tom; with Him it will be easy to skip breakfast, go for runs, be chic, be effortless, accepted, loved. My skin will be impossibly dewy, and people will assume its hue is a tan from wintering in St Lucia, nothing more.

This blood leaving my body and clouding the water, this blood that I now impatiently wipe reminds me that it is almost a year since Tom and I encountered one another. I have been running my hands over His things for a full rotation of the earth around the sun; caressing the ironic football trophy from colleagues, stroking His laptop keyboard, seeking out the shiny spots where the heels of His hands must rest, feeling the rough carpet under my bare feet, bare thighs. I flush, and blood and water are slurped away.

Today, I have spent my time cleaning Tom's windows; His flat is neater than usual – He must have been away over the weekend – why? Where? He hasn't updated anything on social media; His thoughts fly higher than that, swallows in a clear sky. It must have been a weekend of solitude; worn from work and tiring of London, its relentless chewing gum streets, the cloud hanging low over Victorian chimney pots, always threatening rain. He must have taken a cottage in the Yorkshire Dales, taken some novels and a notebook, a weighty fountain pen and navy ink in a pot. Perhaps He wrote poetry, like that in the Seamus Heaney on His shelf, resting, sweetly, next to James Herriot. I imagine His words railing against His life, its constraints and sorrows. O that He knew I could unburden Him, lift the weight two-handed from His rounded shoulders. I would thumb His neck, squeeze the rope of His trapezius muscles with my small hands, kneading until He gasps.

I am cleaning a pane of glass when I see a handprint. His. It is so clear and crisp I almost cry out in wonder. I have seen vague impressions of Him before – an elbow in a cushion, a hand-swipe over a clouded mirror, finger-smudges here and there – but never a hand in its entirety, an atlas for me to study. He must have been on the phone, perhaps, leaning on the glass and looking at His reflection in the dark. It is as if He has left a secret gift. For me. For whom else would He leave it? I attempt to memorise His fingertips, each serpentine line, loving them. I try to take a photo of them, but my phone camera refuses to focus properly on the glass, capturing instead the grey view outside. O it is like He is here with me, more than ever. I look and I look and then I press my hand onto His, our fingers entwining, twin warmth, the click of one wedding band against the other. I have never been the right size for anything but I see that our hands fit perfectly; I can see how purely they align, each of us with a slightly longer ring finger, His only just larger than mine, and beautifully so. I take my hand away, throat thick with tears. I have ruined it. I spray and wipe it clean and I am buoyed anew. We match. It's a sign.

I move quietly around the flat, refolding a tea towel, straightening the post. I fold the ends of the loo roll into a neat point so He will see it and think of me. It's time we met.

5.

THIS IS HOW IT WILL UNFOLD. HE WILL FIND ME. I will turn the ball of twine in my heart, the invisible length between us will tauten, thrumming, drawing us together, our quick hearts beating, until we are breast to breast, breath to breath. This is what happens. I will wait, perhaps, at the bus stop when it is raining and He does not cycle to work; we will huddle apologetically close under the shelter, smiling wryly as yet another bus, not our bus, arrives and the other commuters board, yawning and groaning, all keep-cups and blinking white-lashed eyes, mascara yet to be applied in the juddering neon light, freshly washed hair hanging limply on blazers, dripping, clutching the odd porridge pot or hastily wrapped foil package of almond butter toast. We'll squint into the drizzle, searching for our bus in the gloom; He will notice my smile and wonder what podcast I might be listening to. I'll take out my phone and skip back ten seconds as if to listen to a particular line again, laughing prettily like Lizzy Bennet, all charm and bookishness, and He'll accidentally catch a glimpse of the music podcast I know He listens to at home, each episode stacked up in Spotify, listened, listened, listened. As He smiles in recognition, another bus will pass through a puddle and a fine spray will shower our shoes.

O! I will leap back and stumble into Him, my back on His firm chest, the first time of many we will do this, me leaning back into Him as we contemplate the smoky dark on Bonfire Night, fireworks cracking open and sizzling high above us, spitting embers, a millefleurs tapestry of gunpowder and light. Watching bloody suns slip into oceans, or icing-sugar snow-flakes come to rest in our garden. First frost. I'll hold a mug of tea in both hands, red-nosed, and His cable-knit chest will soften my spine. I will remove my headphones from my ears and apologise, and His hands will gently set me steady.

The bus will arrive and we'll each try to usher the other on first. He will insist so I will step on and trail upstairs, dripping, hoping He will follow me. He does, of course, that engorged and thickening bond in our hearts leading Him. We will sit next to each other and He will turn to me and my stomach will drop and my heart will leap as He says, voice deep and kind: *I'm Tom.*

That is the first way. But there is a second: perhaps it's in a dark room with low tables where we meet, stepping through will-o'-the-wisp candlelight, tables of dark, sleek heads bent towards each other, murmuring voices, shadowy corners and shadows, a low pulsing beat that plucks at the pit of the gut, loosening limbs and His hand holding a glinting bottle of beer – no, tumbler of woodsmoke whisky. I will slide through the tables in grey satin, the grey of a river pearl, an open oyster, spaghetti straps gossamer that will break with the lift of a finger, as He stands to approach the bar, colliding so a few drops of my drink, champagne, I think, fizz onto my skin. They will sparkle and He will briefly think of licking them off my wrist but turn His mind from this thought, ashamed. I will smile as if to say, do not worry, my love. O the things you will do to me. He will smile and apologise, charmed. Perhaps I will raise my wrist to my mouth and with a small pink tongue do that which He wanted to do. *I'm Tom*, he might say, or perhaps, emboldened by His slow looks, I might put my hand in His, gently, and say, *it's me*. And the muffled tattoo of our hearts will beat and beat.

Or – and this will require careful planning – one Wednesday I will wait. I will clean His flat more carefully than ever, each surface will mirror my face, ashen, flushed. I will tuck His size ten shoes snugly side by side under the coat rack, smooth His ties one by one, briefly pulling each tight around my wrists, my throat, scrub stubborn limescale from His taps. Then before He comes home – I don't know exactly when this is, half six, seven, perhaps, tired and with a wrinkled shirt and brow – I will take a wine glass, those stupid curvaceous fishbowls that sing when you tap them lightly. I will tap a little too hard against the sink and that teasingly fragile glass will shatter and perhaps I will be cut or perhaps not but whichever way He will find me on the floor of the kitchen, with a halo of glass, blood seeping from one wrist, one palm. The floor, recently washed so the blood spreads thinly, dangerously, will gleam. *I'm sorry* – I will say, dazedly, as He rushes to my side and puts a hand to my face. *I was washing up – I don't know what happened – I'm sorry* – His face will be concerned and horrified, He will sit me up and wrap my hand in a towel and ask if I hit my head and stop me from getting up and trying to tidy. He will make me a cup of tea without asking how I like it, but it will be milky and sweet, for shock, He will say. I will insist and insist that I am fine and He will compel and compel me to stay, finding a plaster, a bandage, pressing my palm lightly, sweeping up the glass, mopping the floor, a wry role reversal, the bin becoming full of damp and pinkening kitchen towel, shyly asking if I'd like to stay for a proper drink. I will say something along the lines of: *have you got enough wine glasses?* Or: *perhaps I would if you had a spare wine glass!* And we will both laugh. He will say how strange that we've been in each other's lives for so long without meeting, and perhaps He will say He hadn't expected me to be so beautiful. We will talk into the night, our minds crashing and rebounding, each drawn towards the other, unwaveringly.

This has to go smoothly; I want a plan of pale wood in a tight dovetail joint, no need for nails or glue; the flawless sliding of things into place, not a catch or a splinter; a key sliding into an oiled lock. You only meet the love of your life once. Each little thing, each movement, each inch will be the first. The first look, smile, touch. I thrill. I know we are fated to meet and love and wed – this bond between us is drawing us ever closer but I am taking no chances – the path must be cleared, no roots on which to snag a foot, or briars through which to crawl, bloodily. It shall be a stroll through a wildflower meadow, if the universe approves our love, and how could it not – nothing, nothing has been more right. I think of the desperate prayers of my youth, palms pressed, eyes closed, the ferocious, juvenile wishes and bargains – if I shut my eyes for the length of this song – let me be thin – if the next car that passes is black – let him like me – if I hold my breath for as long as it takes for that magpie to fly from this telephone wire to the next – let them all forget – if I scratch at this place on my thigh until it bleeds without stopping – please – please – let me be different. I fulfilled my side of the bargain time and time again – gasping, bleeding – cold gods, the lot of them, but now I feel their gaze on me once more, and think, perhaps, I have suffered enough and they might take pity on me. The path must be cleared and I need my first helper.

Anna in the office is the most posh and therefore the most thick: friendly and empty, like an especially purebred and stupid dog – an Irish setter, perhaps. I turn to her now.

Anna? She looks up, startled, and her front teeth, permanently on show, glisten. Her lipstick, plum to match the accent, so pristine this morning, has faded from the inside out, from endless tea-sipping, and nibbling on her bottom lip, as she is doing now. She knows a minor royal personally; she's supposedly Scottish with her cut-glass accent; yes, she's the kind of girl Tom might have once dated (tell me the secret), but equally, she has a collection of crystals arranged on her desk, probably aligned with her chakras or similar, and her hand jumps to a particularly drab stone that looks to me like coal, but isn't. The crystals started appearing five months or so ago, and she has an infuriating habit of caressing them when she's nervous or speaking to clients on the phone: jagged purple amethyst, a lustrous tiger's eye, a dim knot of fool's gold (I think), one worn smooth and blue, that lump of coal. This is how she is seeking meaning in her insubstantial life, with these energies and influences, along with vaginal steaming, no doubt. I wonder what she feels the coal is imparting upon her, and, despite my scorn, am willing to debase myself in this way, try anything.

Is anything interesting happening with the planets, Anna? I ask her. Her smile, which had tentatively begun to form at my calm tone, falters. She looks to her right, auburn hair whisking, to Natasha, for support, uncertain, but Natasha is not there. The fingers on her crystal stroke, stroke, stroke. She thinks I am mocking her. She's recently engaged (and don't we all know it) to a man whose name I can't summon the energy to remember. It's probably James, let's be honest. It always is; every man my age is called James, and if they aren't, they might as well be. I have long stopped caring; or rather, I offer them as much care as they have shown me.

I just read something about it, I improvise, *and I heard you mention it the other day.* Her face relaxes and her bottom lip is released from its toothy prison. *It sounds really interesting,* I add, encouragingly.

O, terrific! She says. *Let me just check,* she turns to her screen, impatiently minimising an email and (I roll my eyes) going to one of her saved tabs. She starts scrolling officiously.

Star sign? She asks. This is the most efficient I have ever seen her. *Capricorn,* I say. She turns to me and narrows her eyes. *What's this for? I need to know because, like, it changes whether it's to do with your family or job, or relationships . . . ?* She nibbles a fingernail performatively. Her lipstick doesn't stand a chance. I decide to offer a half-truth, the secret, pulsing core of my being muted and obscured, scried through a clouded glass.

I'm supposed to be going on a date with this – man. I want it to go well, so I wondered if there was a particular day— Anna utters

38

a cry of joy and turns back to her computer. I have the impression that this is the most exciting thing to have ever happened to her, and puzzle. Why should she care?

She speaks quickly and seriously as she scrolls: *do you happen to know his—*

Virgo, I say. I am holding my breath. *Wednesdays are best for me. And Him.*

After some minutes of blinking, biting of lip, furrowing of brow, Anna turns to me, smiling, and says, *three weeks today. Wednesday the twenty-second.* She is delighted; I am stricken. Three weeks is twenty-one days, hardly anything when I have been dreaming of Him for so many more. At least I won't have my period then; you never know what might happen, although maybe I should wait, like those loveable women in romantic comedies. Not until the third date, am I right, or is it the fifth? As Anna starts explaining how Saturn is moving into the seventh house, conjuring to me the slow turn of celestial bodies, imperceptible movements rolling these orbs through the heavens, aligning, crossing paths and realigning, each planet on its mysterious course, the quicksilver messenger Mercury; dream-like Venus trifling with poets in the evening sky; Earth, this inconsequential dying planet; rust-red frowning Mars, muscular; the king Jupiter, stately and serene; many-mooned Saturn, ringed by ice and winds; frosty, faceless Uranus and dense blue Neptune, and although demoted, I'll always count little Pluto of my childhood lessons, the blind eye, forgotten and scorned. I imagine these orbiting bodies in an infinite inky space and while I smile at the thought of the movement of these dispassionate dead planets having any impact on me, and Him,

39

and our meeting, I am appalled and cowed by their magnitude and my insignificance. I once heard a recording of the sound of winds on Mars, sent back light years from the scoured, sandy ground to my earphones, a rushing howling wind both familiar and alien and I felt at once terrified and calmed and the most sure I have ever been that, upon death, there is nothing.

Thanks, I say to Anna, who is still talking. I swivel my chair back to my desk, to my work calendar, intending to ignore her, then, struck by a thought, turn my head back to her, wondering at what hidden source this recently engaged couple's journey began before it thickened into this river flowing effortlessly to the sea. A journey to emulate, perhaps, now on shy tributaries, gentle but strong, cutting through rock and earth through aeons to join as one. I ask, as casually as I can, although my voice catches: *by the way – where did you meet your boyfriend?* She smiles eagerly or self-approvingly: *fiancé – god that still feels so weird to say?* She smiles at and fingers the winking diamond at her left knuckle before looking back at me: *actually, on a uni ski trip – we were at different colleges so I hadn't actually met him before, but it turns out we'd both been skiing at this same resort with our families for donkey's years and we'd actually been to the same ski school?*

I turn away and let it wash over the back of my head until she finishes. I nod vacantly, say, *cool* (unsaid: so, unhelpfully, years of privilege was the catalyst behind this encounter) and pretend to read an email. I pray she doesn't speak to me again.

But the date she has given me, the aptness of it: the double digits, twins, 22, two figures curled together in bed. I have to ensure all goes smoothly. I don't believe in it, little rocks altering the this-and-that-way course of life, but I need something – and this is as good a place to start as any. I google *crystals for love* and order a blushing piece of rose quartz from Amazon, a new notebook, and a new pen for good measure: there's nothing quite like those first black marks on a fresh page. I have a lot of planning to do, a journey to chart through the stars and the earth, galaxies colliding, swift rivers converging, a cord of communion between hearts, tautening, growing shorter – I am interrupted by Anna's crisp voice piercing my thoughts as she returns from the kitchen with a mug of steaming tea and a Jammie Dodger: *o, Alice, I was thinking – if it doesn't work out with this guy, let me know – I've got a friend who I think would be great for you. He's really into books – and he's an Aries—*

I smile at her naivety, pityingly, and say, *it will work out.*

6.

TIME SLITHERS BY, DAY BY DREARY DAY. AFTER WORK on Friday I stop by Whole Foods as a treat, intending to buy a salad, some sushi, a fancy bottle of sparkling water, but I am waylaid by the hot pizza counter, with thick, tempting, help-yourself slabs. I do help myself, to two wedges of the vegetable-topped one, at least, and buy a box of four chocolate-chip brown butter cookies so under-baked as to still be wet, delicious dough, and I say to myself I'll save my pizza until I'm home, sitting at the table like a normal person, but I catch the bus home rather than walk so I can sit in traffic and eat it hot, in frantic, gasping bites, both slices, pretending this is all I'll eat, that I've worked hard enough to justify it, but I eat two cookies too, and when I get home Sasha is rummaging in the kitchen, saying guilelessly or calculatingly, *I've made enough supper for you if you want, it's only spag bol* – and I am powerless. *Yes please*, I say, *yes, yes, I'm starving. Long week.* I sit at the kitchen table and watch her, opening and closing drawers, the fridge, short and round but o it suits her. She looks normal. *Are you doing OK?* she asks, as she lifts dripping pasta from a saucepan.

We haven't seen much of you recently. I nod and shrug, say, *I'm fine, just tired* – and let her grate Parmesan on top in a pale mountain, before plunging a fork into the salty, savoury sauce. I twirl and twirl, and eat, nodding while I chew, trying to say without words: thank you, so good. I take the bowl upstairs as the Canadian comes into the kitchen, rubbing his hands and saying: *what do we have here?*

I am so full I feel sick. The two remaining cookies are in my bag and I think, *I'll give both to Sasha to say thank you,* or, later, *I'll save them to share with Mr M tomorrow.* I do, I do save them and save them, for hours, but when it is midnight and I am in bed, teeth freshly brushed, lights out, I get up in the dimness, avoiding looking at my spectral form in the floor-length mirror, take them from my bag and eat them quickly, pleasurelessly, because I know they're there. I lie down again, settling onto my broad back, and nip at my stomach with my nails, raking them into my thighs again and again, until I'm sure I have drawn blood.

The next morning, on the way to Roseacres, I take a photo of the view from the bridge; the remains of the night's mist rising prettily from the water, which I send to my mother and sister: *morning run!* I say. Cass responds within minutes with a sweaty-faced mirror selfie from her insanely expensive gym, kettlebell at her feet – *snap!* [dancing twins emoji]. My mother responds a little later: *well done, sweetheart. Good to move your body! That reminds me – off to Pilates x.* I zoom in on Cass's photo, especially the toned curve of her arm, the straightness of her brows, her hip bones under her leggings, the taut slope of her thighs. The laughing, challenging look in her eyes. I try to take a cute selfie with the river behind me, being careful to hide my non-workout clothes, but I can't get the angle right.

I remember one summer in adolescence skipping meals and drinking can after can of Diet Coke to stave off cravings, licking a single spoonful of peanut butter if my stomach cramped too painfully. I did, I did look more like Cass. One hot day our mother went to London for a conference near the coveted Topshop flagship store on Oxford Circus, brought us back limited edition T-shirts. We squealed in delight, and as she drew them out of the bag playfully slowly and handed them to us, she said, *they're exactly the same, just like when you were little,* but I noted her eyes flick to the size label of each one before she held them out to us, the one in her right hand to Cass, the left to me. I felt my face grow hot, a coal of pain in my gut. Unable to stop myself, I reached out to take the one she was proffering to Cass, and she jerked it away from my grasp. *Don't snatch,* she said, *and this one is Cass's.*

But they're the same, I said. She laughed, lightly: *don't be silly.* I took my T-shirt from her, said *thank you, Mummy* and tried it on, breathing in: it looked quite nice. And then I waited until Cass was in the bathroom before slipping to her room to check the label on hers: yes. The same, but smaller. I went for a jog the next morning, gave up halfway down the road, doubling over, pressing my side, my chest, and returned home to eat and eat and eat.

Now, I continue, flat-footed in my trainers as runners dance by, lightly. Out of habit, I check my work email on my phone and see that Anna emailed me yesterday evening after I had left – *FYI here's the website I use for checking auspicious dates! It's really good. You should also check out this podcast, Soulstis...* I stop reading and I listen instead to an album I saw in Tom's recent Amazon orders as a vinyl, checking the track names every so often so I can mention them effortlessly, trying to decide which His favourites might be. I return my phone to my pocket and concentrate on the notes, the lyrics. One day I will sing a line, absently, as we pass each other in the kitchen, making breakfast, and He will turn to me, amazed – *how did you know? How did you know?* And I will say, *know what?* And He will laugh with wonder and His arms will pull me to Him and—

Mr M is at breakfast when I arrive so I sit in his chair and await his return, running my hands over the worn fabric of the arms and smelling the antibac and shaving soap smell of his room, running my eye over the books on his shelf. There is one on his bedside table with a bookmark – a proper, leather bookmark, the type no one uses any more – halfway through. I crane my neck to read the title without having to get up and make out the word *Treason* in a gold old-fashioned script before hearing footsteps and gentle voices inching up the corridor outside. I stand up and wait, almost nervously. He enters and smiles, unbothered by my presence in his room, among his things. *Good morning, Alice,* he says. *And how was your week?* I am prepared: *lovely, thank you – plotted to blow up Parliament.* I incline my head knowingly at his book and he laughs. *What about you?* I say, and he looks around the room for further inspiration before settling on

46

my loose-weave jumper and saying: *I learned to knit.* Both our answers are boring but we laugh together and he creaks his way past me to sit down with an involuntary gasp of effort or relief.

And what are you reading at the moment, Alice? he asks. The real answer is muddling through a book on economics that I saw in Tom's Amazon order history, but I answer: *Jane Eyre.* He nods approvingly, then surprises me by saying: *do you think, because I am poor, obscure, plain, and little, I am soulless and heartless? You think wrong! – I have as much soul as you, – and full as much heart!*

Goosebumps erupt on my arms and I rub them hastily. I think of Tom. *Wow, yes, exactly,* I say, and he smiles. *My wife's favourite,* he says. *We were married for fifty-seven years.* I don't know what to say to this, whether I should say congratulations for being married so long, or I'm sorry she's dead, and you're alone, so I am silent for a bit then ask, flippantly: *any tips for a happy marriage?* He thinks with a serious expression on his old face, then says, *expect change.*

I look at him.

You don't marry the person they will be in ten or twenty years, he continues. *If you're prepared for that, then the variations, the up-and-down nature of living, of life, can be dealt with without feeling like your marriage will be disrupted.* This feels very profound so I pretend I'm thinking about it deeply, nodding slowly, but really I don't know what to make of it. I want to appear to Tom fully formed, metamorphosing in the chrysalis as I currently am, have been, since that terrible moment when I was sixteen. Mr M smiles at my expression. *Not very romantic or straightforward,* he says. *Perhaps I should have said never go to bed on an argument.* I smile and say, *no, that's great, really, really interesting, thank you.* Then I stand and say, *I'd better be going. Have a good afternoon.*

7.

I AM SO INTENT ON THE MEETING, FOCUSED ON Wednesday the twenty-second, panicked by each sandy minute trickling by, wondering how the distant stars and the dull gods will elbow and nudge His path on that day, how the fates' thread will trip Him my way, how a deity or devil will lift that veil and He will see me; even though I know these things not to be true and all of the magnitude of existence is indifferent to us, I am caught up in this sweet confectionery of wishing and hoping and thinking and praying, even though it's not real it could be, even though crystals are foolish, I am caressing quartz and thinking about how I will wash my hair the night before so it is its tousled loveliest, how I will stop eating the previous morning so I am light-headed and frail-feeling, how I will dress, how I will hold my breath for hours and days, one lungful of air and throat tight, repeating a mantra to the pulsing of my blood – that I almost miss Him.

I am on my way home from work, turning the knot of rose quartz that arrived in a prosaic brown envelope yesterday in one hand, replying to a text from my mother about an old school friend's new baby, my skirt riding up over my thighs as I walk as fast as I can, pulling at my hem every so often, heels tucked in my bag, hair in a dirty day-three bun, when He steps out of the Tube station with two other men, directly into my path: just like that. I stop dead in my tracks and my hand convulsively goes to my hair to pull it free and I want to cry and to be sick and to die and to run to Him; I wish at once I had never been born, that I had been expelled from my mother's womb as a rush of cells, wiped at with tissues, perhaps mourned, perhaps forgotten about, flushed deep into the sewers to emerge into the subtle brine of the English Channel.

This trio of men stops on a corner and one, not Tom, pulls his phone from his pocket and consults it. Gesturing down a side street, they turn, one by one, loping away. There is talk but Tom is not the one speaking, nodding His agreement. I am fascinated by the movement of Tom's body. One of the few times I have seen Him move is one tiny video in the depths of social media, when I scrolled back years and years, one of Him running and jumping off a white boat, narrow rosy soles into a blue sea. I tried to pause each frame, to scrutinise the beauty of His nineteen-year-old limbs, each angle, obtuse, acute, as He curled into His gleaming skin, hair longer than it is now. Salt god of the sea, crowned with coral; those were pearls that were His eyes. The grace shown in that video is still evident now; His motion measured and faultless, surefooted next to the accompanying oafs, slow, ambling with half-witted turns of heads.

I am following, I cannot help it, tugged forwards by that bind, that raspy twine wrapped roughly, tightly around my heart, strung to His. My heart protests, Jane to Edward. My limbs loosen, I try stepping on the very paving stones His have, hopscotching; His legs are long. Hot from the Tube, His coat is folded over one arm and I am so close that I can see the lower-back rumples on His shirt, the colour of the palest sky, the exact shade when the night creeps away in midsummer as an unwelcome guest, that white-washed blue, thin and bright, bringing with it the promise of a cloudless, shimmering-tarmac, buckling-railways, yellow-lawned, glorious, scorching, suffocating day. I can see from these dear creases that He lolls back in His desk chair, sleeves rolled, I can see a signet ring glinting too, and I see at once the wooden dish by His bed, usually empty, into which He must drop it each night, and vow to polish it lovingly, and I want to feel the warmth of that ring, heated with His blood, on my lips. I imagine how it would split those lips. O, how I would die for Him. His voice must be like clear honey, slick olives, rounded words, smooth and deep. I know it.

And it is too late, and I am sweating at my hairline, lip, small of back and backs of knees and I can smell the sudden stink of panic in my armpits and He is about to slip from my eager sight. He stops, stands aside politely, as bodies push past. In waiting, o patience, He glances my way and His glance slides over me like oil on latex. And then He is gone, and it is all wrong and I am betrayed. He has turned into this doorway, dipping His head as if used to small entrances, low ceilings, charming ram-shackle pubs with people who are not me. Can He not hear, not feel the double drum of our hearts? As the door swings shut behind them with a sour blast of golden ale and bitter stout, I see a tableful of people turning to Him, falling over themselves to administer jovial backslaps, gagging with bonhomie, gaping laughing mouths, eyes dark slits of mirth, a glossy girl fucking slut smiling, kittenish, half-standing for a one-armed hug with feigned and insulting indifference. I see Him raise an arm to – perhaps – slip it round her narrow torso, o He must feel her bones, and the door is shut and I am stricken, hollow-tongued, and fearful.

As I walk home, my shins burning, breaking into a run, my head pounds, my pulse beats in my throat. All is not lost – this only proves that the twenty-second is the day it must happen. I was not prepared, I am not prepared, and it will only be my fault if it goes wrong. It's time to go home, proper home, to think. I have avoided it in recent years, for obvious reasons, to avoid reliving the shame of my youth, the obliviousness of my mother, the layers of tainted happy memories. I feign a bustling social calendar and work commitments, harmless lies perpetuated in our family WhatsApp, backed up with the odd ambiguous picture of a restaurant door, a group of smiling girls screenshotted from Instagram, wondering if it is fooling my mother or my sister, whether they scrutinise and screenshot, zooming in, examining, or if they carelessly glance and forget. Neither of them challenges me, so I choose to think that they believe me. But the truth is, despite fleeing the village as soon as I could, I feel more myself there, for all London's anonymity, less hidden and constrained, fewer people to observe my body, my pace, my tread as they walk behind me, to stare in fascinated disgust at my unseemliness. I can breathe out in this familiar old world. A saturated, black sky, long, dry grasses, ribbons of water, and a childhood bed – Cass's things. Perhaps I can pinch up some of her wonderful life for myself, dust myself with the luck that slipped off her skin as she whirled around her room to Katy Perry or whatever. The great love that exists between me and Tom will unite us, but seeing Him has made me realise how easy it is to derail everything. At home, my sight will be keener. I can pull out my notebook away from looking, peering, observing eyes and plan how Tom will love me. I resolve to stop eating, and I crave sleep.

8.

THREE TIMES THIS YEAR, I HAVE TAKEN A SICK DAY. I am never actually ill; no matter how throbbing the headache, wrenching the pain, thick the cold, weak the limbs, oppressive and weighty and anguished the thoughts, I go to work, banking the day as one owed to me – one last-minute, guilt-free day off (for, inexplicably, I know I would feel guilt otherwise), when I wake up and the sky is too blue to stay indoors, or the wind too bitter to go outside, my mind too wretched. I decide that I shall take that day – cashing in last month's pain-cheque – and go home. Ordinarily, I would have set the scene by now: a weak cough or two, an ostentatious snapping of pills out of their plastic beds, the dramatic swig of water, faux-gag, perhaps after the weekend the rueful making of hot soothing drinks, squeezing stiff ropes of honey into a little mug, sharp, fresh lemon, taking small, wincing sips, winding a scarf about my neck. I should have spent all yesterday placing my dry palms upon my forehead, lifting my heavy hair off my neck irritably, shuddering as if too cold, pressing the glands under my chin with weak fingers. Whispering, *is it just me, or is it sweltering in here?* to the temperate office. I should have worked in a cheerful, determined, wet-eyed way, sighing often, and I would have been sent home at lunchtime, with instructions to not come back until I'm completely better. Simpletons. As it happens, my plan to travel home came at such short notice that I have to settle for a text to Marta first thing: *woken up feeling dreadful after a really bad night, so sorry, think will stay at home today as would hate to pass it on. Will log on at lunchtime if feeling up to it but otherwise hopefully see you Monday. Sorry again* [thermometer-in-mouth emoji].

And so, it is Friday morning and I am on the bus to King's Cross and my thoughts are low and determined, my hand in my coat pocket, curled around the colourless, glassy quartz I had taken – borrowed – from Anna's desk, for clarity, you know. My own rose quartz is tucked in my purse, glinting at me meaningfully as I dig out my card to tap in. To my surprise, a man sits next to me. I know I am not his only choice of seatmate as I too scanned the top deck when I sat down, viewed with displeasure the half-full bus, ponytailed young women with Michael Kors handbags on the seat next to them scrolling through their phones, thumbs quick; the young lads with sharp jaws sitting sideways, each in a different row, talking to each other, joking, you know, joshing, in forced voices, eating crisps; a round-spectacled businessman, Nigerian, I guess, leafing through onion-skin-thin scriptures; invisible old women on their way to the British Museum, grey best friends, or sisters, perhaps, prim twins in slacks and jaunty scarves.

But mercifully, really, there are spare double seats. And now, sitting, my small oilcloth overnight bag pressed on the floor, spare seat to my right, worn smooth and thin and faded with the buttocks of ten thousand Londoners, pencil-skirted, jeaned, trouser-suited, I am joined by someone who has scanned the other empty seats and found them lacking. Someone has chosen me. I deliberately don't look, but shift over, acknowledging my neighbour as he sits down solidly, no tentative perch or the insulting sideways slouch of schoolboy, backpack still on, ludicrous key rings jabbing my ribs. He is large and smells unwashed, not unpleasantly so; the sharp sweet smell of sleep, pillowcases and exhalation, and I imagine that feather-rustle of the duvet, and gentle breathing, a heavy arm leaden on my waist. I see grey denim and meaty thighs, a green waxed jacket, musty. His arm and mine are parallel, and touching, and our legs, bent at the knee, feet solidly on the floor, are parallel, and touching. His hands have golden hair on the knuckles and could knit around my wrists. I try to assess the shape of his body through quick, sly glances, and see that he is even larger than I initially thought, perhaps nervous to sit next to me, breathing in, trying in vain to reduce the volume spilling into my seat, over his belt. In truth, I quite like the warm press of solid, soft flesh, the tension in a great body as it struggles to diminish itself, my reassuring smile and the ember-burn of a generous deed done. I imagine his pathetic gratitude and his fantasies about me later, where I gasp and writhe under his bulk. I'm not offended. It makes me feel very little, and dainty, and kind. I close my eyes and thrill, imagin-ing that it is Tom and we are on our way to Cambridgeshire for the weekend (obviously my mother loves Him; the first time they met He charmed her completely with His shy smile, effusive compliments, that funny story He tells about our first date, the way He looks at me. She took me aside before we left the restaurant and told me what a lovely man she thought He was. An insipid comment, you might think, but really, the highest praise you could get from her). I am crying and the woman sitting in front of me removes her Michael Kors bag from the seat next to her and goes downstairs to disembark and the grey-jeaned, wax-jacketed man stands and surprisingly deftly slips into her empty seat. Stung, I stare at the back of his head, well shaped but overdue a haircut, hair running into his collar, otterlike. It is the first time anyone has touched me in weeks. I see the mirror image of my bus, heading south, inching down the road ahead of me and as the two buses draw close the driver gives a thumbs up to our driver, invisible to me downstairs, leans out of the window to shout a greeting, beaming, a crackle of connection in this city of solitude.

We creep to King's Cross and I alight awkwardly; my right ankle feeling a little bruised from its swift rolling last night, when I returned to the pub and crouched, puffing, by the green bins around the corner, waiting, calves hot. The group emerged several hours later, a raucous unkindness; a couple peeling off immediately in the direction of the station, another meandering away to the kebab shop where juicy coils of meat were briskly shaved to lie on chips. I looked and looked. There she was: honey hair, and her broad smile that wrinkled her little nose. She waited with Tom until His Uber came; they talked the whole time but I knew I could read boredom in His expression, eyes roving from His illuminated phone to the street and back, indifference in the touch to her narrow waist and impatience in the kiss He discarded on her cheek, before folding Himself into the car with a wave when it arrived. I didn't exactly have a plan but of course I followed her when she wandered off into residential streets with a clipped determination that spoke of a homeward journey; she trotted in her whimsical heeled boots like Bambi, ostentatiously crossing the road when a man appeared in the distance, speeding up with a concerned wobble. It's worth mentioning, perhaps, that I'd donned a woolly hat and wound a scarf about my face, wondering with detachment what I'd do once I'd caught up with her: spring at her, claw at her smooth skin, dash a bottle to the cement and slip its ragged edge into her flesh. In fact, nothing so admonitory; I said, *excuse me, is this yours?*, relishing the apprehension in her eyes as she turned, keys already warily in her palm, placed my hands on her shoulders, noting even as I did so the fresh scent of her perfume, the softness of her jacket, expensive, the frailty of her shoulders, the slight, yielding bones within, and pushed, hard. She stepped back once, twice, eyes staring, then fell hard on her tailbone, like a toddler. She looked affronted, incredulous. She'll have grazed palms, a bruised coccyx, she'll be fine, and o dear lord I felt so much better. Anyway, I turned and ran, which wasn't terribly dignified, I'll admit, especially when the ankle rolled when turning a corner, making me gasp. It's left me with a fond memory and a little gingerish step that I hope is mysterious and alluring.

I'm picked up at the station, and being driven by my mother transports me into sulky teenagerdom. I look at her smiling face, note the lines under her make-up, her coarsening hair, fading beauty, hate it. I slouch down in my seat and wind the window up and down, finger on the button. My phone buzzes and it's Marta: *Sorry to hear you're unwell. Feel better!* I roll my eyes. *Anything important?* My mother asks, eyes slipping between my phone and the road.

Without waiting for an answer, she continues, *how's Tom?* It is always her second question and heat envelops me. I told her once about Him, one Sunday-afternoon phone call, just to fill the silence, and now I need to remember the lies I have told, the dates I have said we have been on, the conversations we have had. *Fine, thanks.* She continues: *are you two an item, would you say?* I say nothing and roll my eyes again, so hard it hurts, and she smiles and mimes zipping her fading lipstick lips. She tells me about the school at which she sits on the board, not my alma mater, thank god, although she used to teach there, and I try not to listen and only to watch the grey-green monotony of the countryside slip by.

9.

I AM LYING IN THE BATH. MY THOUGHTS CLOUD THE
mirrors, already trickling condensation, teasing the peeling
paint on the ceiling, by the window, softening it. The hot
water, milky with shampoo, slides off my body, my hair is
bladderwrack on a briny bed. With a toe I pull the plug and the
smothering heartbeat silence becomes a muffled sucking, my
floating limbs settling, and I feel as an astronaut returning to
earth, sensing with fear and relief the grim return of gravity,
wondering at the weightiness of a body once so free, and light,
and without bounds. I am disgusted with my heaviness and
spend some time turning this way and that before the obscured
mirror, holding handfuls of flesh, thick fine-haired thighs,
pinkish and dimpled from the water and my soft, striped
stomach already peppered with bruises from my own pitiless
fingers. Tom loves me as I am, I know it, and I cry again because
He is so good to me, to love this, and I resolve to be better.

In my towel I go to the largest bedroom, and lie on the coveted double bed, looking around for signs of Cass. When we
went to university, birds fleeing the nest, she first, a collared

dove, I, a street pigeon, our mother cleared our rooms before our first trip home for Christmas, peeling down my tacked-up film posters, printouts of bearded musicians, mildly subversive leering postcards picked up from contemporary art galleries on day trips to London. My sister was different in that she always seemed to have taste; tidy little gallery walls before they became a thing, mixing photographs and postcards with some sort of skill; her, middle-parted, thin-thighed, in arm-in-arm glee with her little gang of friends; that Frida photo, vivid and green; *Sgt. Pepper's Lonely Hearts Club Band* even though she has never been lonely in her life; a yellowing *Tournée du Chat Noir*, clichéd but not bad for a twelve-year-old on a school trip. This is all gone, although I note with displeasure a pencil sketch of a dog, part of her GCSE art coursework, remains, framed as if it's actual art. It's not even that good; its mournful eyes are askew and its tongue is lifeless, tough. The other room has been sanitised and repurposed as a home-gym-office-space; a spindly exercise bike and a desk with a PC squatting alongside the single bed. My hair is slipping out of its towel turban to rest on the pillows and I can feel the fabric becoming damp and cold. As I loll, I hear a flutter, or rather crinkle, and put my hand beneath the pillow. There is a fold of paper, which I recognise immediately as being from the pad beside the telephone, and on it is my mother's neat handwriting which reads: *Welcome Home Sweetheart! Lots Of Love, Mummy xxx.* She always insisted we call her this; Cass still does. My one small rebellion was to refuse once I turned fifteen. On the note she has drawn a heart and a smiley face as well. I put it back under Cass's pillow and return to my own bedroom to dry my hair. My mother has left her travel hairdryer, black and brittle, in the bathroom, with the cord wrapped round the handle over and over and over. There is nothing under my pillow although I knew there would not be and I hate myself for checking.

When we were younger, Cass and I would sit in dream-laden bedroom forts, to us the pinnacle of luxury, a pillow-strewn floor, uterine duvet walls draped between bed and chair, every soft toy we could find our companions. We'd make these weekly, inventing elaborate games, dropping to once a month as we got older (for sleepovers with schoolmates, history's most feeble truth or dare: *I dare you to pinch Cass! Would you rather kiss James Barrett or Jamie Gardner? Flight or invisibility?* (my answer was always invisibility, Cass wanted flight) and then hardly at all from the age of fifteen, when, every so often, twice a year perhaps, we'd be sitting on Cass's bed, her drawing, reading, me writing, dreaming, Muji candles lit, fairy lights, some album on. Then Cass might ask, holding a pillow on her lap – offering it to me: *shall we?* And I'd take it and we'd move like clockwork, pulling the armchair over just so, the foundation of feathers, structurally unsound. Our thoughts would take on a cosy, confiding quality, like sisters in a film, in books, the Bennets or the Marches, arms tight around corseted waists, and our mother would find us whispering and giggling and say *what are you two laughing about?*, then shake her head at our silence, smiling, leave sandwiches and Diet Coke at a respectful distance. Sometimes I wonder whither this happiness fled and if I can ever claw it back. Then I think again about what happened, coldly, and the gasping raw feeling rises again and I know it's not possible now, not from her.

My mother has invited the neighbours round for supper – *you told me you were coming home with such short notice that I couldn't just cancel*, she'd said, widening her eyes and rolling them about in her skull. She squeezes me quickly and I stiffen: *lovely to have you though.* They arrive at quarter to seven precisely, tapping and scratching at the back door and Wyn steps in first, gold-framed glasses, thickly cropped white hair, limp flapping-sleeved blouse, skin hanging slackly from her upper arms, stockinged feet in little loafers, shortly followed by Martin, shorter than she, with a faded blue-green tattoo on one forearm, an Imperial Leather aroma and a gap-toothed smile. When Cass and I were younger and he and Wyn popped round he used to give us a pound each; instructed us to put our hands out, which we did, smartly, before dropping each coin with mock reverence into our palms. Cass always put hers in her piggy bank, whereas the coin, seductive and cool in my hot hand, spoke of delights and I would dawdle on my way home from school, would buy sweets and eat them furtively, rattling Smarties from their tube, slurping on cherry drops, letting Rolos dissolve on my tongue, licking up the sugar from my hands and feeling hotly shameful, then later bitter and furious when Cass bought a cool thin striped scarf, or a locket from Accessorize, or a purple fountain pen, or a set of nail varnishes, with her savings. Martin grins at me and drops a dry, heavy hand on my shoulder, saying *hello, love, I haven't seen you in years. How are you doing?* I suddenly wonder what his motivations behind the pound coins were when we were little. Can I remember him touching me before, the feel of that warm palm moving over flesh? I smile without showing my teeth, and move away.

Martin follows Wyn into the sitting room where my mother has put out little bowls of Bombay mix in anticipation of us all wanting a pre-supper nibble. *How's Cass?* I hear him ask in a low voice. Of course.

My mother has experimented with Ottolenghi for the evening, not entirely unsuccessfully, though I spend the rest of the night probing at fibrous strands of mango between my teeth, which means I say little and the conversation bumbles along without me. The main course is a silky aubergine curry with a slightly undercooked wild rice, which my mother has scattered artistically with pomegranate seeds. Again, it is surprisingly adventurous for her, she who refused to cook dishes from the entirety of southern Asia for the duration of our childhood, after my father left. I consider this as I chew each mouthful thirty-two times as we used to as teenagers, trying to eat as slowly as possible to let our stomachs register the sensation of fullness so we didn't eat as much, or so our mother said. My stomach feels like a pit never to be filled, yet I cut each morsel of food into minuscule pieces and chew for decades. I drink a glass of green and melony Sauvignon Blanc that I despise and then I pour and drink another. Martin and Wyn have been on holiday to Barbados and have pictures to prove it, showing printed grey photos of a seaweed-dredged beach, both grinning in wraparound sunglasses, Wyn in a baggy beach kaftan showing a cancerous red-bronze chest, Martin's repulsive and grey-furred. I imagine running my hand over it and my mind undoes itself in horror.

I find I am staring at Martin as he daintily eats. Once admonished by Wyn, perhaps, for gobbling his food, he takes his time, pushing morsels of oven-dark vegetables onto the back of his fork, squashing on some rice, anointing the lot with a dab of sauce before posting it, laden, between his gap teeth and chewing with relish, breathing heavily. A severe case of HKLP (Holds Knife Like Pen: an age-old way to uncover commoners), unfortunately, and I note my mother watching him as well, mouth small with disappointment. She never liked him as much as she liked Wyn, and I wonder if this is why, although it may also be to do with his tattoo, a reliable sign of being lower class.

That's an interesting way you're holding your cutlery, Martin, I say, tilting my head at him and looking at him in an open and suggestive manner. He looks at his knife and fork as if he's never seen them before and says, *what's that, love?*, showing us all the roasted aubergine in his mouth, dark with pomegranate molasses, half masticated. I turn to my mother. She looks appalled and is shaking her head at me.

Tell him, Mum, I say. *You smacked us for doing that when we were little.*

I did not, my mother says, eyes wide, at the same time as Wyn, who does not HKLP but is clearly just as bad for not knowing, says, *doing what?*

You're doing all right, Martin, for using the back of your fork, I suppose, I say. *Not upside down.* I demonstrate, elbows akimbo, really hamming it up. My mother is aghast and Martin's cheerful gap-toothed expression is faltering. After an excruciating two or ten seconds, I relent and I say it doesn't matter and my mother is also saying it doesn't matter and that she doesn't know what's got into me. Martin's fingers are lying slack and wondering, knife and fork rolling in his palms. I wonder how Martin holds his penis and whether it's like a pen and I am laughing hysterically and I have to excuse myself and lie down upstairs where I am racked with heaving heavy gasps that make my eyes stream. The tears roll down the curve of my cheeks and settle in the crease of my neck, sticky. I lie on the bed in the dark, holding my mother's note to Cass in a wet hand, listening to the indistinct voices from the kitchen below drifting up the stairs and through the floorboards, initially a low concerned murmur, rising slightly as they no doubt move on from the subject of my madness, strangeness, ugliness. My mother laughs a couple of times and someone rises with a chair-scrape to use the bathroom. I imagine Martin saying *toilet*, or even, god forbid, *the little boys' room*, and my mother fighting (or not) the urge to correct him: *lavatory, or loo*. I hear a stacking of china, the slide of knives and forks on plates being carried to the dishwasher, the creak and thud of the oven door opening and closing, the dull slide of a crumble hitting a trivet on the table. I have eaten and eaten but I am hungry and my eyes fill again with tears of self-pity. I know it's impossible but I swear I can make out the gentle crackle of the serving spoon piercing the topping, the scrape at the bottom of the dish, the wet slap of the sweet stewed fruit hitting the bowls, the creamy slide of custard from the jug, the slippery sound of tongues and saliva on metal, chewing, hums of appreciation. I hear Wyn and Martin getting up, an interminable goodbye, the shuffle of their feet on the gravel as they walk home, a scream of a fox. I wait and wait. I hear my mother locking the back door, tidying in the kitchen, loading the dishwasher, mounting the stairs, brushing her teeth, flushing the loo, quietly stepping down the corridor to her bedroom (pausing outside my door), and going to bed. I wait an extra half hour just in case, and even though it's almost one o'clock and I am exhausted, I creak down the stairs to the larder where the crumble dish lies covered in foil and I peel it back and eat everything that's left, barely registering what kind of fruit it is, what additional spice my mother has added, even though there's enough for two, three, scraping and scraping the dish clean with a teaspoon and crying with relief that there was some left for me.

My mother has definitely not forgotten the incident by the time I enter the kitchen for breakfast the next morning, squeezed into an old school gym T-shirt that is too short, and a pair of ancient, overwashed leggings that bag about my knees and make me feel thin. My ankle stopped hurting so, in celebration, I have painted my nails with my mother's sparkly pink holiday varnish, and my toes look festive and globular against the cool beige kitchen tiles. I am not supposed to be eating too many carbohydrates as I want Tom to feel my ribs when He embraces me but I am exhausted from a restless night of trying to sleep but thinking instead of wire-wool chest hair and pound coins and crumble and a great, suffocating weight so I find a crumpet in the bread bin which I toast and generously butter, licking the plate clean, and then I toast another and eat that too: springy, sweet warmth drowning in fat and salt. My mother watches me over her glasses from the kitchen table where she is laboriously completing a Sudoku grid, in pencil, lightly, so she can rub out the inevitable mistakes.

How's Cass, then? I ask, and she stares at me, running her pink tongue over her teeth, trying to gauge the mirth or malice in my expression. She eventually starts to speak and I deliberately don't listen to her lengthy response, to spite her, to spite both of them who let me be this way, who created this. The only power I have in this fraught relationship is indifference: nothing used to anger Cass more, back when we were friends. A film she loved: *it's fine I guess.* It never failed to make her spit with fury. I smile absently while my mother talks and open the cupboard where the biscuits are kept: half a packet of Garibaldis clipped up with a peg. I tune in again at a yawn of silence, and am appreciating the pebble-beach rustle of trees and the indistinct echo of a solitary car up the lane, when my mother sighs and, before I can close up my ears again says: *I don't understand what happened with you girls. You were so close.* She laughs abruptly. *When you were little, and had just moved into your own rooms, not a morning passed where I wouldn't find you both bundled up in one of your beds or the other.* I sigh in return and say, *yes, well.* I go upstairs, taking the packet with me, even though I hate Garibaldis. My mother reaches out to stroke my arm as I pass but her hand caresses the air, missing me by a few centimetres and I don't stop or slow. My arm vibrates at the absence of the touch.

I can't shake the feeling that I'm looking for something, the real reason I am here. I loiter on the landing, letting my thoughts permeate the house like scent. What titbit of Cass can I take for myself that might help bring me to Tom? I am sure, sure our hearts are seeking each other, but I am taking no chances. I decide that superstition and all that nonsense cannot hurt my cause. Drawn by some guiding force, I am borne to the spare room, where boxes of our things are jumbled in the tall cupboards, only now remembering a pair of matching friendship bracelets Cass and I had in our youth, each beaded with the other's name, how we both pretended to each other that they had special powers of luck, wearing them to juvenile sports matches, exams and the like. We imbued them with power; Cass used to whisper the name of boys she liked while kneeling in front of the mirror and it always seemed to work for her, them glancing at her in lessons, passing notes, where mine was less reliable. I cannot see this bracelet having a place in her polished life today, but she was always a fervent keeper of things, scrapbooks, journals – like me, I suppose, although my bracelet is long gone, thrown away, bitterly – so if it's any-where, it's here. I search through the cupboards, lifting art supplies and dejected soft toys to find a shoebox containing postcards and letters from her stupid, giggling friends and, finally, twisted in the ribbon from a long-lost Pandora box the bracelet. *ALICE*, it says. A proclamation. The colours of the threads were once purple and blue, now they are closer to grey. The black-on-white letters of the name still gleam as I wrap it around my wrist and tie it using the other hand and my teeth. My talisman. A bracelet that gave her luck; look at her perfect life, perfect beauty: my turn. I hope there's some left for me. I take a photo of my wrist, holding my arm aloft, at an angle so it looks as thin as possible, crooking my hand slightly so a wrist bone protrudes, and send it to Cass. She replies: *omg I remember those!!*, then, in quick succession:

are you at home?

that's nice

why?

I take the bracelet to church the next morning, heavy with centuries and filled with fragrant echoes and faded widows. I have sat on these pews countless times, squirming next to Cass, surreptitiously inching the sweets off a Christingle orange (plucking at the red ribbon of blood), nudging each other, fighting off giggles as parishioners doze and snore, sobering up at the sharp elbows of our mother. I remember through sensation, the increasing burn of my sitting bones resting on the dark, scratched wood, the fat nudge of the embroidered cushion hanging at my knee, Cass's thin, juvenile, wiggly, slouchy body next to mine. A glow of loss. And now, I sit next to my enraptured mother, running a finger over each beaded letter absently, and try to pray for this non-existent god to smooth my path, although I just end up thinking about what I shall have for lunch, fat stupid miserable bitch that I am; I hope we're having a decent pudding; sometimes my mother selects a satsuma as if it is a delicious confection and pushes the fruit bowl towards me.

Lunch is cheese on toast, crystalline mature Cheddar and Tabasco on a slab of granary, with the slices of cucumber and halved cherry tomatoes prepared in the same way since we were small. My mother hovers by the kitchen table, wiping it down, and eats my crusts, and a sharp little apple, core and all, while emptying the dishwasher. She surprises me by offering a slice of cake for pudding, baked by Jenny from church and choir, whose husband ran off with a woman from Latvia, poor thing. She doesn't mention, or hasn't noticed, the missing crumble. She keeps trying to ask how I am, and I say fine, and that work's fine, and the house is fine, and my friends are all fine, and, you know, busy, really. She asks how my running is going and then tries to explain barre to me, which she has just started, even though I know what it is. She asks about Tom: *I notice you haven't mentioned Him much, sweetheart, is everything all right with you two?* Tears spring to my eyes and I will them away, carefully scraping my plate for crumbs, pressing them to my lips: *it's all perfect,* I say. *He makes me so happy.* She smiles in relief or triumph. *I am glad,* she says, *after all that unpleasantness at Bristol*... My palms itch and I rub them on my thighs, hard.

I'd love to meet Him, she says, as she takes my plate and adds it to the now-empty dishwasher, carefully. Her deliberate, studied movements make me think: *she doesn't believe me.* I hate her for it. *He's quite busy at the moment,* I say, *with a lot of weekend work too. And we've got plans over the coming weeks, with friends.*

You sure you're not ashamed of your old mother? she smiles, and I imagine Tom knocking at the back door, ducking His head to enter, offering an armful of flowers, a bottle of wine, my mother laughing at His easy jokes. I imagine Him taking in her slenderness, her neatness, her blue eyes and wondering how on earth we could be related. I imagine Him looking at photographs of me and Cass, so alike, and finding the fork in the road where Cass's face elevated to beauty, and mine fell short. Would He still love me? He would, He must. Having wiped the table again, my mother invites me on a walk, *to burn it all off,* she laughs.

By the time I am on the train back to King's Cross, having spent three days with my mother watching police procedurals;

72

listening to her telling me news from the church, from the vegetable garden, from the hairdresser's; watching her stew vats of woody rhubarb; trying on old clothes from our teenage years, the ones that haven't been thrown away, appallingly low-hipped and baggy-legged, trailing frayed ends, straining against my bulk; playing CDs for the first time in a decade, all the way through, not even skipping the tracks I never really liked; sitting under the apple tree in the garden until it got too cold, writing, writing, writing, I think I have our meeting mapped out. As surely as Odysseus nocked an arrow weighted with bronze onto a well-polished bow, drew it back and released it so it flew through twelve shining axe-heads, so shall our first true encounter be: inevitable, momentous, dazzling. This is what will happen: whereas ordinarily I don't much like to think what He does outside of His life with me, for the first time I will properly look at His schedule; beforehand only dreamily half-done and imagined, a wistful, o He is in Kefalonia now, or, tonight is His office Christmas party. I will merge the cryptic notifications on His laptop, which never seem quite up to date, His work schedule, which He is sometimes still logged into when I check, and the paper calendar nailed to His wall only randomly filled in with a delicate scribble, but those wonderfully half-formed thoughts curling from His mind, together with knowing where He works and where He shops and where He sleeps, I will find Him. The twenty-second is a beacon to which I and He are drawn, weary travellers, and I tremble to think of the things that might be in His calendar for that day: perhaps He has taken it as annual leave, sensing the auspicious nature of the date, or perhaps He will take a particular train, or go to a particular bar and I shall be waiting. It is a sorry truth that that precious hum, sounding deep in the cavern of my heart, is not yet audible to Him; He will not cock a head, frown, a dear line appearing on His brow, as He tilts His head to establish its bloody source. I just need to help Him, guide His head to my breast, press His ear to me.

And now, on the train, I am what feels like the only adult in a carriage full of school-age children returning from some appalling excursion, all pungent and screeching, about fourteen years old, and I feel an unexpected pang of wistfulness for those days, of being that age – unaware of one's own innocence. In truth, I hated school; although I tried hard and did moderately well, I found subjects difficult for varying reasons, arachnid numbers skittering away from my head, the drowsy repetitiveness of Latin, the mottled-pink thighs and gym shorts of PE, my shameful body. The teachers disliked me, and said I was secretive (my mother, who thankfully never directly taught me or Cass, asked what they meant; I did not know); I had friends, I suppose, or a friendship group, really – and Cass, up to a point – but preferred to spend my lunchtimes in the library, leafing self-consciously through a prolix dictionary, reading the works of Hardy and the Brontës, all three: rational, loving Charlotte; wild Emily, buried in a coffin sixteen inches wide; and serious, subversive Anne, who used to be my least favourite but now I'm not so sure. Cass would barrel into the library and find me, rolling her eyes at my drab bookishness and insisting I come and sit with her knock-kneed comrades, to alternatively titter and mock-swipe at the pack of white-shirted, backpacked boys, Lynx Africa. It takes you back, doesn't it?

Those squat striped ties, with absurdly fat knots, the grinning triumph of passing an impromptu uniform check with the top button stealthily undone. When everything changed, Cass stopped collecting me, and it took a few weeks before I no longer turned my head every time some chattering thing came into the library's gentle dormancy, expecting to see the dark pennant of her hair.

Everyone in my class returned for a whatever-year reunion; photos surfaced on some social media platform or other, of greased faces pressed side to side in the assembly hall, the football field, smiling, all teachers or solicitors now, probably. One summer evening last year I drank a bottle of rosé and systematically social media stalked everyone in my year and the year above, Cass's year, that I could remember. The profile of one boy – no, a man now – I scrolled through particularly assiduously and I observed coldly the beauty of his girlfriend who looked like she could be South Indian, or Sri Lankan. I googled her in turn and found out she was involved in some sort of AI start-up: of course. Beautiful and clever and rich and he does not deserve her, and does not deserve to be happy and I hope very much that she leaves him or she dies and he is bereft. They live a ninety-seven-minute walk from me and have a French bulldog called Otis. When I scrolled back very far through his timeline, through the neon face paint, Edward Cider-hands, all-nighters in the library university years and those just before, school ties, long fringes, and a white cast appearing on his left arm – his timely stumble down the steps outside the changing rooms – I stopped in a panic. I can see his mocking face, hear the derisive laughter now. The very thought of returning to those sage-green halls makes my cheeks burn.

Now, these children on the train shriek and I can barely tell if they're speaking English or not. I feel old. The girls are laughing and looking at the boys who are pretending not to look back – o nostalgia – and, nauseous, I close my eyes and try my hardest to think not of school, not of my sister, not that boy and his broken arm, and his beautiful new life, but Tom, only Tom.

10.

THE HALLOWED DAY OF THE TWENTY-SECOND SLUNK
by unmarked by anything and anyone apart from the gasping
tears I wept in the work loos, face glazed with salt like a ham,
eyes wet and pink, my heart tugging at my ribs. His calendar
had been empty, the blank square morphing into a mocking
howl. I dragged tissues over my cheeks, taking off half of my
make-up, and went home, where I flipped and slid through a
deck of tarot cards I had found at home, hoping and hoping for
the lovers, the sun, the high priestess, and finding instead the
hermit, judgement, and death, death, death. I had waited in His
flat all morning, having cleaned quickly, briskly, shaking out
my hair and waiting for the gods, the fates, the stars, the planets
to steer Him back to me. It felt as if my heart might swell out of
its cage, seeking its twin. I had been so sure that this would be
the day: He'd forget some important papers and have to dash
back to the flat for them, or something else, anything – book,
birthday present, credit card, *The Economist*, football boots,
gym kit, hat, jumper, keep cup, laptop, mobile charger, packed
lunch, railcard, security pass, train tickets, umbrella, USB stick.

Waterproof jacket. And there I'd be. Except He didn't, and so I wasn't. I returned and waited outside His flat all evening and He didn't materialise; the empty eyes of windows peered at me. I wish I knew what He had been doing, who He was with, what happy-go-lucky last-minute plans had arisen, what genial text had steered His feet away from home, my waiting arms, towards what fickle goddess had lured Him astray. Perhaps I hadn't cleansed my crystals diligently enough, bathed them in sunlight or seawater, or perhaps I had been wrong to trust thick Anna's calculations. I try to stop my thoughts but I cannot help but think of that girl in her boots, my shoving hands. I think of Tom looking at His empty calendar on the twenty-second and feeling an inexplicable void, a longing and, unable to hear the wild song in my heart, texting her instead: *dinner tonight?* I imagine Him kissing her scraped palms, stroking her neck. O I feel each millimetre of that touch and my body is electric.

I was foolish to rely upon others. It has to be me. But tonight, this fateful Friday, His work calendar was marked *V&A LATE*, with no further details other than those six shouted letters, that curlicue a caress. I am here, struggling to hear the hum of my heart over the music, chatter, footsteps, but confident it will lead me to Him. My wish for autonomy didn't stop me texting Cass, always the artistic one of us both: *what should I wear on a date to a V&A late? What should I talk about?* For someone with a high-flying job (my mother's words, not mine), she is always incredibly quick to respond; I imagine her holding up her hand to pause discussion in the middle of a meeting so she can message me at her leisure. Life comes so easily to her. Her answer: *o fun! Normal/cute clothes, say how art makes you feel – don't need any more than that.* I couldn't be bothered to reply to this vaguery but I clicked and a brown thumbs-up emoji appeared in response.

I fight my way around sculptures to the linen-topped bar, catching the eye of a bartender who notices me flatteringly quickly and pours my glass of white wine with aplomb. He winks at me as I tap out my payment and reach for the drink, and I am staggered and uncertain, afraid. I cautiously decide this is a good sign, that my normal/cute clothes are working, and drift away to find a perch in a corner of the entrance hall, and peer at the evening's programme of events in the irritatingly violet shadow. The wine is acid bright on my tongue. I am aware, suddenly, that a body is near mine, firm where I am soft. Masculine. He has sat down next to me, chosen that hollow blank to my left and thought: *I'll sit there. I choose you.* I stiffen in my pose, and think – *surely, surely it can't be* – but it must – and I turn my head and—

No. It is not Him, and I am stupid for thinking it could be, sitting as I am in a prearranged spot for meeting another man – this man, I think, who is looking at me, at my face and my eyes, smiling. Not Him. This man is leonine; with sandy hair, red-gold stubble, a snub, slightly pink nose, round denim eyes.

Are you Alice? he asks. I nod automatically. His voice is rich, posh. I have the impression that he smiles at me again, but he can't have done, because he never stopped smiling in the first place. His smile is refreshed, renewed, at this knowledge that I'm here, and I'm Alice. He looks harmless, kind even, but I wonder if he means to lure me to a dark corner, or to charm me back to his flat and grip me hard by the throat and rape me and possibly kill me, slipping a kitchen blade between my ribs, point touching my protesting heart, semen sliding off my cooling thighs as he wonders how to dispose of my body. He will run his hands through his thick fair hair, most un-Tom-like, then will work to remove my arms and legs and head, perhaps working his way through the knives by his butcher's block, the serrated bread knife carving cleanly under his weight, popping knobble-headed bones out of sockets with a pointed and flexing filleting knife. Is a meat cleaver too dramatic? Possibly. Before bundling these slack limbs, the hollow bowling ball of my head, into black bags, unsure what to do with the flabby trunk of my body, breasts flat, blood-smeared and grey. Whatever he decides, I will end up in some secret corner of the river, or a canal, weighted down with yellow London stone, chipped bricks, trapped under the khaki Thames by a shopping trolley. Aldi, rather than Waitrose. I wonder how long it will take for anyone to notice I am dead. My housemates might wonder, assume I've gone home. A week, perhaps, before a colleague might text, then call, then alert the police. They will search my flat and find my box of Tom under the bed. That will not do; when I get home, if I get home, I should move it somewhere safer.

You must be James, I say, and I wonder where on earth this composed, normal-sounding first sentence came from. He smiles and puts out a large hand to shake; I take it, warm, dry, and my hand feels little. *Glad I found the right corner of the gallery*, he says, gesturing at our seats, and then at the enormous tangle of glass suspended from the ceiling. *When your text said the north-west corner, I almost got out my compass.* He smiles to show he is joking, I think. My heart is racing, and I wish I had never come here, even though this is what I wanted: a date, a handsome one at that, so that when I see Tom, I seem appealing and in demand, shielding my friendlessness and forsakenness. Terrified of silence, and of James's lingering or fading smile, I say: *so how do you know Anna?* (even though I know the answer) *Durham,* he says. *Or rather, I played rugby with Wadders – James Waddesdon, her boyfriend – and we became friends too. She's great.*

Yes, great, I say.

After a brief pause we both say: *so do you—* then stop, then laugh. *Do you come here a lot?* James says. *Not much,* I say. *I love it here though.* He nods at the programme in my hand. *Fancy going to the dance performance in the Raphael gallery, I think it is?* I shrug, then nod, and feel as if I am in a film. Not once has this felt so easy – perhaps I should have asked Anna to introduce us sooner, practised harder, honed my light, carefree conversation over weeks and months rather than days. I remember the sick feeling of dread when I turned my chair to Anna at work, said casually: *that friend you mentioned. Is he still single?*

I had expected a scathing look, a poorly disguised titter, but she had clasped her hands to her bosom and radiated happiness or triumph my way: *o my GOD this has made my life! He's honestly so so nice, you'll like him so much! He's got like, an edge to him? I think you'll get on.* She did not refer to the twenty-second, or my previous questions about the stars, and I didn't know whether to be hurt or grateful.

The gold glint of a ring on his little finger as he raises his glass (red wine) to his lips and stands. My eyes travel from his hand to his arm to his chest to his groin, and as I stand too I think again of his rough knee forcing my legs apart, slick hand pressed on teeth, saliva, breath catching in my throat, wild terror, and follow him. He's tall and walks in that way they do, you know. Lazily, proudly. *Shall we?* he asks. Yes. There is a silence as we weave through the thunderous crowd.

The dancer is a Dalí shadow of a man, all creeping tiptoeing limbs, spindly and unnerving. His face turns away from the lights, and the back of his head is finely shaped, hair plastered in waves, his skull fragile, with hollows behind the ears like a child. He stalks backwards, fingers loose and long. As I watch his body I am aware of my body, the heat rising in my cheeks. James's head is cocked to one side in a studied way as he watches the writhing performance piece splitting shadows. His expression is neutral, arms folded, chin up, eyes half-lidded. I will go home with him if he asks, or assumes, I know that. My eyes slip around the circle of voyeurs, hoping one will look up, drag their dark, bright eyes from the mesmerising twisting display to eye me, just for a second, so they know I was here, in case they read about my murder in a few days. No one notices my look; they are all gaping at the dancer, joylessly, blankly. I am working up the courage to put my hand on James's golden arm, half-turning to do so, when to my hideous shock, by some miracle – although I know it is meant to be – I see Tom through a doorway. He is passing along a corridor running parallel to the darkened gallery in which I am standing, striding past an archway, shrugging on His jacket (soft denim, with folded faded receipts in the pockets, my hands have often curled in there, sweating), looking curiously in at the sinuous dancer, who is now slipping among the discomfited spectators.

We are perhaps three metres apart. My soul exhales in a great rush of joy and it is as if a puzzle piece, one that until now has seemed misshapen and ill-favoured, has been cautiously rotated and proven a perfect fit. My lungs are leather. My heart beats a tattoo and I feel so clearly the string somewhere under my left ribs, tightly and inextricably knotted, from the soft cavity in my chest, vibrating between us, and if I were to reach out and brush it, it would resonate beautifully, like a lyre. Would the note be clear, light, or rich, round? My hand raises itself to both smooth and tousle my hair, I turn away from James and towards Tom and for the first time our eyes meet and I am stunned by the humanity of Him, the repose in His face, the wave of His hair. I go to Him.

Hello. Slipping through the doorway I walk alongside Him, as I have longed to do. I cannot comprehend His nearness; I am in tremulous ecstasy. Surely I do not imagine the heat radiating from His body to be absorbed by mine, the answering call of His heart to my own? As pain bursts with delicious familiarity in my breast, my mind unfolds with imaginings so familiar and dear to me they feel like memory: o the times we will walk side by side like this, checking my impatient steps to match His calm stride: squeezing hands as we emerge from a festoon-lit barn into a burst of biodegradable confetti and shining faces; barrelling hungrily into our favourite restaurant from a tempest, collapsing umbrellas and pushing back wet hair, His hand lightly guiding me to the little table at the back; lazily, luxuriously along a wide Mauritian beach, fingers grazing, sun like lava on skin. I am emboldened by these thoughts to reach and brush the arm of His jacket with shy fingers as I repeat the word He has not heard over the echo of my heart – *hello.*

He turns His face to me and I am blessed with the force of His beauty, those eyes look dark in the dim light but they are looking at me, at me, and I am looking at Him and I am jubilant. His face moves rapidly from surprise to confusion to wry amusement. *Hello?* His voice lilts with question and I want to suck words from His mouth and roll them around with my tongue.

You're Tom, aren't you? I ask, and His brow furrows a little and I can see He is trying to place me. I will Him to hear the twin drumming of our hearts and to realise the magnitude of our love and how small and neat my hand will feel in His, my face in His neck. Memories and wonder spool in His brain as He puzzles: am I a childhood playmate, forced together by our mothers to sit across from each other in nappies, crossly snatching building blocks in the shade? A school acquaintance whose glossy hair, like a magpie's wing, caught His eye across a sprawling exam hall, a crowded assembly? A friend of his sister's, gawky and bespotted once but now a breathless, strange beauty? A one-night stand (I flush) at university, intoxicated, clashing teeth on a dance floor, hands moving? A stranger on a shared commuter carriage who struck up conversation, just once, or who smiled every now and then, as if she knew Him? Or, that rarity, true love, drawn through time and space to Him.

Hang on, have we met? His voice is warmer and scratchier than on His voicemail message, a rich curl of peanut butter on wholemeal toast. I open my mouth, unsure of what I should say next. The bouquet of words in my throat, once watered and luscious, pollen-dusted and fertile, rattles, dry. *I love you*, I want to say, *I know you.*

Yes, I say.

Unsaid: I run my hands over your things like they are your body; I know which poems move you to dog-ear pages, I have learned them breathlessly by heart; I know your nicknames for your shallow friends and theirs for you too; your standard takeaway order from stapled receipts; your preferred brand of toothpaste, shampoo, soft moisturiser; how often you trim your delicate nails, run a trimmer over a bristled chin; which crisps you leave until last in a multipack – I know whether you have slept poorly or well, eaten poorly or well, felt poorly or well; I know your charming peccadillos: balancing knives half-off the work surface, forgetting your multivitamins, leaving the milk out on the counter, lid off, not picking up your post for days, these are forgiven for I love you – Tom – o I know your thoughts better than you do, and know that no two are more suited than we.

I open my mouth again, the booming bass lulls and my phone shrills. Irritated, I pull it from my jacket pocket and glance at it: *Cass*, it says. *You can get that*, Tom says encouragingly. WhatsApp chat aside, Cass hasn't tried to call me in about five years, and I think of my mother, and dither, anguished, before wondering if she's checking up on me on my date and becoming infuriated.

Tom smiles at me, draws His own phone from a loose pocket and checks it. He says, *sorry, I'm late for—* He waves His hands, expansively. *I'll see you around.* He walks away – He walks away from me. I stand there, phone vibrating in my hand. I decline the call, and it rings again. I decline once more, set my phone to do not disturb. James has followed me, hands in his pockets, hanging back respectfully until now. By arranging to meet James here, I had hoped that Tom's first sight of me, smiling easily with another, would awaken a burst of jealousy or possessiveness, would fill Him with hunger to know, to have me, would electrify, jolt awake the quiet cord connecting our hearts. I don't think Tom even noticed him. I am looking at Tom's back, broad, retreating from me, away from warmth, and me, into the brisk evening. He doesn't hesitate, doesn't look back at me. He didn't know me. The whole encounter had lasted maybe ten seconds. A slipping open of the glass doors and He is gone and I take James's hand from his pocket and hold it, bold, and stalk away, pulling him with me, pushing into the crowds, shouldering, elbowing, heeling, toeing. We came here for a date so we'll have one.

We are seated in the round and a poet is speaking words quietly and fiercely; they roll from her lips and splash onto the floor, run towards my toes. I inch them backwards. James's hand is on the seam of my waist and hip, his lips have brushed my neck three times as he has whispered to me and chilled me. He points out a middle-aged man in a fleece gilet who has nodded off across from us, and I smile but am distracted: I cannot shake Tom from my mind. I am gazing at the poet and her expressive, anguished eyebrows, hands creatures. I rise and James springs up too, no doubt hoping his hour has come, that we can cease frowning and nodding respectfully and leave, stop pretending these words cast at us are anything more than clumsy, wielded imprecisely: *Mother*, the poet spits, *you made me.*

As I head for the exit, James trailing behind, I see it clearly now, this test set for me by the gods: I see that I am still woefully unprepared for Tom, despite my silly little notebook, barely worthy, despite our twin souls – I had the chance to captivate, to charm, and my thoughts were stupidly and shamefully dull and my tongue out of practice. I need more experience, in mind and in body, to be ready for Him. Our walk is circuitous and, conscious of my need to practise the art of conversation, I point half-heartedly at some sculptures I like. James talks about this and that. *Mm*, I say, nodding. *Mm*. I really can't think of what else to say. We pass under the Edmund de Waal and I numbly absorb its curvature, white teeth in red gums and then we are outside and I am silent, thinking, James looking at me guardedly or with hostility. *That guy*, he says, putting his hands into his jacket pockets with finality, *is he a friend of yours? No*, I say, and press my mouth to his.

11.

I BECOME SENSIBLE OF THE PEACH GLOW SLIPPING through my eyelids, one that changes to the flat white light of an overcast sky as I open my eyes. My head pounds, fist on a door; it feels as if the swollen tangle of my brain is slowly turning in its cerebrospinal fluid, knocking each curve of my skull as it drifts. Last night I took James by the hand and we went in a taxi to his house, in Balham, shared with others, although I didn't see or hear them. We took a bottle of wine from the cupboard and drank from crystal glasses cloudy from London's calcified water. I knew a cloth dipped in white vinegar would fix the ghostly tint and opened my mouth to say so, but James put his hand in my hair so I drank the wine, body temperature and spicy. When we went upstairs I turned the light off when he turned it on and I lost myself. My lips crackle. Rolling over (my brain knocks on bone and I gasp) I see that I am in my own bed. I don't remember coming home, just a cadaver heaviness and a rolling head spin, mouthfuls of sour wine, making him turn away as I undressed and slipped under the covers and utter, consuming emptiness. The clock rolls round and round and I put my hand on my soft stomach, wondering if I'm pregnant. I briefly imagine a flicker of life there, germinating, a wriggling white larva, blind. Nausea seeps through me and I am disgusted although the rational part of me protests that I would no longer be alone.

Last night under James's hands (callused where his fingers met his palm, leaving faint white scratches where he ran them up my body) I closed my eyes and opened my mouth and thought of Tom. Perhaps I moaned, moved. How had He not felt each heart tugging towards its twin – each ruby knot of muscle aching to cleave to the other? Our eyes had met, light bending through the crystal lens, the thin tissue of the retina, through the optic nerves to the pearlescent brain where thoughts shiver, and He did not know me. I feel foolish and run the meeting through my mind. I try to recall the precise words He said, as He looked at me: *hello, have we met?* No, that's wrong. His jacket was the colour of His eyes which are the colour of His sofa which is the colour of the sea. No – denim, with the receipts – chewing gum, chicken breasts, beansprouts, a net bag of sweet clementines. He is slipping away. I imagine His hands, soft, on my thighs and close my eyes, re-memorise the fumbling antics of last night, changing the scuffed, soft bed to the pristine flat I know so well, James's golden head darkening to Tom's. By the time I've thought it through, four, five, times, the memory is delicately set. I turn to the wall and sleep.

It is strange but I dream of Cass and it too is a memory, her hair or my hair tickling my cheek as we crouch together, examining a dead vole on gravel. Small and almost completely round it looks unharmed, velvet, and we cannot think what might have killed it. A deadly disease, old age, fright. *Can voles have heart attacks?* We each poke it with a concerned finger and it is cold and stiff and so void of life we stifle screams. When I wake I lie, trying to grasp the dream as it slinks away, thinking I have gripped its tail only to open my triumphant clenched fist and find nothing.

I slope down to the kitchen, first waiting for Sasha to head out for brunch with her stupid, vacuous coven of friends. The tea I brew is so brown and strong it has a bitter edge; I add still more milk until it is a flat, opaque tan, unpleasantly cooled, a faint iridescent scum settling on the filmy surface and gathering at the edges: low tide. Once I interned in an office where a woman smilingly asked me to make her a cup of tea the colour of my skin; keen not to misstep, I held my forearm to the steaming mug in the office kitchenette to compare – I have managed it perfectly now, without even trying. Funny. My phone, re-trieved from the pocket of my coat, is dead: battery expired and screen black, scratched and malign. I wonder about my movements, the last second the police would have been able to track me had I died last night: they say London is the most spied-on city in the world, unblinking eyeglasses dispassion-ately and thoroughly recording our slim, sorry lives. Would they have been able to find me in the security files of the V&A, a murky figure with James, or in the stop-motion footage of the wide roads of South Kensington, inky against the orange radiance of the night? Plugged in, my phone awakens and I see six missed calls, four voicemails, and three texts, all from Cass. I ignore them. Like I said, indifference infuriates her. As the tea coats my tongue, an oil slick, and I scrutinise the kitchen tiles, their freckling of sauce spatter, I see in the corner of my vision another text arrive: James. *Hope you got home OK. I'm in a sorry state! Off to Dublin for work tomorrow for a week but let's have a drink when I'm back. Next Friday? X.* It leaves me cold, but I resolve to be good, and respond: *Sounds great!* [blowing a tiny kiss emoji]. I can't bear the thought of reading a response and being drawn into an interminable conversation so I consider that I have done my bit for the day and put my phone on do not disturb again, sullenly drawn back to my bitter bed, where I spend the rest of the afternoon, crunching vitamin C pills to dust and guzzling water, reading Tom's messages to me in the cleaning app. He thanks me every week; tips me £2.

I spend two hours on Sunday morning at Roseacres, still somehow nauseous and dehydrated from Friday night. My age, I suppose, and I feel the bloom in me withering, despite – or perhaps because of – the dotage of my current companions. Ironically, given last week's fake sick day, I can also feel the beginnings of a cold scratching at my throat and curling up in my head. I remember those revolting teenagers on the train and know for certain that they guffawed their viruses my way, finely sprayed from their cherry lips and freckled, upturned noses. The gods have decreed: my turn. I kill time being Elsie with Dorothy, trudging down history's most boring memory lane: *remember when we picked blackberries in the garden, Elsie?* All right, Seamus Heaney. I smile and nod. *Lovely, weren't they, Dot?* She talks about Mr Drabble at school, and his pocket watch or whatever, and to spice things up I ask: *remember when*

Mr Drabble touched you inappropriately, Dorothy? She is not as perturbed as I would have supposed she'd be, but she says: *o no, Elsie, he were ever so kind.*

Mr M isn't in his chair when I reach his room, although I expected this – he will be at lunch, supping at today's offering, perhaps having moved on eagerly to pudding, despite it only being midday. One glass of green sherry per resident per meal. I check the corridor, then go to his water glass and lick the rim, all around. I cough on his pillow, hard. I spit on his toothbrush. I don't want to hurt him, I just want him to catch my cold, boost the pathos, encourage visits from his family. I can imagine the phone call now: *how's my grandfather getting on, nurse?* A high Irish lilt: *o he's not well at all, the poor dote – to be sure, he'd appreciate a visit – that's grand.* I may be overdoing the accent. But surely this must come to pass – Mr M in bed with hot honey and lemon, Vicks, grandchildren at his bedside, in the lamp's glow. I gaze at the photographs in their silver frames.

Shit. A shuffling tread and the gentle burble of old voices – lunch is over. I must look horribly guilty when I turn and see Mr M walking hunchedly and steadily in, but he seems unbothered by my presence, and in fact, smiles and accepts with a dry warm hand my help into his seat. I am careful to speak close to him – *what have I been up to?* I see the book on Everest on his bedside table and put my hands on my hips, heart pounding. *Scaling mountains, you know, the usual.* His response: *tea with the Queen.* Laughter, trying earnestly to cast my disease and hangover over him for that means a tickle, a wheeze, and visits and visits and visits. Bowed heads around a bedside, a fortuitous corridor encounter: *o you've met my ministering angel, have you? I thought you two would get on.* A cough, a twinkle, a recovery. A laughing reference in the wedding speech: *a few of you will know it all started when my dear grandfather caught a cold . . .* A hand around my waist, smiling, smiling, smiling, giddy with champagne.

I spend the afternoon in bed trying not to eat then giving in and ordering a pizza which I tell myself I'll save half of but I eat it all. I eat it all. I cry, scratch and pull at my stomach until it stings, then I haul myself upright and plunge my hands under the bed, recognising by its smoothness and pulling out a bright orange shoebox taken from Tom's recycling. I open it and sift through the contents, pawing at scraps of paper, secreted from the notebook He keeps by His bed, of His hazy night-time thoughts, some so scrawled and veering that He mustn't have turned on the light at all. I like these best; I trace my fingers over these barely legible scribblings, longing for the night that all they will read is *Alice, Alice, Alice.* Also in this box is a tissue I sprayed with His cologne and sealed in a clear plastic bag: almost six months old, the scent is fading, and I ration myself. I bought a new bottle of it, it sits on my bedside table, but it's not the same, somehow. An old toothbrush I found in His bathroom bin that I trail, scratchily, across my skin. Most riskily, a Polaroid photo, presumably from a night out, that He'd pinned up with a weak magnet (a bottle opener from Mexico) that shot to the floor as soon as I opened the fridge. The magnet had bounced, the photo had dropped and slid itself under the fridge and I fished it out (I thought: *I must find a way to sweep up this gritty mess of desiccated defrosted peas and dust – a dampened cloth on a ruler perhaps*; I brought one the next week) and almost put it back on the fridge before seeing Tom's face and putting it in my pocket. At home I scratched out the faces of the three people accompanying Him in the photo: two carefree, thin girls and a shorn-headed man pouting, so He remains the only open, handsome face in that dark room, smiling, surrounded by ghosts. I push the box back under the bed, glimpsing the others behind it. Different memories. I lie down again, pulling the covers up to my chin. I can smell the sharp miasma of my body under its T-shirt, one taken from the back of Tom's chest of drawers, unloved and rumpled, clearly unworn for years. I refolded each remaining T-shirt, arranging everything as immaculately as possible and was touched to see He tried to maintain this neatness for several weeks afterwards, attentively trying to replicate the folding it had taken me three YouTube videos to perfect. Tears roll from the corners of my eyes and salt my hair. I ring my mother and regret it immediately: *o you don't sound well at all, have you been taking your vitamins?* I pull the covers entirely over my head and answer in monosyllables.

Wednesday again. The key catches in the lock but I am hasty and it takes me several tries to pass that bland gloss-paint barrier; unyielding metal grates and clicks. I breathe. I am terrified that His flat, always a haven, as familiar and kind as a well-worn pair of jeans, will have shifted, become menacing and hostile to my loving touch, now that our eyes have met and He did not know me. Inside, I set down my bucket and breathe in; the air is warm with the scent of Him and soft and silent and my vision wavers with tears. All is the same; a solo toothbrush, its foamy spray on the mirror; His pillow smells the same; His gym shoes are slightly askew where He toed them off, exhausted (I rearrange with care); solitary cardboard sleeves in the recycling; a new book on His bedside table, the bookshop receipt used as a bookmark twelve densely typed pages in and I am glad. It was nothing, that meeting, a prelude to the piece. My eyes take in the slight shifts of His space, noting each, reading them – a half-empty packet of cold relief pills and a glass of water sit on His bedside table; we, my love, so alike, sickening together. How He would press a dry hand to my damp face, tenderly. How gently He might kiss my head, how softly He would step to my bedside table bearing a honey and lemon, or buttered rum, blackcurrant throat pastilles and Bronchostop. I lift the glass to my lips, swill water in my mouth and let it fall back into the glass. I want Him to swallow me. I open the tall cupboard where His clothes hang and crawl in to slump with relief in the bottom of it, where some of His shoes lie, along with a pair of novelty slippers – large slabs of salmon nigiri – which I detest for their crass optimism, which I just know were a present from someone – his mother, perhaps, offering them to her rueful handsome son with a forced jollity – *you like sushi, don't you darling? I thought they were rather fun!* He would have smiled generously and said, *I love them, Mum, thank you*, despite their hideousness, and kept them because of loyalty and love and goodness and guilt, because He is better than I will ever be.

I close the cupboard door and all is crepuscular, a beige darkness lit by the line of light in its hinges. My face is caressed by His shirt tails and the hems of His coats, the odd woollen jumper He doesn't wear. I tug one, waffle-knit and slack, and it slides reluctantly from the hanger and into my clutching hands. I bring it to my face, willing myself to feel how it would on His chest, how it would feel to be held by Him wearing this, the soft-rough texture under my cheek as we embrace. I daydream of resting here in the dark indefinitely, of slumbering until He gets home, until days pass, and long nights, until I die here, buried in His things.

By the time I emerge I have ten minutes remaining from my hour to clean the flat, which I do in a flustering panic, snottily, perspiring, cleaning the surfaces most visible, the bathroom mirror, shower floor (dear, damp toe-prints in the bathmat), kitchen worktop, toaster crumbs swept into my palm, running the vacuum over the sitting room rug, pinching up the dust in the corners. As I swing the bin bag into the communal bins downstairs, temples damp with sweat, I remember the glinting rim of a coffee cup in His sink that I have neglected to pick up, rinse, upend. I close my eyes and try to remember: was it just the one mug? It is most unlike me not to check, but then again I do not feel myself. I am halfway up the stairs again, trembling, when I stop and think: no, I must be mistaken – and in any event, perhaps it will be good to remind Him I exist, that I am here to serve Him but I am human. The next morning, when His rating for the job I have done comes through on the app, four stars, rather than my usual five (additional comments: *thanks alice! :) Tom.*), I stand up abruptly from my desk, blood-less (a cocked head and a simper from Nina, who is sipping from a narrow can: *you OK, Al?*) and walk in silence to the women's loos where I shut myself into a cubicle and I am sick and I cry and spit, the chemical lemon scent only just masking the earth and acrid stink of humanity.

When I return to my desk with a glass of water, Nina glances at me slyly or with worry, but I look fixedly away, put in my earphones and navigate to a playlist of Tom's, copied to my own account with painstaking precision click by click, so my ears can receive the same mellow notes His do. I take comfort in the shuffling drums until my nausea has faded, and I rejoice in the empty feeling in my stomach and feel pleasingly thin. I turn to Nina and she looks back, smiling. *All right?* she says.

Unusually for me, instead of springing from my desk at 5.23 and hurrying home, I hang about, doing a little fake work, my change in rhythm meaning looks shoot above my head like chemtrails. It's quarter to six when I fish my diary out of my bag and start hand-writing notes, by which time the others around me are beginning to log out or unzipping little make-up bags and applying powder and lipstick, and at ten to they're still drifting about, popping to the loo or just checking something, quickly. At 6 o'clock Nina says, tentatively, *you coming, Alice?* and they all pause, a pack, at the doorway, security passes in hand. *Coming where?* I say. *Pub!* they chorus. *Come!* they chorus. I don't know if it's my commitment to practising my social skills for Tom, helped by the fact I didn't have a completely dire time with James, or my wanting to delay the return to my room, and loneliness, but I decide to go. Unlike them, I'm efficient, so it's only a minute later we're traipsing down the stairs in loafers, seeing as that's literally how long it takes to log out and put a coat on for Christ's sake.

How come you've never come with us before? Rebecca asks me once we're squashed into a booth with a couple more faces from our floor. *Didn't know I was invited,* I say resentfully, and Anna says: *omg please say I remembered to put you in the calendar invite?* She picks her phone up from where it's respectfully face down on the table and opens her work calendar, nails clicking. *O phew, yes, thank god.* She shows us all her screen as proof as if we're the FBI and I remember receiving the invitation months ago, a rolling fortnightly appointment 6–9 p.m. entitled *DRANKS,* one which I'd sighed at and swiftly deleted before the last wisps of my exhalation had exited my lungs. I wonder if I regret doing this, of missing weeks of female acquaintance-ship, or friendship, and decide not, while smiling gamely at Natasha casting aside the comically large menu saying, *fuck it, shall we just get a couple of bottles of Picpoul?* I don't know what Picpoul is.

I struggle to keep up, smiling a fraction too late at funny stories and mishearing questions, nodding stupidly. Rebecca is going to be a bridesmaid at her sister's wedding and *absolutely detests her dress:* she shows us pictures. Everyone says how hot she'll look but I silently agree: she will indeed look awful. Conversation gallops on. I enjoy us all agreeing how dire the director of our company is, how clearly clueless he is, and Natasha laughs and touches my arm when I say something biting about his hairline. My fingers brush Nina's when we both pick our glasses up – Picpoul de Pinet, an acidic white wine, googled under the table – at the same time. Rebecca puts her hand on my shoulder to indicate she wants to squeeze out to go to the loo. My pathetic lonely body tremors at these thought-less taps and prods, and, pretending to text, I take a quick photo of the table crowded with glasses so I can look at it later, and perhaps send it to my mother and Cass with a cheerful note: *work drinks!* or perhaps: *work pals!* The conversation moves on to things I can't follow, so I get up to leave after a respectful period of time feeling overwhelmed and tired. How do people do it? Rebecca has only been here for a couple of months and seems fully assimilated, part of the in-joke already when they all shout *Tory!* at the mention of a particular partner, which sounds fun although I note the uncertainty of posh Anna's smile and think about outing her but I'm too exhausted. I squeeze myself from the booth and as I turn my back and walk away there is an eruption of laughter. I'm not sure which is worse: that they are laughing at me (I spit on them), my awkwardness, ugliness, bulk, colouring – or that maybe they have already moved on, my departure quite forgotten.

I flush with shame as I remember the less than perfect job I did for Tom this morning. I scratch a star into the crook of my elbow with one nail as I watch suburban couples holding hands mosey along the pavement, content.

12.

I PERCH ON HIS SOFA, HAVING FIRST STRUCK AND
knocked it to smooth plumpness and relished in the downy
give of the cushion under my bare legs. My clothes pool about
my ankles. I am mouthing a poem, imagining a moment in the
near future where I am curled, His fingers tracing my spine,
whispering these words to Him: *Wild nights – Wild nights!*
Dickinson's an obvious one, breathless, obsessive, virginal,
etc. But o how the words speak to my hopeful heart. *Rowing in
Eden – Ah – the Sea! Might I but moor – tonight – In thee!*

I am aware that I'm somewhat in denial. A girl, that girl,
she whom I toppled like a bowling pin outside the pub, and
hopefully injured in some meaningful way, has been creeping
into Tom's social media presence, one stunning head-tilt and
strobe-lit dance-floor Instagram story at a time. Is she inching
into His thoughts the same way? I cannot tell you the number
of minutes I spent on the first glimpse of her, a bare knee in
a photo. I barely glanced at Tom, the sun-like subject of the
image, instead screenshotting and zooming in, assessing.
The knee is thin to the extent you can see the flat shape of the

patella, clean and smooth beneath her skin. I look at my own, shapeless. I imagine Tom's warm hand on my knee as it rests on hers in subsequent photos and vow to epilate once home, stinging pinpricks, following with tweezers, working at the tough skin to loosen ingrown hairs, drawing dark blood. I open my phone again to scroll through the latest updates. I loathe them and I look forward to the day that it will be me: me jostling elbows around a too-small pub table, me being invited round houses, on holidays, to be best friends, bridesmaid, godmother. My heart longs for its other half and I feel sure He must hear it soon.

I scour His flat for evidence of the girl – Tiggy (her ridiculous name, of course, short for Antigone, because her parents are posh twats too) – squeezing my eyes shut at the kitchen sink, not bearing to look at the two empty coffee cups waiting there, not matching, as I'd initially imagined might be the case, but one thin-rimmed porcelain and His the usual thick textured clay from John Lewis, thus proving their incompatibility. The bed seems the same but perhaps the sheet more vigorously rumpled. I press my face to the cotton and breathe in deeply. I save the bathroom bin until last, methodically lifting out tissues until – yes. Yes. One, two used condoms. I feel numb, scientific. I hold them in my hand and imagine them in my body, feeling a dull spasm of desire and pain. Do I imagine they are still warm? My palm is wet with lube and secretions and I look closely at His ejaculate, white and glistening in latex. Is there any way this does not mean He had sex with her? I consider, desperately, then decide not. I can't decide if I'm angry with Him, then remember the slap of James's hard thighs on mine, my panting passivity, sweating, weathering the storm. Mr Rochester had Bertha, after all, and Jane had St John, sort of. We're square. This is a relationship of equals, both using others to prepare. I am shuddering with adrenaline, sick, as I wrap the condoms in squares of loo roll, pocket them. I touch my palm to my dry lips, lick. Now they are away, invisible, I feel better, almost cheerful as I tumble the remaining contents of the bathroom bin into the black bag. I can deal with it.

His laptop is open and shining on the coffee table I polished earlier: removing the thin brown stack of post lazily half-opened, two coasters (marble, to match His tooth mug), a saucer that once held something buttery (I smell its sunshine), an unopened Amazon parcel the size and weight of a bottle of spirits (peaty whisky, mellow rum, small-batch mineral gin? A quick search in His inbox will reveal the answer; I vow to buy some too), sweeping toasty crumbs and a little dust, a hair, into a palm and eating them up; misting the cleared wood with disinfectant; wiping it; bringing out a tub of beeswax polish I have bought especially; timidly dipping a clean cloth, making small neat circles, waiting, buffing to soft luminescence. And then, having replaced the parcel, coasters, post, neatly, squaring them with the edges of the table so He knows I have been here, that I have tidied, bringing His laptop from His bedside table and opening it, ready to check His calendar updates, prune His inbox of junk, and read whatever little missives His sister has sent Him over the past week, at my leisure.

I sink back into the cushions and skim the titles of His emails. One, from His sister, is headed *PARIS woo!* And my heart leaps to press my throat and I click on it. I scroll through the chain and see that their mother's birthday is approaching and they have, over the last two days, decided that a surprise day trip to Paris might be nice – lunch and a gallery to spoil the old dear. His sister is being boring about sorting childcare with her husband and Tom is charmingly non-committal. I know Tom spent time in Paris when he was younger, at least a few months, learning French. Screenshotted on my phone is an old social media post which shows Tom in a bar there, La Meduse, glassy-eyed and gaunt, ironically drinking pastis. In the photo a girl is pressed to His side, low-lidded and sulky like Léa Seydoux. Their fingers are linked and I know the precise, beautiful, casual tangling by heart, how His thumb rests over hers, His index finger loosely curled, her answering grip, her slender, lovely hands dwarfed by His, caged. How I have contorted my arms to replicate it. I see online that she is an investment banker now, probably absolutely rolling in it, with expensive highlights and dressed in Chloé. I wonder what shape their conversation took as they smoked cigarettes in bed, both thin and young; did they speak lumpy English, her scratchy voice catching on an *h* or *th*, or perhaps He whispered to her in French: *je te désire, déesse*. Perhaps they did not have much cause to talk.

His sister has sent a proposed date – the only date that she can guarantee her husband is available to babysit his own child. It is a Saturday a month from now and I feel, I feel so surely that this is it. I open the calendar on my phone even though of course I don't have any plans. My stomach writhes with nerves at the thought of what can, what must unfold – in Paris, of all places. I think of future questions: *so where did you two meet,* and our shy response, embarrassed by its picturesqueness, its perfection: *actually, we met in Paris, quite by chance—*

My smile fades as I check and see Tom's calendar has an appointment that evening – some kind of boys' dinner is scheduled, a gathering of Jameses and my own sweet Tom. This plan, Paris, feels so right, I can't explain it. I navigate to the website that Anna sent me and enter the proposed day: and before I click 'enter' I know the result before I see it, I sense it in my very bones. Sure enough, it is ideal for a wedding and for a first meeting. A sign. I thumb the quartz in my pocket as I look at Tom's calendar again, heart beating hard. I hesitate, poised to cross a bridge that until now I did not know I had stretched across the uncertain currents of my brain, then quickly move the dinner appointment to the following day, Sunday. Then, before I can stop myself, I 'like' his sister's most recent email, something easily done with a slip of the thumb. Hopefully she will take this as permission to proceed, to book. Tom will see His blank calendar and will only discover the inaccuracy once trains have been booked, lunch arranged, and the plan is impossible to unwind.

The scent of honey and turpentine from the freshly polished table is making me feel nauseous; I need to clear my head. I step over my clothes and as I go to the kitchen to get some water I find myself opening His fridge and looking at a bottle of pale wine in the door. It's orange, French – a sign – and intimidating. The gold sun on the label looks at me knowingly. The bottle is almost full so I take it and open it, meaning to take a sip so I can know what tastes blaze on His tongue. I realise too late that it was unopened and my wet grasp has broken the coppery seal for the first time. There is a release of adrenaline some-where in my gut and I tremble, then put the bottle to my lips and drink. Just a sip. Earl Grey and honeysuckle. I replace the lid as tightly as I can, my knucklebones straining through my skin, return the bottle to the fridge door trying not to look at the level of wine remaining and retrace my steps to the laptop. I have barely had any but I feel giddy with this transgression, drunk and watery-legged as I look again at his sister's mes-sages – Emily, I suppose I should call her, as we will meet soon, she will hug me to her and call me the sister she never had but always wanted, she will be smiling in our wedding photos, aunt of our children, probably some sort of legal guardian to them should Tom and I die together, blissful, clinging to each other at thirty thousand feet or ablaze in a tumbling car—

I allow myself ten minutes of free-fall into horror, my undo-ing, pressing the heels of my hands hard into my eye sockets until I see bursts of light – imagining Emily asking for confir-mation, or Tom realising the dinner date has been moved, or noticing the small thumbs up linked to his sister's email, look-ing at the time stamp, perhaps tracing the IP address somehow, to his laptop, his home, Wednesday morning, when His cleaner comes ... My fingerprints whirling with His. I wipe the key-board, and try to visualise this scenario working out well for me: perhaps He would understand I was desperate to meet Him, to expedite our love, and be grateful for this small trans-gression. For the first time, I arrange His matchless features into an expression of anger, and shudder. I close the laptop and place it fastidiously on the table, neatly, wiping the top of prints so it is immediately obvious I have been here, so when

He arrives He will think: *I am cared for.* I always look forward to Wednesday mornings, but I know the wait this time will be unbearable. I tried once to guess the password to His account at home, so I could read His thoughts from the comfort of my own bed, tapping in all the variations I could think of, even, in a thrilling moment, trying my own name, but these, as well as I know Him, these depths of His mind elude me. I am glad He is security conscious; He will keep us safe.

A buzz and my phone lights up. James. *Hope you're having a good morning. Back to back meetings so on coffee three lol. Still on for Friday?* and it feels wrong, grubby, that his little words are here, polluting this sacred space. I deliberately wait until I've dressed and taken the bins out before responding: *Ha, all good for Friday. See you then. X.*

I suppose I could have put more effort in, but I have much more important things to do.

13.

MY MOTHER ONCE TOLD ME A STORY, AND I CAN
remember her clean face-cream smell and her cool hand on my
forehead; I must have been ill, home from school, as it's a rare
memory of it being just the two of us. She had coddled two soft
eggs, salted them and brought them to me in bed, a rare treat,
with buttered toast fingers and a mug of hot Ribena that I drib-
bled down my flannelette pyjamas in vivid blotches. She talked
of how in her twenties she and a friend (and I felt sure then it
was my father, although I did not ask and still have not) went to
a restaurant in a town just outside Stockholm. The only English
people in this pine-panelled, candlelit (perhaps I imagine these
details) room full of convivial Swedes, they quietly chattered of
the day's adventures, then noticed, one by one, like ripples in
a pond, the tables around them discreetly switching their own
conversations from musical Swedish to prosaic English. Soon
the whole restaurant was conversing in their second language
for this hapless duo, and they laughingly thanked their neighbours, insisting it was fine, they needn't abandon their mother
tongue for their sake. *We want to*, said a mother and her angular

teenage son, seated next to them, eating delicate fillets of fish fronded with dill, *it is polite*. I always loved this story, asking her to tell it often. This courtesy – natural, intrinsic – outshines my mother's exalted list of U and non-U words, and I always think of it when I am on a crowded Underground train, as I am now.

A single woman leans on the yellow pole by the Tube doors, cavernous handbag projecting from her shoulder, heavy panel of hair swinging, absorbed in some godawful book with a cat on the cover, pressed to this pole shoulder to hip and preventing the nervous-looking man behind her – and anyone else for that matter – from holding onto it. Such rudeness. I squeeze myself forwards and doggedly wedge my fingers around the pole, roughly level with her not unsizeable bosom, and she leaps upright, affronted and gawping. I gaze at her expressionlessly and she returns her eyes to her book, now holding on daintily with one small hand. There is one woman in this carriage larger than me, although she is tall, and carries it well. I look at her smooth face, high cheekbones, and hate her. James has been texting me, almost every day (I refuse to listen to the voicemails from Cass, she who ruined my first meeting with Tom), and I have been responding dutifully, wishing I didn't have to but knowing my work with him is not complete. I am aware that I need to hone my dating practice, for although when Tom and I are together we will be as one, knowing each other's thoughts before we have even begun to express them, I need to work on my romantically inclined small talk, as well as more general social chit-chat for the sake of Tom and the first time I am invited to His mother's house for a Sunday roast (I will be polite and say how delicious it is, but while we're sitting at the table Tom will whisper: *yours is better*, His hand slipping to my knee, and I will shake my head and swat at Him playfully and He'll wink and I'll shiver). For the latter I have been attempting to join in with Nina and Anna's conversations about their foolish weekend plans, with Rebecca's opinions on Beyoncé (good), on the Royal Family (bad), going so far as offering to make tea, coffee, hot chocolate to open conversation, even if it's to furrow my brow thoughtfully and say *hmm* at Anna asking Rebecca: *so when do you think he's going to propose?*

Dear god is there not more to life than this? I sit and I watch others living their silly little lives, and I am ashamed to be a woman sometimes, though it is no wonder this is all we have: a desire to be small, to stay small. I know it well, from looking, from scorning, from wishing it were me. Berry-pickers, baby-raisers. Chaste and childlike. Burned at the stake. Ducked in the pond. Hanged by the neck. Stays, stomachers, corsets, girdles, Spanx, SKIMS; whalebone then steel then rubber then spandex, bodies winched into letters V and S, or numbers 1 and 8, gaining and losing value through body weight, beauty, and biological clocks. Mysterious, veering, treacherous codes: long, loose hair is innocent, until it's whoreish; tanned flesh is lowly, until it's exotic; cleverness is charming, until it's embarrassing. With everything we give, we get smaller – and if we don't, men take it anyway, pinching and nipping and penetrating. We pat creams around our eyes, cover upper arms, as men coarsen and grey good-naturedly.

But I refuse to be diminished now I have Tom. Plato said that humans were once one double body: four legs, four arms, one head and two faces – two hearts. Threatened by this power, the gods tore them asunder, leaving each half-creature desolate and searching for its other. O, believe me when I say Tom is mine, and when we are together I will be complete and shiningly whole, my immensity and ugliness dimmed by His brilliance, and it will be perfect and I will be happy.

It is for Tom that I am on this long Tube journey, sneaking out early on a Friday I travel to a French delicatessen at the top end of the Northern Line. It is a little game I play with Him, we play together, that I top up the jar of cornichons in His fridge, a specific kind usually found only in France, crunchy bursts of sweet vinegar that I (and He) delight in. I am so glad He introduced them to me; appearing ten months ago in His fridge after a skiing trip, together with an overripe Reblochon that He had loosely bagged up in an attempt to control its pungence. After slicing off a tiny triangle, and sucking it from my fingers, I added a foil layer and placed it in a Tupperware and knew He would smile at my conscientiousness for Him. I searched and searched online for these cornichons, and found them not readily available, apart from at this little French deli-catessen all the way across London. I travelled there, bought some more for Him, for us, have revelled in carefully dividing a jar between Him and me, counting aloud, dropping each into the jar already there, sometimes sucking the sharpness from one or two before adding them, playfully. He must know I do this, for how else would He continue to pluck each morsel from the fridge yet never run out? I cannot wait for the day He thanks me: *I wanted to thank you before, my love, but I didn't know how, I was too shy.* I shiver with anticipation, mouth watering, as I buy two jars, together with a block of creamy chèvre that is wrapped lightly in paper, which I press onto a torn fresh baguette from next door's bakery, topping with a few sharp cornichons, and eat on a concrete bench, wishing I was in Paris, in a light, sandy square surrounded by pruned linden trees, embellished with fountains and neat lawns. But soon. I open the white boulangerie box by my side, where pastries lie crowded. I take a picture and send it to my mother and sister, with the caption: *afternoon thé!* Cass responds with a dribbling emoji and a few minutes later Mum says: *Looks yummy! Tea for you and Tom perhaps?* I put my phone away and select a glossy éclair, and bite. Cream blooms. I want us to go to Paris together every year, perhaps for my birthday, or His, and step by step I will erase all His associations of Paris with this other girl, this woman, with His youth and laughter and any days He has spent before me. Next I choose a plump religieuse, eating her choux head whole, then pull the body apart, ravenous. I will become everything to Him as He is everything to me: true love. I eat a praline-cream-filled Paris-Brest and then a crisp millefeuille, pastry shattering and crème pâtissière dripping down my chin. I feel sick, disgusted with myself, but I carry on: two delicate raspberry macarons, and lastly a fragrant, custardy canelé. He will love me.

I make my long way back down to Clapham on the Tube; two cornichon jars clink in my backpack. My reflection in the opposite window looks insubstantial, lonely. I sit and look at the evening crowd: on their way to supper, to drinks, to revel and converse and bicker and debate. Hand-holding, seat-kicking children dressed in finery for the theatre, anxious out-of-towners needlessly pressing the button to open the doors, teenagers returning from Brick Lane clutching vintage-wear and paper bags stuffed with beigels.

On the high street I weave through flocks of friends on their way to fun drinks, and I pretend I'm on the way to a friend's house, a birthday dinner, with a bag of presents for my host, and the gentle clinking is bottles of wine, Picpoul de Pinet. I notice how much space they leave as they float apart to let me pass, annoyed by their carelessness if they don't move enough, insulted if they move too much. I find the cold, clinical outside of a beauty parlour, aware that I'm cutting it fine, but mercifully once I'm inside the process is anonymous and quick; the beautician, *Yassmina* her badge says, asks me a couple of questions about holiday plans before taking the hint and then only speaks again to ask me to move a leg, or hold a particular mass of flesh taut to minimise pain. The wax is too hot, punishing, but I don't mind.

James is sitting in a darkened corner of a discreet bar off the high street, still sandy-haired and red-stubbled. Two glasses of water sit on the table. He stands up as I approach and gives me a kiss on the cheek, for which I cannot fault him but it disgusts me nonetheless. I disguise the babyish wiping of my cheek with a hair-tuck. I look at James and remember that night, his freckled shoulders, the unTomness of him, thick where Tom is slight, fair where He is dark. *Good to see you again*, he is saying, smilingly. *You too*, I reply, each word a betrayal, *how was Dublin?* And we're off, and I am stunned by how easy it is, how quick he is to smile and find my reluctant, awkward words amusing, or interesting, or worthy of note. I suppose posh people are good at that sort of thing. Every time I fear we will lapse into a frosty silence he is ready with an easy question, nothing too personal, although I take giddy delight in responding to: *do you have any siblings*, with, *my sister died when I was sixteen; do you mind if we don't talk about it?* I stroke my bracelet. He has ordered us both gin and tonics, with a seaside, rosemary tang and I try wondering again, coldly: is he luring me into a net, lulling me, will he rape me and kill me, and close his fingers around my soft neck and stifle my throat-sore sobs with a rough mouth – but my heart isn't in it.

We're two drinks in when he stands, smiling, to lollop off to the bathroom like a Labrador and I feel a sense of panic that I haven't drunk enough. Taking a gamble, it isn't terribly busy yet, I approach the bar and order four shots of tequila: two each, that's a fun, cool, thing to do, isn't it? I contemplate for a moment how to convey them back to our table, where James's jacket lies, shrugged off, on the banquette, before I drink one sharp mouthful, then a second. I am carrying the two remaining shots back to the table, one in each clawed hand, when James slides back into his seat and leans back, looking appreciatively at me. I already feel light-headed. *Sláinte*, he says, after I have handed him a glass that looks comically small in his grip. Bet he's got a single Irish grandmammy and a pending Irish passport application. *Shaad baash*, I say, with an ironic eyebrow raise, and sip this shot daintily. I'm guessing he needs to be drunk too, if we're doing this. I'm thankful for the subdued lighting, the candles lending an airbrushed and apricot shine to our cheeks, making my eyes glitter, lips wet. James leans forwards, and although I was asking for it with my internet Urdu (I should have gone with *Yamas*, I've been allocated Greek before) I am weary when he says: *so, where are you from? I wait. I mean, where are your parents from?* he presses.

Just north of Cambridge, I say glibly, *how about you?* The unanswered question slips over his face and away, and I just know Tom wouldn't ask, but I would tell Him anyway, and He would look into my eyes and understand me. James loosens as we drink more and I practise my behaviour, laughing urgently when he tells a funny story, not recoiling when his knee brushes mine; sucking in my stomach so much I feel breathless and ill, making sure he never sees me from behind, or from the side. He looks at me with seriousness sometimes, as if he thinks I'm worth looking at, listening to, and I hate the intensity of his gaze, sure he must be mocking. Finally, we leave and I say: *your place or mine,* because I thought that's what people say, and I am disarmed by him laughing as if I have made a joke. *You're an intriguing woman,* James says, putting an arm round my shoulder and squeezing. The sensation is weighty and lovely. He slides his hand down my arm and takes my hand and I snatch it away, pretending to look for something in my bag. I would deign to have sex with him, sure, but hand-in-hand moonlit strolls I am saving for Tom. I'm sure even I can't ruin that without a trial run. I run my thumb across my palm.

Do you not want to— I say. *Yes, I do,* he replies, and so we walk to his house, the half-hour walk taking far longer as we stop every so often to mechanically and sloppily embrace, James pressing his burgeoning erection into my impassive groin, my hands limply on his shoulders, unsure as to where else they should go. Dizzily, we pant into each other's open mouths, and stagger to his front door, up the fraying stairwell, and into his bed where I keep my bra and socks on and his jeans pool around his ankles, belt flapping. His warm body presses into my cool flesh and I hate how his eyes and hands stroke my body. *You're so fucking hot,* James says, and I roll onto all fours to stop him looking. I know he's lying. The relief of allowing my stomach to hang with gravity, hidden, to stop holding it in and tensing my core, is immense until James's hands move from my hips and round to my front and I can't bear the thought of him discovering the soft, bruised, juddering underbelly that rests there so I say, *no – pull my hair,* and he grabs a thick handful at once, coiling it around his wrist so my head is pinned back, jerkily, throat tight. It hurts. It doesn't feel particularly stimulating or erotic so I shut my eyes and wait for it to end. And eventually, it does.

I do feel like someone in a film, which is nice, when I wake several hours later to James's curved, freckled back and rasping breath, and rise, like a phantom. Those heroines tiptoe charmingly, lifting a gauzy undergarment with a finger from the floor, perhaps faux-clumsily stubbing their pretty little toes, where I slide from the bed, head thumping, gathering the clothes I think might be mine, hurriedly pulling them on in the dim light of the landing. The stars are still doing their best as I start the long walk home, but the sun is pushing at the horizon with such sorbet industry that I feel optimism even as my head throbs. I am metropolitan and appealing, despite my relatively modest outfit – dark jeans and a once crisp shirt, boots – it is undeniably apparent I am on a so-called walk of shame, not that I feel it, for once. Once home, I pull my notebook to me and write down all that has passed. Reaching for my laptop, I search: *hair pull sex* and several pornography websites come up. I click on one and watch a few videos carefully, pausing them to add to my notes every so often. It looks about right. In fact, James was much more gentle than these muscled homunculi, who wish to tear the extensions (shorn from my people) from the scalps of these young girls. I ape their expressions, squealing quietly. I go to the bathroom, peel off my jeans and knickers, crouch in the bath and look at my vulva, hitching the broad mass of my stomach aside. My heart pounds and I feel dizzy as I look. Hairless and animal, I now know James is a liar. I sit down, and run the tap punishingly cold, rinsing myself briskly, shivering. I return to my room in a towel and, opening Netflix, watch two or three romantic comedies in succession, paying extra attention to date scenes, rich with witticisms and knowing looks, loose curls, gleaming décolletage, rib and arm bones apparent. The sex scenes are tender, well lit and face to face, choreographed. I couldn't bear that, the pale eyes roaming over flesh, genitals bared and glistening. When I have finished I open the Fenty Beauty website, sit by the window and click methodically through the shade finder, looking from my lifeless, round cheek to the glowing beauties on my screen. I impatiently scroll past the milk-skinned maidens, their eyes glacial, the heart-shaped white beauty of ancient China, and pause on the middle rungs of colour, looking at each. I know them off by heart: a freckled white woman, tanned; a heavy-browed Mediterranean goddess; a South Asian fawn of high caste, I'm guessing; three light-skinned Black or mixed-race women, of varying warm tones, cheekbones luminous. I hold my hand up to the screen, moving it from face to face, comparing. I think today I rest neatly between Greek and pale Pakistani, a kind of made-you-look exoticism, nothing too threatening. In summer it's a different story. I stare at my face in the hand mirror and then go and get my tweezers.

It's midday and I am eating chocolate digestives in bed, seven, eight, when I see James has sent a text: *I'd have made you breakfast you know* [winky face]. I curl my lip but dutifully respond, faithful to the plan: *you can next time.* I know his stupid response before it forms in his head: *next time?* [winky face]. He is typing again, and I try, unsuccessfully, to picture his face, frowning in concentration as large fingers paw at the screen, signet ring gleaming: *pub lunch tomorrow?* So soon – I am thrown. I open my calendar even though I know it is empty, decide to leave him on read for a bit. I put my phone down and try to wait an *I'm busy* hour or two to text back, but I have nothing better to do, no one to talk to. I pick up my book – Sylvia Plath – but find myself reaching for my phone before I've made it down a page. Despite my annoyance at Cass, I message the family WhatsApp a picture of this morning's sunrise, captioned with *morning run!*, then without waiting for a response navigate to James's message again. I truly don't understand why he is so insistent on seeing me again: he's not unattractive, he's posh and nice, I suppose, and I am – well. I wish I had thought to date around a bit more, you know, be a single professional in the city; a Charlotte, sadly, with a saucy hint of Samantha. That way I could speak breezily of exes and not sound so desperately lonely when I tell Tom: I have only ever loved you.

14.

I MAKE IT TO MY SATURDAY-MORNING SESSION AT Roseacres an hour or so late, but no one marks me. Jess is away from her post when I arrive, so after signing in I take two chocolates from the tub at reception and push them both into my mouth at once. I chose poorly, the potent fragrance of a strawberry creme masking the taste of my favourite: thick sweet caramel. I'm aggrieved to see Dorothy has a visitor, so I slip into the room next door without bothering to knock, meaning I can eavesdrop and sit with poor old Alfred, suffering from dementia, but not really. I drag the visitors' chair closer to the open door and sit down.

Hello Alf, I say, probing at the caramel lodged in one of my molars. He nods courteously, looks elsewhere. At least they're mostly nice, even though no one ever knows who on earth I am. Next door, some relative of Dot's is speaking very loudly about school fees, probably aiming for a bigger percentage in her will, a Boden-clad vulture. I turn my attention to Alf again. *How's your mental wellbeing?* He smiles at me. I look around the room, scanning for things to comment upon, something to say.

I clear my throat, toss my hair, pretend I'm my sister. *So what do you do, Alfred? That's a nice name, very Anglo-Saxon, and strong. It must mean something quite masculine, like warrior, or ...*

I flag, pull out my phone, tap. *Wise counsellor, good enough.* An intellectual then. Alfred nods at me. I nod back. *It's a nice day outside*, I say, and he obediently turns to look. *Yes, 'tis*, he says, his voice high and with a touch of south London to it. I giggle in a coquettish manner, then say, *what is it you used to do, Alf?* I am mentally lining up a list of questions to ask next, before he even opens his mouth again to answer, afraid of the blankety silence that can settle on conversations. With the oldies it's fine, they're often quite happy to sit, mute, retreating into their capacious, tired old heads, but this is a practice session, after all, so by the time I am with Tom I will have learned the skills of repartee and ease.

I was in the army, Alf tells me, *Burma*. I presume he's talking about the Second World War, so nod fervently. *Gosh*, I say, *how interesting. That must have been interesting*. I need different words. I try to imagine the young man, with twinkly eyes and one of those Clark Gable moustaches, although that's more First World War flying aces. How about: strong hands, sinew, a jawline streaked with mud, sweat, hair falling into eyes. Enthused, I continue: *and how are you finding things here?* He doesn't answer at first and I wonder if he's heard me, then he leans forwards. I practically hear his joints creak, treated to a close-up vision of his antiquity. The wet smack of his lips parting: *the nurses take my things.* I suppress a fervent roll of my eyes and sit back. Here we go. *They're thieves*, he clarifies. *O no, that's terrible*, I say mechanically. Bet it's just the non-white ones. There is a pause where he sits back heavily, eyes locked on mine with an air of triumph. I decide this has gone on long enough: *let me tell you about me: I've got a date tomorrow, with this guy. Can we role-play?*

I have a final half hour to kill and so I find myself loitering outside Mr M's room, pretending to be on my phone. I listen to the noises he makes, trying to discern if the virus I spread in his room, as if a curse, had wrought its magic. He makes usual sounds of the aged, rustling and creaking like an armchair, or a ship, but then he coughs several times in an irritated, impatient manner, then thunderously blows his nose, probably into the white handkerchief I have seen him pull out of his pocket in the past. My plan worked; he's ill. I feel a distant flick of guilt, but it is just a cold, and he lives somewhere with 24-hour medical care. I look up at everyone who turns into the corridor, hoping his family will tumble round the corner, riotously, or, better still, one slim figure will stride towards me with purpose, Mr M reaching to take my hand: *this is Alice, she's looked after me marvellously.* I realise I have done no such thing so I knock and enter his room at the same time. *Hello, there,* I say. I'm slightly shocked to see how unwell he looks, one or two days' worth of white stubble on his usually neat chin, his thin hair unbrushed. I'd also envisioned him sitting in his usual chair, reading his book, or a paper, but he's sitting up in bed, doing nothing but holding his white handkerchief. I avert my gaze from the photograph on the wall, the beauty that crowds there.

Hello, Alice, he says, hoarsely, smiling. *It must be Saturday! I've rather lost track.* I gawp. *Are you OK?* I say, *do you want me to get a carer?* He smiles at my horrified expression. *I'm quite well, thank you. I must look a sight!*

Poor you, I say, weakly. *Have your family been here cheering you up? O no,* he says, busily resettling the sheets over his knees, *I wouldn't want to worry them. Fuck,* I think. Out loud, I say, *I'm so sorry, I really hope you feel better soon.* The words feel fake and ugly in my mouth, as if I'm spitting out single-use plastics, littering virgin soil. He nods. *That's very kind. I'm sure I'll feel right as rain in no time.* I dither, standing inert. He looks tired but he folds his hands and looks at me interestedly. *And what have you been up to?* he asks. I rack my brains, looking round the room for inspiration. My eye lands on his wallet, tucked onto a wooden tray. I wonder what he uses it for, what little purchases he makes. *I robbed a bank,* I say lamely. He smiles kindly. *How exciting!*

You? I say. He thinks, and gives up, shaking his head smilingly. *But how are you, really, Alice,* he says. *O don't worry about me,* I say, feeling dreadful. *You look,* Mr M pauses and considers: *unsettled,* he concludes. My hands spring up to smooth my hair, my clothes. I suck my stomach in and sit up straighter. *O,* I say, unsure. *I suppose I am. Work's getting a bit on top of me, and, you know, I'm lonely.* I laugh. *I don't know why I said that.* Mr M is nodding gravely, really looking at me. *It's very common,* he says, *I was reading about it the other day. The loneliness epidemic.* He smiles in a way that makes me want to cry. He gestures towards his armchair and finally I sit down, powerless.

Tell me about your family, I say. The photograph on the wall wavers and pulses at the edge of my vision. I concentrate hard on Mr M's face. He smiles again, warmly. *Why not tell me about yours*, he says. *O*, I say. *There's not much to say. It's just my mum, and me. And my sister. Cassandra.* A silence while he processes this. *And your father?* he asks. *Not in the picture*, I say tightly. He nods. *Are you close with your mother and sister?* he asks.

I am silent and I think of texts and the phone calls and how I haven't hugged my mother properly since I was sixteen. I think about holding hands with my sister, as we walked to the school bus stop, the village shop, anywhere, for longer than is usual with children I feel, wordlessly releasing each other's hot fingers just round the corner from our destination in case anyone saw us. We pretended to be annoyed about the matching Laura Ashley dresses our mother bought us to wear to church on Christmas Day but I loved it, I loved it – as I loved when people thought we were twins or mixed us up. I think about the chasm between us now – that sickening yawning darkness that erupted, and across which I cannot, will not, pass.

So, I continue. *That's me. What about you? And your grandchildren? How's Tom?* Mr M frowns slightly.

Tom? Do you mean Jamie? he asks. He gestures to the photograph and I allow my head to turn, relieved to stop fighting the urge. I look at the young man I know to be Tom, a few years ago. I have never let myself look at it so openly and it feels illicit, being so close to the glass I can see the moons of my eyes haloing their faces. I frown. It's Him. Is it Him? But now I'm not sure, and it feels as if a veil has been lifted – I see that this young man's features, though fine, don't display the symmetrical perfection of Tom's, and the gentle golden tan from holidays in Greece is not quite the same shade, Dulux rather than Farrow & Ball, the glinting signet ring is silver not gold, the smile less poised, more carefree. I feel cold. How did I miss this? I mentally flip through all of the old men at Roseacres, a venerable carousel – Mr M is the only one he could have been. He is saying pleasedly: *and my granddaughters are Georgina, Rose and Sophie.* He ticks them off on his fingers. I look at them numbly. Is Mr M just an ordinary old man? Is Tom's grandfather not here after all? Had I simply assumed that his Roseacres was the same as mine? I pull out my phone and google *roseacres care home,* see there are at least ten in the south of England alone. One near Tom's parents' village in Surrey. How appallingly careless of me, how utterly stupid. My stomach plummets as I think of the wasted hours, all that time, then – no matter, no matter, I have other ways to ensure I bring Tom to me. *Yes, Jamie,* I manage, from a distance. *He's very well, I think,* Mr M says. *He got a promotion last year so I understand he's very busy indeed.*

Mr M talks for a few more minutes about his grandchildren who never visit. He finally quietens and looks exhausted, breathless. I press a glass of water into his hand and slouch away and seize the arm of the first carer I see. *Look after Mr M,* I say, *he looks like shit.* Alarmed by my fervour, he nods. *I'll check on him now,* he says, and lopes off. I don't feel better although in retrospect that carer was quite handsome, eyes shiny and dark, his warm forearm firm beneath my grip.

Sunday is fine: after eating folds of brown and pink beef and a Yorkshire pudding saturated in salty gravy (James, a triumphant curl of battered fish), having conversations about this and that, and a walk on a waterlogged common, it looks like we're about to have too-sober sex in daylight on the sad sofa in James's sitting room (*my housemates are out, it's fine,* he pants). This time, one hand full of the flab of my hip, he winds the length of my hair around the other and pulls without asking and asks me if I'm a dirty bitch, to which I respond, arms trembling: *yes, yes.* He tries to turn me round to face him but I resist, pressing my face to the cushions so that I leave stamps of saliva, tears. I think of Tom.

Afterwards, we watch an old episode of *Blue Planet* on TV; David Attenborough's voice soothes as I watch mysterious creatures suspended in oceans. James shifts beside me and offers to make me a cup of tea. I say: *yes.* I stay until night starts closing in and James leans in to kiss me as I leave and says, *bye, Alice,* and I have to repress the shudder that threatens to make itself known on my skin, a great, bone-rattling convulsion. *See you next week, if you're free?* he says, smiling. *Dinner?* I nod quickly although I'm not so sure. But perhaps he is practising for his soulmate too.

On the long walk home I realise a familiar low ache is encroaching in my abdomen, a kneading of pliant dough. I decide to risk it and continue my slow way, defiantly passing a Boots, a little family pharmacy, a Tesco Express where I could buy sanitary products if I so desired, mitigate the risk of blood soaking into my knickers, my jeans. When I get home, panting, sweating, Sasha is having a bath and listening to Taylor Swift, which means she'll be ages, so I check my knickers in my bedroom and see a picturesque streak of blood, a symmetrical inkblot, like in an advertisement. I fold tissues into my knickers and, as it's Sunday, get into bed to call my mother. I roll my eyes at the ten seconds of rustling while she fumbles with her mobile and puts it to her ear. *It's later than usual,* she greets me, *been doing anything nice?*

Pub lunch with Tom, then went to His for the afternoon. O lovely, she says, *what did you have for lunch? Just a Caesar salad,* I say, and hear her nod her approval. I lie on the bed, thinking of the sticky toffee pudding moated with custard that I'd eaten after my roast, and pinch and pinch the flesh of my stomach, each gouge and twist mirroring the growing agony of my womb.

After the usual exchange about her week, church, tutoring, there is a silence, then: *I spoke to Cassandra,* and the unpleasant jolt I feel hearing her name lurches through my body and I pinch harder. Mum continues: *she says she's having trouble getting hold of you – she really would like to speak to you, soon. It's important.*

Well, you know me, I've been so busy— I begin. *Sweetheart,* my mother interrupts, *please will you just call her – or perhaps you girls can arrange to have lunch? Or I could come down for the day and we could all have lunch?*

Irritation flares. How could she countenance us having an agreeable little lunch together – an untouched breadbasket, salads, a shared pudding if we're lucky – as if everything is fine?

Why now? I say. My mother sighs and I hear the tinkle of her bracelets as she flaps a hand with indecisiveness or impatience. *I daren't tell you as Cass made me promise, and you know how she gets – but it's her health—*

It's late, I should go . . . I say. *A networking breakfast tomorrow. Speak next week, bye.*

Call her, my mother says. *Bye, sweetheart. Love—*

I hang up.

By now I have scraped away a layer of skin from the part of my abdomen most easily reached by my idle left hand, had been plucking and scratching during every word spoken. No blood has been drawn but I know from experience it will scab, like a graze, a dark mark mocking me in the mirror, cracking and stretching with every movement of my body, making itself known. I heave myself to my feet and find I have bled through the makeshift padding of tissues in my knickers, and my trousers, into my sheets, just. The dark blot mocks me as I strip the bed and take the linens downstairs to soak.

15.

TWO MUGS IN THE KITCHEN SINK AGAIN, AND AGAIN, and again. The tracks of this bitch are spreading throughout His flat, have been doing so, like an infection, over this past couple of weeks. It means I have had to monitor the situation closely, building to an almost daily check-up.

I'm not stupid, I knock first, heart swelling bloodily in mouth, to ensure no one is in, and am never there longer than five minutes – ten. I quickly walk from room to room, barely marking Tom's activities except to look for His laptop, strangely missing, turning my face from its infuriating absence (had He found me out?), looking instead for signs, crude ciphers left by her carelessly, knots of hair in the drain, a small fingerprint here or there, a wisp of scent. Lying next to His sweet blue manual toothbrush: a rose gold electric one comes and goes. I use it to scrub the embedded black mould by the base of the shower – not a reflection on my cleaning abilities, truly – I have tried everything. I also try to masturbate with it, over my clothes, listening over its insistent hum for the rattle of the front door, but it runs out of charge after a weak minute or so. A carton of soya milk appears in the fridge, to which I add a high-calorie powder from Holland & Barrett. She left a pair of work shoes, which I reluctantly love and try on, stepping nonchalantly here and there, pleased to have the same size feet, eventually looking them up and laughing out loud at the price. I know she works at an art gallery, and have extended my lunch break a few times by half an hour or so, so I can slip onto the Tube for fifteen minutes and walk repeatedly past the floor-to-ceiling windows and watch her tapping officiously at a MacBook in an empty room. I almost went in, but saw you had to press a buzzer to be admitted and I couldn't bear the thought of her assessing eyes raking me from head to toe, a decision to make, her smooth fingertip hovering over the door release to admit me, leaving a print identical to those I now buff from His bedside table, light switches. Those fingers probably stroke His hair, link with His, grip His cock.

This morning, I arrive twenty minutes late to work having spent time unwrapping the two wax-paper wrapped steaks chilling in His fridge, studying them, and noting the dramatic decrease in the number of cornichons in the jar, but I think only Nina has noticed my slipping punctuality, peering at me over her morning Red Bull innocently while I unpack my work laptop, notebook, an apple I will not eat, a Tupperware containing more Sasha-baked Bundt cake.

I have been thinking about Tiggy all morning, imagining their supper tonight; carving through those steaks, pink, plates puddled with myoglobin and Béarnaise. Perhaps they will snack on cornichons while the beef sears in the pan. I feel sick and hungry, stressed, so at lunch I walk to the street market nearby that sells arancini and cannoli. I buy two of each and eat them absently, licking my fingers. The food settles in my stomach but does nothing to deaden the growing anxiety that He is turning, a lighthouse, His love is shining elsewhere. I decide I can't return to work, texting Nina: *can you tell Marta I've gone home – not well* [green-faced about-to-vomit emoji], and drawn by an invisible thread I am at the Tube station, getting out my card to tap in, knowing that the ticket gate and stairs and Underground will lead me to her gallery again. I arrive. I look at the art in the window, then drift away, return. Despite her laptop screen being tilted discreetly away from the window, from a certain angle I can see it. It looks like she is actually working, which surprises me; she types brief emails and occasionally refers to a spreadsheet with various tabs along the bottom through which she clicks decisively. She picks up the phone and I can see from the shape of the mouth as she speaks that she is a massive toff, or possibly German. *Yah*, her mouth goes, and she nods: *OK yah, sure.* Her skin is so pale it seems lit from within, her eyeshadow is glossy and terracotta and her cheekbones gleam with dewy highlighter. I watch impassively from a bus stop opposite, but not one person enters the gallery all afternoon. No commission then, no more extortionate exquisite shoes. At 5 o'clock on the dot she puts her water bottle in a handbag (Loewe) and closes the laptop. I loiter, scrolling through my phone as she locks up. My bones ache, but I follow her home. Men look at her as she sways on the Tube, her slim legs in stretchy flares, try to catch her eye. She listens to music and reads *Metro* while I idly compose a text to James, ready to send when I emerge above ground. We really don't live that far away from each other, forty minutes' walk or so, but of course her house is a chi-chi two-up two-down white terraced cottage that looks plucked from the back streets of Chelsea, with a boot scraper on the porch for all those country walks she's doing in London, for god's sake.

I imagine us being friends, knocking on her door with a bottle of wine under one arm, or a phone note of bad-but-good films to watch on Netflix or Prime, or a novel she had lent me, or that I would lend her. I imagine the feel of a tight hug hello, the press of her little body, hair soft on my cheek, the way she might touch my arm to emphasise a point, or laugh very hard at a joke I had made. I imagine her swatting at my knee when I say something outrageous, or rolling her eyes fondly. I see an upstairs light click on and I start. I make a note of the address and walk back to mine. I click through my phone, signing her up to a few catalogue mailing lists, including one for dowdy eveningwear, and one for presents for children from fun aunts and uncles.

Even though it's later than usual, I surprise myself and pop into Roseacres on the walk home, sticking my head around Mr M's door with a big smile, brandishing a packet of jelly babies that I have seen him eat once and so picked up from Tesco, not even minding the enormous queue. I look at the treacherous photo and feel nothing – I should have known Tom would have visited, visited every week. I am half-witted. These wasted weeks – but I've prepared a good answer for Mr M's usual question: *well, I was approached by MI6 to join the secret service.* I've seen him reading a book on the Cambridge Five so it might tickle him. Even though he isn't Tom's grandfather, my ticket to His heart, I feel oddly responsible for him, attached, even. I see that he's asleep, glasses folded on his bedside table, and despite knocking on the open door gently then harder, then checking his chest was still rising and falling, he remains asleep. His lungs rattle and catch very quietly. I put the jelly babies by his armchair without leaving a note and tiptoe out.

16.

I AM MANY THINGS AND HAVE BEEN CALLED DOZENS of names but what I am right now is clever, or lucky, or something. I have seized the wheel of fortune, arrested with impossible strength its slow revolution and spun it my way, for once. I cannot believe I've pulled it off. I feel my heartstrings tugging me forwards with such urgency, sharp in their eagerness to join with His, to be bound in a snug lover's knot. My breath is ragged and I feel elated and wild.

A week has rolled by during which I cleaned Tom's flat numbly and well – noting His wellies were caked in fresh mud – country rambles, perhaps, and the takeaway boxes taking over His fridge – no more steaks picked up from the butcher since that first time – she doesn't cook for Him, then; He doesn't cook for her – and His laptop was still devastatingly absent, so I briefly cried before worrying further and I went to work and was silent in meetings and I went to Roseacres and Mr M was out having his hair cut when I arrived so I spoke to Alf who had forgotten me from last time and practised how I would be with Tom with him. I texted James every other day, asking him about work and remembering that his dad recently had a knee operation. At night I lay awake and wondered what it would be like to stay in Tom's flat past the usual time, to hide under the bed, listening to Him making supper, watching TV, brushing His teeth, to feel the eventual sag of the mattress on my stiff body, His somnolent rollings, to hear His night-time murmurs and steady breathing, a drowsy, whispered *Alice* ... Perhaps to hear and feel her slip in with Him, lightly, the wet suck of their kisses, their fucking, the pulsing mattress pushing the air from my lungs, smothering me.

And now it is Wednesday again and I was so anxious and desperate and yearning that I arrived at Tom's flat at 7 o'clock, and skulked up and down His street, furtively, seeing suspicion in the eyes of the schoolchildren trailing out of their front gates with scooters, their hard-eyed, distracted mothers holding book bags and muslins; the whiskery old woman walking a sandy little pompom that strained with button eyes to sniff my shoes; office workers doing the low-key jog-walk of someone about to miss their train but trying to maintain nonchalance. As runners gusted by me, I breathed in their slipstream of detergent, deodorant, sweat, thinking: *will I ever not be lonely?* After strolling back and forth as casually as I could (eyes watching), bucket swinging, I perched at a bus stop a hundred yards away, eyes trained on the door of Tom's block of flats, straining. Twice I jumped up, thinking it was Him but it was not, another pale-blue shirt (Oxford), another pair of boots (Chelsea), another tousled head. At quarter to eight – finally – I saw Him leave, tucking His keys back in His pocket, jacket over His arm. I couldn't be sure but His hair looked still damp from the shower, with breathtaking, clean comb marks and a darkened collar. It looked like rain so no bike today. He turned towards the station, that dear, loping stride, shrugging on His jacket, and, finally, I walked to His flat and pressed the Trade button on the silver panel (the door clicked), into the chilly entryway, up the stairs to the first floor and then to the door I love so well, where I took my key from my bra where it rests, always, warm as my blood, and slotted it into the round lock.

The door opened with the reassuring resistance of fire safety and I let it slam behind me. Dropped the key on the table. Silence, and I felt as if I were in a church. My usual hours are 9 until 10, so I have never entered this hallowed space so soon after He has left it, in so unhurried and peaceful a manner. The space felt, feels, charged. I slowly moved about, savouring the now-rare single mug in the sink, delighting in the sheen of water still pooling in the shower, the dampness, no, wetness, of the towel once wrapped around a narrow waist, the unmade bed even more recently vacated and nest-like than usual. Pressing my hand to the kettle, tears sprang to find its residual warmth. Dear Tom.

I remembered why I'd arrived so early, and hurried to the sitting room, the coffee table, a laptop, finally, miraculously there – I see now that it is brand new (o He had been upgrading), fresh from its box discarded on the floor, which I am careful to put into the recycling bin before I allow myself to sit down, slowly open the screen – still no password, my sweet love – and navigate in trepidation to His inbox. My heart almost stops when I see the most recent email at the top, a merry few lines from Emily:

PARIS HERE WE COME! Saturday 30th – 9.22, return at 20.13. Let's meet by M&S at St P at 8 to be safe? Remember DON'T TELL MUM. Excited! Have locked it in James's diary that he's having Ottilie for the day ahaha xx ps you owe me £239 for your ticket plus £119.50 for half of mum's (we're going standard premier woo! Sorry not sorry).

She is insufferable, really, but in this moment I love Emily's sweet, idiotic simplicity and organisation. My fingers slip across the trackpad, pressing lightly. I see that after I had liked her email suggesting the date, she had proposed precise train times, and Tom had sweetly responded with *I'm free, looks good, thanks Em.* I see the forwarded Eurostar ticket. I see Emily suggesting a variety of lunch and gallery combinations, and Tom ignoring these. He must sense that there is more to this trip than the celebration of their mother; He must be trying to silence her pointless chatter, cut through the noise, divine the true meaning of the day. Perhaps He can already feel, hear the tug of my heart.

I have longer in the flat than usual because I arrived so much earlier; I relish it and open a few more tabs on Tom's laptop, clicking idly then with intent, while waiting for the kettle to boil, and then the coffee to steep. I lie on His bed, smiling and serene, sunlight slipping over my skin. I loosen my hair and it spills cool onto my shoulders and His pillow. I take a fistful and pull, hard. O to lie here with Him by my side. For once, for once, I feel radiant, beautiful.

*

I have left it even later than usual and I know I have been here too long when the sun is no longer a slanted laziness but more insistent and stark, shadows shortening. I am due at work now, no, a minute ago, and the flat is untidied, and I am sorry for it. Soon Tom will be my only priority; I long for the day I no longer have to balance work and my love, pouring all my being and effort into Him, only Him. I pull on my clothes and snag a wilted leg of my tights, hurry to pin up my hair, to make the bed. I text my boss: *Hi Marta! Sorry, just left the therapist's, it was a difficult one.* I choose a single-teared crying emoji, then I delete it, feeling it's probably too much, before selecting a downcast sort of emoji with dejected, sorrowful eyebrows that will be right up her street, and sending it. I can imagine the little wrinkle in her brow as she reads it: *o, Alice, poor thing.* A minute later, as I am hurriedly tying the fluttering tops of the bin bag, my phone buzzes and Marta has said: *No worries. Poor you. See you later.* I struggle to decipher the tone, the full stops, but don't think I'm in trouble. Nevertheless, I must leave, which I do, looking back at the flat as I reverse out, and thinking it looks not too bad, no, surely He won't notice the crumbs on the surface (I swipe at them), the unwashed mugs (I rinse), that I haven't scoured the soapy tideline of the bath, or dusted the tops of his books, Heaney and Herriot. He's a clean and tidy one, really, the flat's never that bad. He won't know, surely He won't. I trace my name on His worktop, His bathroom mirror that has lost its dreamy fug. I snatch up my key, tuck it to my chest. Bins: I hold my breath.

I arrive at work less than half an hour late, sweat gathering at the base of my spine, ostentatiously waving at Marta through the glass of her office door so she knows I've been relatively punctual. She's on the phone, twisting the cord like a teenager in a nineties coming-of-age movie, but raises her eyebrows at me in what I think is a friendly greeting. I am in a distracted daze all morning, and spend almost half an hour in the kitchen slowly making coffee and eating the caramel chocolates from a box that someone has left there.

I am aware it is lunchtime by the fact everyone is sitting back down again around me with Itsu bags and cracking apart chopsticks. I feel a blaze of pride that I have not furtively left my desk at quarter to one as usual, having been thinking about food since eleven o'clock, and get up slowly, revelling in apparent indifference, to buy myself a little something as a treat. I return twenty minutes later with a rice bowl and some miso soup, and two plump balls of mochi. I sit and I eat, chewing and chewing, trying to feel full. I turn to Anna, recalling overhearing a conversation about a two-and-a-half-week holiday to St Lucia. Practise, practise. *All packed?* I say, and she smiles. *Yes, just about! The flight's at 8.45 tomorrow morning, which I'm slightly regretting now!* I laugh politely, then, after trying and failing to find a natural segue, just come out with it: *do you know anyone called Antigone – Tiggy?* Anna thinks for a couple of seconds, and gets out her phone to search on Instagram before saying *O yes – Tiggy Mackintosh?* I nod, my eyes drawn to the grid of photos glowing on her phone, so many pale faces, so many celebratory occasions to document. Is that the wave of Tom's hair, the line of His nose, His jaw? Her phone screen goes dark with unuse, and I drag my eyes away.

What do you think of her? I ask. *I don't actually know her very well,* Anna says, *she's the little sister of one of my besties from school, so I've seen her at a few parties, and we've got lots of mutuals and I obviously follow on Insta but she's really nice I think! Why do you ask?*

O, I say loftily, *I was hoping to buy some art and I love this little gallery in South Ken and she's the gallery assistant or something. Just figured you might know her.*

O that makes sense, says Anna, *I knew she'd interned at Christie's. Fun!* She wrinkles her nose at me. *Small world – say hi to her for me!* I will do no such thing but I nod and as I am turning away Anna says, leaning forwards, hand lightly on my sleeve – *by the way, guess who I saw last night?* I look at her questioningly, my mind jumping to the one in my thoughts, all my thoughts, even though it's not possible – *Tom Tom Tom* – and she widens her eyes exaggeratedly and says: *James? He says it's going well . . . ?* She dimples, knowingly. *O right, yes,* I say, breathing deeply, trying to regulate my disorderly heart. *Just call me Cupid!* Anna says, as she turns back to her computer.

17.

THE NEXT DAY TOM HAS RATED MY SERVICES: FOUR
bright stars and I am giddy with relief. I vow to do an impeccable job next week; perhaps I could arrange some flowers in a
vase, although He does not have one – His cream ceramic jug
will do – some daffodils, seasonal and cheery, or yellow roses.
That I'm still falling short of five stars stings but I rationalise:
perhaps on some level He has recognised the promise of our
life together. I am smiling so much at my phone that Nina swivels towards me, away from her Oliver Bonas monogram mug
of curdled-looking low-calorie hot chocolate from a sachet,
and says: *who's that* in a knowing tone, and I turn to her as the
weeks unroll in my head: next Wednesday, impeccable, yellow
flowers, cream jug; Paris: where we shall meet, properly, and
will be in love, and then I will move in and He will marvel
at how well I know the flat, and He will say, *I always used to
wonder about you*, or, *the flat always felt more like home when
you had visited*, or, *I wish you'd stayed behind so I could have
met you sooner*, or, *I wish I'd met you years ago*, and: *my life was
meaningless without you.*

My boyfriend, I say, attempting to sound casual but unable to hide the smile creeping in behind the words, the giddy shiver of anticipation coming through. Nina shrieks, *o my god Alice I didn't know you had a boyfriend!* She cups her hot chocolate in both hands and sips, eyes greedy. I hear the earring-swing of Rebecca turning to me. *What's his name?* she calls, and I swivel my chair to face her, pleasantly. *Tom,* I say. There really must be a dearth of gossip at the moment, but I feel shy and elated nevertheless. Anna, thankfully, is halfway to St Lucia, so when Nina asks: *is this the friend Anna set you up with?* I shake my head coyly and continue to field their questions: *what does He do, what does He look like, have you got a* photo? *Where did you meet? O wow my cousin just got engaged and they met on the internet too! Don't worry – it's totally not embarrassing any more. We should all do drinks!* This babbling conference is broken by Nina's phone ringing, she pops on her headset and answers, voice clipped and infantile: *this is Nina, how can I help?* and I swivel back to my computer. I type and click lethargically for the rest of the afternoon. Maybe we will do drinks. We will do drinks, and dinners, and weddings, and holidays. I am soon to be in one of those couples, invited to sup with other couples, cosily grinning at each other in candlelight and sawing at a sponge-fleshed rack of lamb crusted with breadcrumbs, flaky salt and parsley. Sodden, boozy tiramisu for pudding, coffee and an Uber. Tumbling in from the cold night to our waxy bed soon warmed by our limbs, the sacred pressing of our bodies.

The days between Wednesdays pass as a dream – now, more than ever seeming a half-life. Work, Whole Foods, hours pass.

Buying Sasha a bottle of nice olive oil that she seems so over-the-top excited by, gasping and turning it this way and that, reaching out to hug me, that I wonder if she is being sarcastic. Eating, eating, pinching, twisting. Sitting in my room, listening to the burble of the TV pass up through the floorboards, or the sound of Sasha drying her hair in her room, or of the Canadian rattling cereal into a bowl at two o'clock in the morning, letting the fridge door slam shut, mounting the stairs slowly, creaking past my door. I go to Roseacres to see Mr M, and he asks how I am; he looks very bundled up and thin and is holding the book he was reading last time, but it is closed and resting on his knees, bookmark about a third in. He seems better even if he is perplexed when I tell him, with forced jollity, that I've been dancing the Charleston with his grandson, and I find it too hard to remind him of our game. I've looked before but I'm pretty sure there aren't CCTV cameras in the residents' rooms, only in the odd corridor, the entrances, that sort of thing. I remember spreading my germs gaily about his room, then think worriedly that there must be footage somewhere of me entering when I knew he was at lunch, and staying there for several minutes before exiting, shiftily. I doubt it would be a murder charge; manslaughter, perhaps? Still, Mr M does seem better though, even if when he returns my wave as I leave it looks an effort. I dutifully call my mother on Sunday and she tells me about her life: church, book club. I update her on my life: I'm fine, I'm busy, I'm happy, I work, I run, I volunteer. I'm going to Paris with Tom. She avoids mentioning my sister, clearly trying a new tactic, and I take pleasure in it. I lie in bed for hours and hours, and I imagine four blank prison walls shuddering towards me.

Wednesday: at last, at last. I follow through on my promise and His flat has never been more immaculate. Daffodils stand in a cream jug on His kitchen table. My stomach feels fleshy and sore; my period returned in the night with triumphant vigour; irregular and unpredictable, like me. My mother once called it a red-ribboned gift from Mother Nature although I have never envisaged this a present from a benevolent and maternal earth goddess but a cold sort of maiden aunt, thin-faced, spinsterish and bitter, doling out pain to women in cruel doses: this moon-driven blood-letting which curls us around hot water bottles, the dispassionate dice throw of fertility, threatening the horror of pregnancy through the soft and blissful days of youth before whisking it away once the indistinct idea of motherhood is embraced; for some, the body-splitting and bloody terror of childbirth followed by treacherous, leaking breasts and orifices and, finally, the malicious slipping away of womanhood, accompanied not with faded dignity but with humiliation, uncontrollable, raging fevers, an unpeopled dryness where once we were lush valleys, and a withering into insignificance. I watch this all unfold, neighbours, colleagues, acquaintances. It feels like men breeze through life with comedy erections.

I spend ten minutes snapping His sheets taut, smoothing His duvet and arranging the squashy pillows; I don't even think of getting in, of tucking myself up as I have become accustomed to – cleaning today, only cleaning, and tidying. This time, I can't afford to fall into a reverie over every palm print on the table, lip print on a glass, imprint on the sofa, His phone notes that sync to His laptop: *barbell shoulder press four (ten), 30kg, Arnold presses, four (six), 14kg, shoulder circuit: front, eight,*

side, eight, 8kg, three, shrugs, three (eight), slow, two (24). Cardio.
I know it must be a workout routine but I delight in its coded poetry, the way His mouth must move over these words, the sibilance of shrugs, the sensuousness of slow. He writes little reminders to Himself: non-fiction titles, films recommended by idiot friends, once the name of a nearby Mexican bar, where I waited every evening for a week, apprehensively slurping salty margaritas, desperate, and half-hoping not to see Him after all.

I relent once: I put my face to His pillow and breathe in deeply.

I wash everything up (a pair of reedy chopsticks, a noodle-stuck wok, a sauced plate, a jumble of coffee cups whose number I do not count), dry it, and put it away. I am fast but efficient; no time to count His multivitamins (I shake the bottle and ascertain from the rattle, rolling my eyes fondly, that He has not been taking them. I put them pointedly by the kettle so He will remember). After an hour I am dazzled and sweating, and aware now of how I have been shirking over the past months, idling, running fingers through and over and in His things when I should have been honouring our contract and earning my keep and making Him proud. He must give me five stars this time. He must know how I feel.

I check His email, the lunch reservation, the timings, everything. Tempting though it is to while away time sifting through His life online, I must get on.

I'm halfway through tying the handles of the rustling bin bag, averting my face from its stewing contents, when my uterus clenches and I feel a pulse of clotted blood pushing past the tampon I put in earlier. I let the bag sag to the floor, take a green sanitary tube from my open bag and dart to the loo, pulling down my tights and knickers in an undignified roll with one hand and lifting my skirt with the other. After a token show of stubbornness at my tug, the tampon slides out slickly and I swaddle it with tissue and put it on the floor so I remember to put it into the bin bag when I'm done. Blood swirls, settles, and my womb is tender, blood slips from my body. I think again of the babies Tom and I would make, of little croissant arms and soft caramel hair and gently stroke away the blood from between my legs, unwrapping the green packet and pushing its contents into place with a grimace. The wrapper I put next to the loo-roll bundle. Mustn't forget. I've washed my hands, checked my appearance, removed my fingerprints from the gleaming tap and am almost at the door with the bin bag when I remember, with a stomach-plummet, the foul detritus on the bathroom floor. I rush back and collect it, smile broadly with pleasure. The flat is perfect. All is well.

18.

ONE STAR. I STARE AT IT. ONE SHINING BLUE STAR, four faint outlines of ghost-stars beside it, unclicked. No message. No tip. A slip of the thumb? It could not have been deliberate: I do not understand it. Tom is usually so precise; I have barely seen a mistake in our messages. Now, phone on my desk, I wait. The usual follow-up text, which lets me know that next week I will be returning to clean His flat, 9 o'clock until 10 o'clock, top to bottom, has not arrived. Comments: none. I think of the pristine rooms, walking through them in my mind, key, twist, trick, shoulder to front door, bucket down, into the small hallway which opens into the sitting room, the kitchen just to the side, the bedroom through that door, the bathroom through the other. Windows, sofa, eyes. The duvet snapped flat, the kettle descaled. Daffodils in a cream jug. I am stunned, too confused to cry.

Thinking hard, I open the app and go to the section setting out jobs: the weekly rota stretching far into infinity: Wednesday, Wednesday, Wednesday has changed; its usual brightness, with eager little 'suggest edit' buttons and 'contact

Tom' is now muted and unclickable. My wrist goes limp and my phone falls to the desk. I turn to gape at the window beyond Nina; I hadn't noticed that the branches on show have grown pale green buds so I gaze at them and try to empty my mind. My phone buzzes so I look, just quickly, to check if it's Tom although I know it's not, it couldn't be. I know His number off by heart but have never had the chance to give Him mine. It's Cass, of course. I turn my phone off, put it in my desk drawer and shut it with a vehemence that has Nina looking at me askance. *The fuck do you want*, I mutter, but very quietly so I don't think she will hear me. I see her raised eyebrows from the edge of my vision suggesting otherwise, as does her sudden flurry of typing. Imagine her words: *omg did u hear that?* I edit: *omfg did u hear what that fat bitch just said to me???* I shrug compulsively, act as if I am both stretching and pulling my thin blazer onto my shoulders more securely. I get my cafetière for one from my drawer and slouch to the kitchen.

In the kitchen I feel the side of the kettle, still hot, and as soon as I click the button it starts rumbling promisingly quickly. There is a third of a supermarket coffee and walnut cake on a plate – someone's birthday – and, after checking no one is about to enter, I eat it quickly. I brush crumbs from my chest and busily scoop ground coffee into my waiting cafetière, bringing the kettle off its base just as the boil begins and pour. The silty black water soothes me and I think of Tom's cup in His sink – just one – and I am hot with longing.

I can think rationally now, stirring the coffee and deciding, uncharacteristically, as I am alone in the kitchen, to add both sugar and milk. Tom has ended our relationship as cleaner and employer – He has become uncomfortable with the perception of me being His subordinate and thus intends to start a new life with us as equals, peers, lovers, husband, wife, companions. Levelling things before we meet, properly, in Paris. The one star was a slip of the thumb in His attempt to end the old way and start the new, I feel it in my marrow. I sip and the coffee is so warm and sweet and lovely, loving, that I close my eyes like every airhead in a noughties yoghurt advertisement.

Fortified, I return to my desk. Nina doesn't look at me as she usually does, displeasure radiating from her like her split ends, but I smile vaguely and say, *anyone doing anything nice this weekend?* even though it's only Thursday, and she turns to me, softens, to say *we're going to a wedding in Northern Ireland where we literally don't know anyone, apart from the bride and groom of course, you?* I'm due to see James tonight for dinner at a Nepalese place, which I tell Nina, omitting the name of my date. Let them think it's with Tom; it should be.

Earlier today I looked at the menu and have been dreaming ever since of buttery parathas, thick, hot dumplings, soft bites of spiced chicken, fragrant rice and snowy mountain air. *Let me know how it is,* said Rebecca imperiously from her desk behind me: *I walk past it like, every day. Sure,* I say. If I must. The restaurant is so near James's house that it's clear he's hoping that, again, we'll seize this opportunity to practise further sexual techniques. Blood is still leaking morosely from my vagina so it's unlikely, but not entirely off the table, I suppose.

I look at Anna's Instagram and see she's still drinking piña coladas under palm trees in some ridiculous resort in St Lucia. I feel oddly fond of her and wonder if we can be friends, she and her fiancé, me and Tom, perhaps holidaying with our young children in future summers.

I feel almost shy as I leave work the next day to a chorus of *have fun!* and *see you tomorrow!* Do I have friends? I find myself wishing them a happy weekend in return and almost meaning it. James and I meet inside the restaurant; ushered to a high-backed chair by a smiling waiter, I'm early and he's on time, which seems to put him on edge; our conversation goes like this: *hey, how are you doing? Fine thanks, you? Good, you?* etc. He works in some sort of tech role in a start-up to do with investing; he initially glossed over the details but now we are better acquainted he is beginning to tell stories of JJ and James 'Fitzie' Fitzgerald from work and I smile a lot and nod. I read an article about how to be good on dates and it told me that everyone is interesting, you just have to let them show it. James is doing his best. He gets on well with his parents, he says, as if I might be interested. He writes poetry, he tells me, shyly, and I nod thoughtfully. We're having a nice time, I suppose. I still can't fathom why James enjoys our time together so much, looking so merrily into my eyes and repeatedly reaching across the heavy white tablecloth to brush my fingertips with his. We're drinking, as is tradition, and when we're two sheets to the wind and James lurches to his feet to go to the bathroom, I make a decision. I pick up his phone which he has left face down on the table, trustingly, and unlock it with the pin I have seen him enter before: *1604* – I would bet money – my life – it's his birthday, it must be – a fair and bonny spring baby. I delete our WhatsApp messages, then find my number in his contacts – *Alice* – and delete my number from there too. I lock his phone, and slip it into the pocket of his jacket hanging on the back of his chair, deflated. I wish I could pay but I don't have time, and who has cash any more? I flip through the cards in my wallet and leave a fully stamped coffee shop loyalty card I had been saving. I rise and leave swiftly, stepping into the night through the Friday-evening pavement drifters, drinkers towards the bus stop. As the cement shocks my warm, tipsy feet, hot hands in pockets, I envision him running after me – catching my hand – and speed up. I must look comical, ridiculous, in my post-work date-night clothes, hot-footing it in the dusk like a wind-up toy. I think of James, good natured, smiling at the thought of returning to our snug table for two, empty plates scraped clean, my dark eyes, perhaps contemplating a coffee, then his confusion at my empty chair, the panic as he looks for his phone – swiftly followed by relief as he finds it – then his attempts to text me: *everything OK?* only to discover I have vanished completely like a spirit. How long will he wait for me, wondering if I will return?

I really do mean to go into work on Friday, getting up early, showering, sliding on black tights, a smart black dress, loafers, but when I step outside I find myself wandering towards Big Tesco, thinking I will stop by Roseacres to lay eyes on Mr M who will probably cheer me up with his gentle questions and interest. I text Marta: *have dentist appointment this morning, sorry just remembered* [tooth emoji]. It's not like she'll be in on a Friday morning anyway. I buy some fronds of eucalyptus from a florist still setting up, because I have thought of a cheerful lie to tell Mr M based on the book about ancient woods I have been carrying around in my bag to give him: *I have been forest-bathing, talking to the trees.* I hope the image of dappled light and ancient bark will cheer him, together with the memory of the stupendous crashing and stirring of thousands of leaves overhead, the subtle creaking of twigs underfoot. Will he ever see a forest again? Signing in, I am greeted by Jess with some surprise. *It's not the weekend, is it, hun?* she says, looking at her ugly analogue watch as if the answer would lie there, and then the paper desk calendar right in front of her face. *No, I just wanted to visit Mr M*, I say, glancing at the time and entering it precisely into the logbook: 09.03. *Check he's better.* I look behind me, as if he'll be shuffling along the corridor on his frame now, blue cardigan over his square, stooped shoulders, although of course he'll be settled in his room, post-breakfast, possibly having a snooze. There's an odd, eiderdown pause and I look up from the dotted line upon which I am busily signing my name. Jess opens her mouth and time bends sickeningly; I know what she is going to say before she says it, before her mouth becomes minuscule and sad, before her brow furrows in sympathy, her head tilts to one side. *O hun*, she says. *I am sorry. I know you two got on.* Her hot hand touches mine, still holding the pen. I drop it so it swings from a string, clattering impotently against the sides of the counter. I walk to his room, ignoring Jess's call of *hun*, then, *Alice*. I did not know she knew my name. His door is shut, and when I push it open the room behind is naked-looking and glaring. I half expected ghostly squares on the wall where his photos had hung, but there are none. The walls are white, the bed is bare. I try to cry, but nothing. I bolt, almost knocking over a carer holding a bingo cage and a handful of bingo dabbers. Pens and balls drop to the floor and skitter and ricochet. Two fat ladies.

I find myself back with Jess, and her head tilts on its axis again. *I'm so sorry hun*, she says, reaching forwards, hand on my forearm. *He passed away on Wednesday night.* (Died, my mother corrects her in my head. *Passed away is euphemistic and common.*) I shake her damp hand off my arm.

Was it his cold, that caused it, I ask. *Yes,* says Jess. *It was a particularly nasty strain, that one. His lungs just couldn't cope.*

But he was old, I say. *Yeah, I suppose,* she says. *But still, it's sad. He was particularly full of life, wasn't he?*

I walk numbly and slowly, stopping briefly when a middle-aged woman in gym gear and a Dryrobe says with concern, *are you all right, love?* I remove my hand from where it has been pressed to my chest and smile stiffly. *You're really pale,* she continues, *you feeling all right?* I don't bother responding and I walk to work, on autopilot, despite my fake dentist appointment affording me at least another hour off. I find the office is empty, as Nina and the others are at some all-staff meeting that I can't bring myself to join, even though I'm only 15 minutes late for it. I sit heavily at my desk, tuck myself in tightly until it is digging into my stomach and I feel nauseous. I google the statistics of dying from a common cold, and the age expectancy of UK citizens. Three-quarters of an hour later desks around me are filling again. *O hi Alice! You missed such drama with the trade union vote,* Rebecca says. I put my earphones in.

Was it his cold, that caused it, I ask. *O no, he'd quite recovered from that,* says Jess. *He had a massive stroke, which is common at his age, and unfortunately never woke up.*

19.

I TAKE THE NOW FAMILIAR ROUTE FROM WORK TO Tiggy's gallery in a self-granted extended lunch break, and, for once, slowly, raise my finger to the buzzer. I am emboldened, possibly artificially so, after an illicit glass of wine from the pub around the corner, but I feel a desire to see her up close, scrutinise her in the flesh, read her thoughts. After a pause, I press it. Her head snaps round, hair flying then settling, and with an encouraging smile, she leans forwards to grant me admittance. I have worn my smartest clothes, so as not to be too out of place, although the offering wasn't great: an old COS blazer, a cast-off of Cass's found on a visit to my mum, unstructured and androgynous on her narrow shoulders, fitted along mine. A shift dress. A vintage leather bag that looks a bit Anya Hindmarch. I have middle-parted my hair in an attempt to follow the trend, but a lifetime of side parting has strands marking their desire to return to their habitual position, so my hands are constantly tucking and re-tucking them in place. *Good afternoon!* Tiggy says, standing up, straight, white teeth on show, nose wrinkling charmingly like she hasn't a care in the world. As cut-glass as

I'd expected: *I'm Tiggy. Would you like me to take you round, or would you prefer to just have a browse?* My throat is so dry that when I open my mouth to respond, nothing comes out. She looks at me politely and I feel my cheeks flush hot, my stomach contract. Yes, I want to appraise her, see if I can spot signs of sorrow and self-hatred in her glance, but had forgotten that, in turn, she would be able to appraise me, scan my body with her eyes. I hide behind my hair, gesture vaguely at the room and she nods conspiratorially, as if we are best friends already. *You take your time,* she says, and sits down again. *Let me know if I can help you with anything.* The last time we were this close I bruised her coccyx. I concentrate on being confident and artistic, chin up, stepping boldly, standing in front of paintings for indefinite periods of time.

When I leave, forty-five minutes later, she engages me in some chit-chat as she digs out an embossed business card and hands it to me, asking about my existing art collection (*developing,* I say vaguely), my plans for the rest of the week. I tell her I am going to Paris for the weekend, scrutinising her face but she doesn't react other than to smile and say, *o I simply adore Paris, have you been before?* I say, airily, *o, two or three times* and she smiles kindly or patronisingly as if that isn't very many. I have, of course been to Paris before on a couple of regimented school trips, and my sister and I had gone with our mother one sweltering August, slipping under the city's dozens of bridges on a bateau-mouche, the blessed relief of echoes and shade.

Countless times I looked at Tiggy's face as I drifted about in front of the art, trying to discern her thoughts, to see if she was on edge, if she leapt unduly quickly to check her phone when it buzzed, to see if hurt or despair settled around her mouth in repose, to see if my actions had caused her pain. She seemed calm and professional, untroubled by life. I wished to find fault in her symmetrical face, and settled on the thinness of her lashes, something that the coatings of mascara could not hide.

I've said it before, many times, but: it's time, it's truly, truly time. The clock rolls. Now. When I saw Tom's Eurostar ticket I wavered over booking a seat on the same train, the same carriage so I could glimpse the back of His head, or His noble profile, His easy manner with His plain sister and mother. Then, I wanted to be in Paris before Him, to have Him enter my space, colonial; to wait at Gare du Nord and look for Him, to welcome Him. I'm travelling in on the Friday mid-morning train, suitcase wedged at my feet. I have booked a studio Airbnb for two nights in Le Marais, tucked in a golden side street near the Musée Picasso. I walked these streets all last night on Google Maps, tracking the bright, tree-lined boulevard south from the station, where I will trot, pulling my suitcase through the flat colourless expanse of the Place de la République, dodging skateboarders who might call to me, coarsely, before I melt into the yellow and twisting labyrinth of cobbles and dead ends (culs-de-sac), shabby bakeries with crooked lines of people outside. My French is middling but I can count to one hundred, so I do that, silently, mouthing the bulbous words, over and over.

I find no pleasure in the faded streaks of countryside through milky glass, the soothing vibrations of the train wobbling my bones, the mellifluous French voices around me, the bitter gusts of steam from coffee cup lids removed, the snap-hiss of M&S tinnies for breakfast (what else but pink gin and tonics for the depressing collection of hens at the end of the carriage, one in a limp veil; I also hear the muted pop of a cork and a discordant, bright *woo!*, the tapping together of celebratory plastic cups), the light patter of commuters' keyboards, the dark-eyed, pink-cheeked baby looking loftily at me through the gap between the seats. Giddy anticipation has been replaced with a sluggish worry. I twist a strand of hair around my finger and feel it become soft and oily. I chew it into a wet point and absently paint trails of saliva onto my hand with it, babyish and coy. Even though I won't see Him until tomorrow I'm wearing my new silken skirt, soft jumper, my sensible heels, and have spent half an hour sweeping on and wiping off a matte blue-red lipstick so my lips feel dry and raw, a faint pink around my mouth from various rubbings – although the lines seem neat in my round pocket-mirror, not too clownish and smudged, or slutty. My head is clouded with subtle traces of grapefruit, rosemary and sea minerals, the scent unfamiliar, having stopped at a Space NK after leaving the gallery to buy the perfume Tiggy wears, the one I saw in Tom's bathroom once. I am jittery, I haven't eaten since breakfast, when I gnawed listlessly at a terrible croissant (to get in the mood) at my desk, scattering bronze flakes onto my lap and causing Nina to pointedly brush off her desk, and my stomach feels hollow and withered, past hunger. I hope I look as dainty as I feel.

I listen to Tom's music as the train rages under the Channel, emerging into the peaceful poppy fields of Normandy, pylons slipping away, electric cables dipping and rising and dipping and rising. Radiohead. Time swerves so the journey seems interminable, yet when we arrive it feels much too soon to be at Gare du Nord; I'm not ready, not prepared, ill-equipped and flustered. I follow the shuffling *hommes d'affaires* to the roiling gut of the city, the Métro, breathing in its swelling scent, little cottonball mice hiding beneath railings and cheeping fearfully with an accent.

I emerge into the damp air, panting at the stairs I have just mounted two at a time, skirting a trembling, prostrate beggar, dirty empty palms held aloft, a young mother pulling a pushchair backwards up the steps, headscarf slipping, into Paris, white sky, glorious sunshine façades concealing tall and crooked buildings with sloping roofs and perilous staircases.

My Airbnb looked light-filled and airy online but, after collecting the key from the safe outside, letting myself into the building, and climbing three floors of shallow stone steps, historic no doubt, it feels sullen and foreboding, the bed soft and lone, the armoire hunkered down by the window, casting a long muted shadow in the flat daylight, and emitting a rush of woody perfume when I open a door. Mothballs spin. There is a locked cupboard of the owner's belongings which I immediately want to open; this is a rare Airbnb that actually appears to be lived in. My eye skims over the shoddy cleaning job, thirty euros extra according to the invoice: the watermarks on the carelessly wiped mirror, ragged balls of hair and dust in the very corners of the room, under the bed. I see the white spines of poetry, and a fragrant booklet of Papier d'Arménie, which I bring to my nose and sniff. The apartment owner's mother, I think, smiles languidly from an old-fashioned photo, with red lips in a sepia studio, Algerian perhaps: Berber. Her eyebrows are cleanly arched, and long, in a style somewhat démodé, elegantly trailing to fine points. My own are threaded in an overlit shopping centre every few weeks for eight pounds by an abrupt Indian woman who I like to imagine is my grandmother. Every time, she turns my chin with rough fingers, tutting, before clenching white thread between strong teeth and conjuring even, unremarkable brows on my smarting face. Our mother, as English as they come, tall, athletic, fair, with good genes, seemingly didn't think to tell me or Cass about the practicalities of removing body hair beyond basic leg- and armpit-shaving, staying tactful and silent as our half-Asian blood and adolescence brought forth faint and silky moustaches, coarse sideburns, and feathering, cumbersome brows. After Jamie Gardner turned meaningfully to me during a choice PSHE lesson with his index finger wedged horizontally under his nose, Hitlerish, as Miss O'Brien wrote 'body hair' on the whiteboard under the heading 'puberty', I ran to Cass in the playground, whispering hotly in her ear, each clutching sweating hands. She took me to Boots after school and bought a tub of hair removal cream and a pair of tweezers, and thenceforth our upper lips were a hairless waxy pink, our eyebrows two distinct entities. Cass had an eye for it, plucking her own into fine arches that filled out as fashion dictated, offering to do mine too, but I was embarrassed and stubborn, misjudged, and they never looked quite right. I was always ashamed of the verdant growth of my dark body, creeping like knotweed from the normal places to the abnormal, the sickening trails of hair here and there, the knowledge that this was disgusting to others, but once I reached the anonymity of London I walked right into a salon and had every hair on my body removed with brusque violence. If this North African siren had been my mother, perhaps everything would be different.

Dropping my bags, pausing to bounce experimentally on the bed, I take a photo of the view from the window, which I send to my mother and sister: *city break!* There are no distinguishing landmarks visible, but it is still unmistakably Paris. I wait for a response (Cass sends a French flag emoji, nothing from my mother), check my lipstick, then turn and head outside into the silver morning.

I walk here and there, stopping at a row of stationers near the river and popping into one, then another, and another, finally buying a notebook that is vastly more expensive than I would usually allow, but I keep thinking of Dante's words, *in the book of my memory – the part of it before which not much is legible – there is the heading: here begins the new life.* This, this trip, tomorrow, Tom, this is the beginning of new life for me. I no longer have any doubts about arriving here before Him, this is the time for me to plan my first words to Him, imagine His response, to sit, pensively, pen in limp grasp, ordering another coffee with the lift of a finger and a red smile. I do just that, I walk and I see the river, wide and green, and the islands nestled like doves within it, and I walk past the Bouquinistes and their plastic-wrapped treasures and I stop and I look at a little carousel of postcards, almost buying one for Mr M before remembering. I walk again, and walk, and find the café I have been searching for – half full, grey-headed Frenchmen with cigarettes, two espressos each, beauties that look at once twelve and thirty, gap-toothed and long-limbed and knowing, a couple of tourists in anoraks, one navy, one yellow, puzzling over a phone map and pouring too much sugar-water into citrons pressés.

I read once that Hemingway wrote here, impoverished, ravenous, and I follow the waiter's gesture and sit, holding my breath, on the terrace, exhaling and inhaling as I open up my notebook, hoping to absorb whatever he left here of his talent, his intensity, his ability to love fiercely, furiously.

Hours pass, and the heater above me burns. I have two coffees, grainy with sugar, by which time it is lunch, when I order a glass of red wine and steak tartare, piquant and yielding and sweet, accompanied by salty, scalding chips – frites – and a bitter, frilly salad, followed by a crème brûlée, which I gamely tap with a spoon like Amélie. I write and I write, and I imagine someone, Him, sitting a few tables away, watching me, amused, wry, perhaps, wondering what it is that I write. I am pleased by this imaginary voyeur, run my hand through my hair, chew the pen suggestively, crossing my legs. I look up, daringly, inviting a gaze, and am met only with the backs of heads, laughing profiles. I know He would watch me, hungrily. I write of my life, how it will be. The words we will say, the touches we will share, the ring He will buy me, the way He will grip my hair at the nape of my neck, and I will hold my breath. Time slinks by and the afternoon is violet. My wrist burns, my fingers cramped and small. I order another glass of wine, vinegar. I look down at what I've been writing, pages and pages: *Tom, Tom, Tom.*

*

Morning slips in, silken. Before returning to the Airbnb last night I bought two bottles of red wine from a supermarket, found those cornichons, cheese. One bottle is for tonight, of course, with Tom, the other I uncorked yesterday with gusto, slopping it into a glass and dancing self-consciously to a record I found on a shelf, Mahalia Jackson, feeling like a heroine in a romcom and wondering if people could see me from the street. I imagined Tom standing at the window, spread, pliant butter, on the bed. Restlessness, agitation – and I washed it away with the wine. Take, drink, for this is my blood. I flipped the same record countless times, wore down the needle. Folded myself. Slept.

I unclose my eyes and a bright square of window glares. Now, of course, the apartment looks how it should have yesterday, lemony light pooling and my head o my head. I go to the tiny bathroom and find an acid and Pinot bowlful of vomit in the loo, a foul tideline, which I flush before heaving into the rushing water again. I have somehow ruined today already and my head feels sickly loose on its stalk. I pluck pills from my handbag and take two paracetamol and two ibuprofen, upending my silicon-clad glass bottle so violently that water courses down my chin and into the neckline of my jumper. I stop, mouth slack. My jumper. I am wearing my soft, soft jumper and my silken skirt, now rumpled and smelling of sweat and – o. I look at myself in the neat, propped mirror and raise both hands to my stomach, grip it hard, my eyes look at my eyes and I say, *you are a fat, appalling, stupid fucking bitch and no one will ever love you.* And then I look at the time on my phone which I have miraculously plugged in to charge, together with its adapter, and have a shower, sluicing off the evening, shuddering. My shower gel is an exact match for Tom's; it's as if we are getting ready together, soaping limbs. Tom's train is due at 12.52 and everything rests on this.

I had a vision, like Joseph; spun from light and played and replayed on the inside of my eyelids. Slow-motion crowds in Gare du Nord, He steps down from the train, pushing His hair from His eyes, helping His mother frailly disembark, looking up as the roguish French overhead announcer breathes into the air. The hypnotic ebb of the throng interspersed with the unmistakable oafish shamble of the English, turning heads. Our eyes meet and the thread lying dormant in His chest shakes awake, taut. He walks to me, His mother calling imperiously after Him, *but darling—*; *it's you*, He will say.

Or, I will be standing with studied insouciance outside the restaurant at which they will have lunch as though waiting for someone (Him, Him) and He will look at me and wonder, then I will sit at a table in His eyeline and order a single chilled glass and wait, and wait, perhaps pulling out a novel or a book of poetry and reading, or, yes, writing, and He will wonder why I am lunching alone, and His gaze will snag mine and I'll give a rueful shrug and smile. And He will come to me. And— enough.

I miss my turning, confusing this cobbled side street for that, turning *à gauche* too late, *trop tard*, committing to this windy street, foolishly seeking my original path, only to circle, lost. All this means my journey is not the honeyed stroll I had envisaged, checking myself out, coquette, in windowpanes, the slink of silk – my pace quickens and the beginning of dampness rises at the base of my bra and the slope of my spine. Despite a frantic scrubbing and hair-drying, my clothes from last night are beyond saving and I am standing in front of the mirror with my Sunday-morning attire laid out: Breton and blue. I think of Tom's love for me and I could appear in sackcloth and hessian, feet wrapped in rags, hair stiff with grime, and He would know me, and touch my face, and pull me to Him. I am ashamed of my vanity and when getting ready, scratched at my thighs and stomach to rid myself of it, then pulled on my jeans and top roughly, skin stinging.

The morning was glorious, yes, after last night's deluge, but now brisk clouds are kite-like in the sky, ribbons trailing. Rain will follow. I rise to a trot, eyeing the sky, shivering with my hangover and anticipation.

Was it his cold, that caused it, I ask. O no, he'd quite recovered from that, says Jess. He unfortunately found and drank all the sherry in the kitchens and died of alcohol poisoning. Thin blood, you see.

—and I am there, with only a few minutes to choose where to stand. I scan the scene before me and I swear to god it is how I envisioned it; dreamlike swirling crowds (a hiss and billow of steam accompanied the stirring strings in my head), my eyes finding Him, pinning Him, catching like wool on barbed wire, the minute He becomes visible, smiling at something one of the women at His side says. I know when I see Him I won't say anything now but will take pleasure in trailing in His gorgeous wake, a quick pilot fish. I keep a respectful distance as we stream into the Métro, then, noting this trio's self-absorption, venture close enough to see the multitude of colours in His wavy hair which strokes His collar, to smell the powdery fug of His mother's perfume. The carriage is packed; I wedge myself to His back which is warm and jacketed and feel my body slacken with relief. Pressed thus, I thrill as I hear His voice and I think, I really do, I think I feel the vibration of His voice through His back, seductive, and hear the answering pain in my breast. I never was a pretty crier so I turn my head from Him, fumbling for my powder compact and little round mirror which falls swiftly and is beautifully cracked under His heel as He steps back to steady Himself.

I silently follow Him, to the ends of the earth for all I care, taking turns to sip and drink at Him, His dark head, tender and pale behind the ears, scuffed shoes, the ones I have slipped onto my own feet and shuffled in. I bide my time, waiting for the perfect moment to rest a light hand on Him, to tap that shoulder, call His name.

20.

AS I FOLLOW TOM, MY HEART SHRILL, AGONISING, pressing both hands to my breastbone, I think of the haunting, creeping games Cass and I used to play around our grand-mother's darkening house; elastic shadows. Standing in front of Dorothea Tanning's *Eine Kleine Nachtmusik* at the Tate a few years ago, absorbing the ripe, fleshy sunflower and the trailing rags, the curve of a belly, hair lifting off the neck – a visceral dread crept up my limbs and I sat down on a nearby bench, fearful and nostalgic. Our games were childish fancy, shot through with panicked laughter, but we felt real terror, our imaginations conjuring villains and finding comfort in each other's sweaty grip. Holding our breaths, listening, the whites of eyes shining, crouching under the bottom shelf in the larder, by the pasta shapes, in the garage by the logs, watching woodlice beetle their way about, alert.

After waiting and waiting for Tom to realise Tiggy was not for Him, and after a few, long, late nights numbly scrolling through more Instagram shots of arms around waists and hands in hands and heads on shoulders, following, finding those same arms, waists, hands, heads, those careful, careless touches from a different angle, I knew it was time to take matters into my own hands – we are meant for each other, we are, we are, but as with the planets, gods, crystals, prayers, the path must be smoothed for I am impatient and have waited long enough. And so, I'm quite good at subterfuge, at knowing when to slacken pace, when to dart forth, how to loiter at a shop window, peering interestedly, how to trail behind a larger group with a half-smile as if part of them, connected by years of friendship and flat-shares and get-togethers and drunken arguments and laughter and crushing hugs, of careless I love yous and text me when you get homes. My skills don't end there; I've perfected Tom's handwriting – to a layperson's eye, that is – as proven by the note I scratched, slowly, into the pad by Tom's bed with Tom's pen in Tom's letters, *Returning these to you. T x.* I had pre-prepared the contents of this parcel – a pair of ostentatious lace knickers, clearly not hers, if His laundry basket is anything to go by, and much cheaper than any she would deign to wear, a size or two too big, the ultimate insult, with the contents of the condom I had been saving for this very purpose smeared into the gusset, finger painting for perverts. I added an earring pocketed a week ago, her stupid toothbrush, a half-used box of green tea, two hair ties (beige, for blondes), an Invisibobble, the soothing rose hand lotion she'd taken to leaving on one side of the bed, a gym-branded padlock I knew wasn't Tom's. I popped it all in a box, for poetry. I knew He wouldn't notice the disappearance of these trivial things. But it did the trick, once she found it on her doorstep a few days ago. I'd been hoping she'd open the parcel there and then, so

I could witness the surprise, the superior smile at expecting a little present, a well-deserved little treat, the confusion at the knickers, the note, her trinkets, the sorrow, the anger, the tears carving lines in her porcelain make-up, dripping milkily off her chin. Instead, she took it inside immediately, neutral, expressionless, as if she receives unexpected parcels all the time, is showered with gifts and love regularly. To make things certain, to clear the path for our love and deaden the noise so He can hear me, were the tabs left open in Tom's laptop, in private browser mode for extra points: nearest STD clinic, symptoms of chlamydia. He won't touch her again. How I wish I could have been a fly on the wall, to see her mascara-streaked face, shaking the underwear at Him in fury, or sadness, or defiance, sick with the unfairness of it all. Or maybe she just texted Him: *we're done*, and unfollowed Him on Instagram. I hope He was kind to her. I know He was.

I hang back as Tom slows, waiting by His sister who is navigating using her phone, finger raised. I know where the restaurant they are looking for is, a little further down this road, its sign temporarily obscured by the unlovely bars of scaffolding scaling a wall ahead. How I would love to take His hand, to lead Him there. I need Him on His own, somehow. I fiddle briefly with my phone: perhaps I too am steering myself to a fun destination, friends, companionship, then glance at my reflection in bowed glass and am disfigured, grotesque, my furrowed brow and disquieted expression stretching and spreading, lending me the look of an anguished Greek mask of tragedy. Grant me courage o Melpomene. My whole being trembles at the thought of the end of my loneliness, my skin singing at the promise of touch. With this next moment my life, my tainted, ugly life will be made new. The sensation in my heart is true pain, torment; my hands ache with His absence. I can end this now. I suck in my stomach, then release – He will love me as I am.

I start forwards, and tap Him on the shoulder, His sister ahead in nose-to-phone intensity, mother stepping round-shouldered and ponderously behind, shawls flapping. Tom turns and my heart is on fire.

My planned speech, written and rewritten in my notebook, flutters duplicitously from my memory. *Sorry, you dropped*, I begin, and then stop because of course He hasn't dropped a thing. *Hello*, I say. *Sorry*. I make my accent as posh as possible: *We've met before, Tom, a few weeks ago at the museum – the Victoria – I recognise you from then, or, rather, from before. We know each other. It's funny, actually, seeing you here, what are the odds, it's like fate*. A weak laugh. *Another funny thing, that, after I saw you, then, in the dark, I kept thinking I knew you and I couldn't stop thinking about you, and your face, and your – and I couldn't work out where I knew you from, school, university, the gym, maybe we'd even been on a date once* (another laugh, a blush) *or I'd seen you somewhere: a bar, a club, in the park, in the pub, on the street, on the bus, or Tube, on stairs at a station, at work, or crossing at Piccadilly Circus or queuing in Pret or – But then I thought I've seen your picture, you know, I kept seeing this one image of you in my mind, you're smiling, and squinting a bit in bright sun, your hair gentle on your forehead – so I realised we hadn't met in person, I must have seen a photo, so I thought: OK then, have I seen Him – you – in print: the papers or on the back*

*of a book, or, then it hit me: online, website, news site, I wondered
if we'd chatted on a dating app* (breath-laugh, cheeks hot) *or
something, and then, this is where it gets weird, I realised I actually
know where you live, because I clean as a part-time job – it's not
my real job, don't worry – and I think I clean your flat? Sorry is
that weird, but I think I've been cleaning your flat for about a year
so I know the place really well, and so, well, you.* Silence. *O sorry*
(hair tuck), *I'm Alice.*

Unsaid: Even now I can feel the grip of your hand in my hair,
and on hip, o I would turn to face you; you could look and look
at me. Your body would worship my body and my body would
worship you and o I would do anything, literally anything that
you wanted me to do. With you I will be beautiful, with you I
will be loved, with you I will not be lonely. It is my heart's desire
to hear you say – *Alice* – o my soul's joy.

Tom's face is wrong. It's not smiling in recognition, or even
amusedly uncertain, the beginnings of light puzzlement, of
charm building in that brow, a barely perceptible crinkling
at the corner of the eyes. His soft mouth is not lifting, no, nor
opening with a moist unsticking, promisingly, to speak, to
kiss – it is becoming firm, a downturn at the edges, a wariness
springing forth as He steps back. I look and look at Him desperately, trying to make sense of the expression that is forming,
one so different from the one I wrote of yesterday in my new
notebook, the one I closed my eyes and dreamed of.

He speaks. *Sorry.* Clears His gorgeous scratchy throat.
Did you say you're *my cleaner? Or perhaps, you're my* cleaner?
Incredulity and scorn – this can be understood, I'm sure.
Perhaps even as shame – she's handled my underwear (o I

have done more than that, my love), seen my bathroom bin, my unmade bed. If he knew. My eyes rove His handsome face, the faint smile lines scoring the hard plane of His cheek. He steps back again, away from me. His eyes rake the expanse of my body. My heart feels as if it will spring roughly from me. His hawkish mother and sister break from their huddled conference and tiptoe to His back, broad as oceans. *Darling*, they chorus – o but He is *my* darling. He looks wary, but joy bursts in my chest as He holds His hand up and stops the progress of these two harpies. He steps away, almost into the road, and I follow, as I would follow Him anywhere, thrilled that I am to be let into His confidence.

Now we are alone, I begin to tell Him, falteringly, about the dates we've been on, the V&A late, the feel of His hand lifting the hair from the nape of my neck, His fingers looping around my hair, the tug so wonderfully a mirroring of our love, our bound hearts. Disgust rises in His face and He interrupts before I get any further than *O Tom, I—*

Stop talking, He says. His voice is clipped; I vow to neaten mine. *Listen to me.* I am attentive and overjoyed, a disciple. *Why did you leave* – He lowers His voice – *blood* – my stomach drops and I think back to the dazzlingly clean flat, as I left it, the scooped-up wrapper safely in the bin bag. What had I done – what had I done – Had it fallen out somehow? Surely not. As I replay my efficient dance around the flat, I remember in a sick, wet moment the gentle strands of uterine lining and thick menstrual pollution clouding the freshly bleached bowl. I had not flushed. The silence is charged and ugly as I think of what to say, what I should say, how I should mend this.

I am sorry, I begin. *I was unwell.*

His sea eyes leave my face and He looks above my head, as if gazing into the eyes of another divine being exactly His height, thinking, and I have the honour of scanning His lovely face, jaw already showing the fine, even shading of stubble disrupted by the delicate scar on His chin I had not noticed in photographs. He smiles slightly and says: *right*. The *t* lands hard. Encouraged, I say, *let us go then, you and I – let me apologise – have some of that orange wine you like – talk—*

I have said the wrong thing and I am fascinated and dismayed to see the range of emotion sweeping over His features, like so many ripples of wind through long grass. I struggle to interpret them, without a dictionary when I thought I would be effortlessly fluent. Thoughtful or bewildered, exasperated or angered? The silence is devastating, but I sense that while it lasts, there is still hope, so I pray it lasts for ever, that I can spend infinity looking at His changeable, expressive face, loving Him. My heart is agony, it hammers and I feel sweat spring to my brow. I listen to the unpredictable bursts and lulls of traffic, eruptions of music from car windows, the calls of children at play, and closer, the murmurs of His sister and mother, soon to be my family too. I imagine their arms hooked through mine on holidays, walks along clifftops, Mr Whippys, salty chips and vinegar.

Then. *Do you take my stuff?* Tom asks – wonderingly. I jump. His voice becomes louder. *Do you drink my wine? Eat my food?* I flinch at these words, darts. I have only ever nibbled at crusts, popped a sweet cherry tomato into my mouth, sipped at organic milk, tweaked off the foil lids of leftovers, just to taste them. I have only ever taken scraps of paper, Waitrose receipts, unimportant photos, small items of clothing, tiny trinkets, the periphery of a beautiful life. Barely anything. I am silent. I cannot lie to Him. He nods His magnificent head several times and then, I don't know how or when, He is shaking His head, eyes lowered. *I thought I was imagining it,* He says, slowly. I look and look at Him, the realness of Him. And then – I know the next question before His mobile, soft mouth forms it and ready my own to plead, *no,* but I underestimate in my imagination the drawing of His brows, the aggressive lilt to His question: *are you – are you fucking following me?* I shake my head, stung, and tears render my vision watercolour, scaffolding bending wildly, the pretty Paris balconies veering in towards us, and Tom, tall, His face smeared and monstrous.

The harpies rustle their wings and sneer. *What's going on, darling?* they chant, at His shoulders, at His back. Tom shakes His head again, slowly, teeth bared, and turns to join them, to resume the pleasant day of lunch and a gallery. Their faces peer at me with curiosity and wonder, as I stand, nose running, throat hard and swollen with a sob I am battling to keep in. His hands, slender-fingered, go so naturally to the backs of His mother and sister, between their shoulder blades (harpies' wings) to turn them away from me that I feel a tearing inside me of grief. He pauses, and turns back, and comes to me, embraces me, my head cradled to His chest, hearts beating as one.

No—

He turns back, and comes to me, and His hand reaches for me and my sweating hand unfurls ready, so ready, to link long fingers but He grips my wrist, hard, so hard I feel bones shift, a bloom of pain and says: *don't you ever – ever – come near me or my family again. If you do, I will call the police. Do you understand?* He squeezes harder and I find I am smiling desperately, longing to prolong this touch, cherishing it, the brilliant heat of His fingers, the neat crescents of His nails, o the sweet clippings of which I have kept in twists of paper, sinking into my skin. Without waiting for a response He lets go, turns again and leaves. My arm flops to my side. *Fucking crazy bitch*, He says under His breath, and it is as if a needle has lodged in my heart. *But don't you love me*, I say. Moi non plus, hisses the breeze.

I sit on the pavement and howl and a well-to-do French couple, sleekly dressed, discreetly circumnavigate me without breaking their pace or gesticulated conversation. I search in my bag, then I scrub at my face with a tissue. It comes away glutinous; fawn and black. The tears will not stop, I feel as though I will drown in them. I carry on down the road, feeling dramatic and raw, past the red and gold bistrot, looking in without appearing to look in: escargots de Bourgogne, hampe de boeuf. I see Him immediately. I was expecting an air of distraction, perhaps a chilling conference of lowered heads and brows, perhaps reflecting on our encounter, and registering the ache in His heart for me – but He is smiling, carefree, arm slung around the back of the chair next to Him in which His sister is perched, His mother looking on fondly as He sips His drink. Champagne for her stupid birthday: one thousand today. I think of all of the things I have done for Him, loving Him, thinking of Him always, buying each book He has read;

noting where He has marked His place each week and vowing to read no more until He has. Sometimes the days inched by and I would sneak in an extra page, quick-fingered, eager to learn the words, stories, that must surely be crawling into His brain, only to feel guilt-ridden and sorrowful if I found those pages unread in His copy, found that I had traitorously slipped ahead of Him. I would punish myself by pinching up fat handfuls of my thighs, my stomach, and twisting. I must have not done enough, not punished myself enough. My nails dig sickles into the padding of my palms.

I have stopped my casual stroll and am staring in at the window. Perhaps this interruption of the gentle to-ing and fro-ing of Paris life outside the glass draws His gaze to mine, or perhaps – can you imagine, now of all times – He has registered for the first time the true tone of my heart, a plucked string, inexorably bound to His? We look at each other and I imagine the bolt of love, this *coup de coeur* springing to life in Paris, leaping from me to Him, and I see a loosening of His expression of hostility, a change. He is afraid of me. I look at Him a while longer, bathing in His anxious gaze, surely, to Him, a terrible deity, miraculous, omniscient, omnipotent, directing His next step before He has even thought it, worthy of worship – offerings and sacrifice. I press a palm to the glass, a mirroring of that sign He left me in His flat all those weeks ago. A lunching family close to the window look first at me with curiosity, then, following my gaze, glance at Tom. His smooth cheek is developing a heightened colour, a painterly hue worthy of Caravaggio, both that of the blushing fruit and the boy holding the basket. He half-stands, His chin firm and I realise that

I understand Him better than anyone. He just needs time; I need to better prepare myself. I gather wild thoughts, turn and walk away from Him – just for now – something I thought I would never do.

21.

I'M BACK IN MY AIRBNB, LOOKING AT THE TWO WINE glasses I had left out, next to a black bottle of red. Twins. I don't know if I want to laugh or cry or scream until my voice dies. If this were a film I would pick the glasses up and throw them, shattering them against the wall, but I think of the scuff mark they might leave on the oaty wallpaper, the gritty needly slivers that would lodge in my palms as I swept them up. I feel bruised; not my body, but my being, aching and soft and numb. He had looked at me, yes, but not with love, or desire, or even civility. I pour myself a glass of wine for something to do, but I don't drink it.

My train home isn't until tomorrow morning; I had envisioned Tom turning to His mother: *I'm sorry, enjoy the rest of your birthday treat, I'll call you tomorrow.* Taking my hand and strolling as Paris is meant to be strolled, peering into serene courtyards and gazing at the river. Riveting, the infinitesimal stroking of a thumb on the palm, or I imagine so, as no one has done it to me but myself, closing my eyes, stupidly, dully willing the hand caressing my other to be anyone's but my own. I raise my right palm to my left cheek, my fingers sliding into my hairline, curling round my neck, thumb on soft skin. My hand is small and damp; not His. I wait for the customary tears to leak from my eyes but they don't come. I feel utterly numb, like I have died, like I am dead. My throat stings from the upward rush of wine and bile so I drink water, slide off my shoes which are beginning to rub at my heels, and get into bed revelling in the strangeness of still being clothed, the friction of denim and cotton.

I have just dozed off into a shallow, troubled dream when like clockwork, my phone rings. Two-thirty French time, half one back home. Cass, on her lunch break, although as our mother reprovingly or proudly said, once, *she never takes her full hour* – just darts down the coiling stairway, I suppose, or stands in the sleek humming lift to Pret. *And she eats takeaways in the evening sometimes, paid for by the firm,* smiled Mother: *you'd never know, she's so slim.* I feel so wretched I almost answer it so I can listen to Cass's unbearably posh voice, amped up to monstrosity by first Oxford and then her Magic Circle office, each *a* a caricaturish combination of seemingly all of the vowels, every *t* landing with precision, no glottal stops at all, they being the spoken equivalent of joggers and an oversized sweatshirt: heaven forbid. By the time I have roused myself to maybe, perhaps, answer her, she has rung off. I imagine she no longer expects me to answer, that she calls out of habit, phone pressed to ear as she impatiently queues, Pret salad (or soup, for a real treat) in hand, smiling extra hard at the servers who hold the promise of a free latte.

Cass has left a voicemail message and so, unusually downcast and fragile feeling, haunted by Tom's exquisite look of disgust, disdain, of fear tinged with hostility, I listen, rather than automatically deleting. *Just call me, please, OK, thanks, bye,* she says. She sounds well, but harried and I think I detect a chattering in the background, of *next,* or, *do you have any allergies,* or, *extra hot oat latte?*, but it could equally be the dreary hum of an office: *this is Nina, how can I help?* I play it seven times then delete it. My phone is a tranquil haven; I erase everything I receive (apart from His messages, still in the cleaning app inbox; I hastily screenshot them all now, just in case). Cass's voice, committed to memory, laps at me. I can't place the edge in tone: I, who used to know her better than anyone, as well as she once knew me. We used to call downstairs for attention and our mother wouldn't know which of us was speaking.

I feel an overwhelming urge to call back, to break the silence between us, stretched thin and brittle over the years. I am not curious to find out the reason behind her persistence; I would much rather not know – but I remember so clearly the ticklewhisper of her voice when we illicitly called each other on our new mobile phones after we were supposed to be in bed, the hysterical laughter that threatened to alert our mother to our transgression.

I have avoided thinking about it all this time. It's been crouched in my thoughts, outside of my line of sight, a gorgon to be circumnavigated with eyes lowered, shield raised. Whenever the urge to look is strong, Pippin with Saruman's palantír, I am adept at thinking very hard and determinedly about something else. But now it's time to drop the veils, a heaving-bellied, tossing-thighed Salome. Now it's time to look at the shame coiled so hotly in my belly. I pretend I am a newcomer being inducted as to why I am how I am: picture the advent of camera phones, sleek pills you could split and flip, end conversations with a snap. iPhones were small, heavy, pixelated, owned only by those whose dads could afford it. Cass and I, in each other's pockets – she was older, by a year, but people often assumed we were twins – wriggling in and out of jeans, crop tops, trainers, swapping those unsightly spiralling chokers, neon or velvet scrunchies, beaded bracelets that meant something or other: love, friendship, sisterhood.

Here it is. A camera phone, an explicit shot of a vulva, labyrinthine labial folds, a teenage mat of unkempt pubic hair, brown thighs, sent round our insular, gossipy year groups, only two people it could be, ethnically ambiguous in our largely white school, etc. etc. I can hardly bother to spell it out: boys will be boys, etc., that girl was a skank and/or sket, and/or slag, and/or slapper, and/or slut. Such sibilance. It was me – stupid, unlovely – getting carried away and Cass neither confirmed nor denied but rolled her eyes and tucked my arm tightly into hers as we walked down hallways, but I, when pressed by my classmates, her classmates, I smilingly said it was her, not me, that it was her genitals that were deformed, disgusting, monstrous, obscene. Cass, snapping back in front of the aforementioned cluster of bobbing Adam's apples and lip-glossed gum-chewers, despite the prohibition of said items in the school corridors, announced: *look, I don't have cellulite, OK*. Hem provocatively raised to display her smooth leg, upper thigh, downy and unmarked, brown but tanned, tawny, made for stroking, squeezing. I like to think I rose above such behaviour, smiled serenely to myself, turned away, hair swishing, as if I knew better, but I knew well the dimpled flesh to which she was referring, the uneven accumulation of fat cells beneath the skin puckering, easing the beginnings of silvery stretch marks, and my mouth gaped, and all I could say was: *no*. My friends wrinkled their little noses, gum lodged in their shiny molars. *Also*, Cass added, witheringly, *I wax*.

Did I ever speak to anyone again? Ever touch anyone again? Coolly gathered my things, drifted away from the group of now howling boys: grabbing one another's shoulders and bending at the waist from the sheer, incomprehensible hilarity of it. The boy I'd sent the picture to grinning, shaking his head. I'd thought he would cherish it, love me.

Cass assured me, some time afterwards, that everyone had forgotten about it, but even if this was the case, I had not. I lived the next years of school half-heartedly half absent, library-bound and reading, reading, desperate to leave. My mother did try, to give her credit, but in the worst way, blissfully ignorant of the true source of my pain, the way that only a beautiful blonde mother can misunderstand her plain dark daughter: excruciating, polite meetings at school about my grades, studiedly casual questions about boys and friends, and: *you two don't seem to be getting on – how about a nice girls' day out?* Each misfire made me retreat further.

My thoughts slip giddily to my university years – I am unable to stop the sickening flushes of embarrassment sweeping up my body, squeezing my heart, which thuds torturously. Such calamitous unrequited love, crippling shame. My mother's emphasis on class, of being well bred, well mannered, like a flat-nosed dog or a horse with steaming flanks, made a fool of me – I thought that knowing to say napkin: not serviette, or what: not pardon, nestled me into this gang of Mitfords, made me part of them. Our mid-range private school was no match for the people I encountered, and from whom I was immediately, carelessly, excluded. I remember freshers' week; the crowd of Home Counties girls who established friendships bewilderingly quickly. I think I lost my ability to be – without Cass I was a ghost.

Lost and aimless, I joined a drama society, and met, or rather saw, a boy, the flame around which we, dull moths, amassed. I suppose he had shades of Tom, a pale, boyish imitation, with long fingers I thought trailed so gracefully in the air as he spoke, described, explained. My heart tremored when I saw him, heard him; his voice so measured and clear – well spoken. He'd say to the fair-haired wisp of a Perdita, *when you do dance, I wish you a wave o' th' sea, that you might ever do nothing but that.* She, a poor actor, would sway and smile but I knew those words were meant for me, that during the clumsy courtly dances choreographed by a grad student, that when he pressed palms with Perdita that he longed for that palm, those small steps, that upturned face to be mine. My part, a shepherdess, had no lines but smilingly took from him a bundle of flowers at the sheep shearing. In early rehearsals this was imagined; he would bow and exaggeratedly present me with a bouquet of air, his hands so expressive I saw the flowers shimmering there. I would take them and if our fingertips brushed electricity would course through my veins and I'd know he felt it too. The first time he winked at me, another time he pretended to drop the ghostly bouquet and I stumbled to catch it and he laughed with me, with me. When the prop assistant conjured up a real, rustling sheaf of lavender and rosemary I was heartbroken; our playful pretence became real, clouded with scent, but I reassured myself that our love could now become real, become known. Night after night he said his line, *when once she is my wife*, holding the hands of another, but he looked over her head, to me, to me, to me. Our final performance was euphoric; we bowed to the sparse audience of friends and the odd parent and as the curtains swung back into place my heart beat and beat and I could hear his heart beating too, beating the same frenetic tempo as mine and he smiled at me and I, a swollen river breaching a bank, I ran, I flowed to him and embraced him, pressed my heart to his, at last. His hands came to my shoulders and patted, pressed lightly, and I could feel the answering heat of his body. I clung and clung and hid my face in his chest then turned it to his, ready to say, to hear, *when you speak, sweet, I'd have you do it ever*, I saw him looking at the others, his face in a comic expression that even I could read; incredulity, a droll sort of alarm, wonder, amusement. His hands uncurled my fingers from his costume, he stepped back and said, putting on a hideously comic voice: *now, now*. And Perdita said clearly, for all to hear: *o wow*, and I was alone. Outside, having fled, my heart convulsed, in agonies, and someone walking by said: *are you OK?* But I ignored them and walked as best I could to my room, repeating to myself: *I have tremor cordis on me: my heart dances; but not for joy; not joy—*

The less said about these aborted university days, the better, really. Much of my time was spent reading and reading and hiding. But know a box of things: props, scripts, photos, a diary, survives. I used to sift through it daily, then weekly, thumbing pencil-annotated pages with a purr, breathing the paper-scented gusts, remembering the wildness, then fear, in his eyes as he saw me waiting one night, two years later, half-hidden in the dark, the fizzing anticipation of my palms and the cautious, steady beat of my heart that stayed calm even as I raised my hands to touch, to grip – I have not looked at it in years.

London would be different – and o it still can be. I am suddenly desperate to return home, sick of Paris and its promise of beauty but delivering instead only pain.

The silence in the apartment is brutal, broken by the odd harsh cry outside, workmen, rattling. I sit and look at the detritus of the past twenty-four hours cast on the floor and see crumpled by my shoes the receipt from yesterday's lunch at the bistrot, where I had been so careful to plan. I stretch and capture it between two fingers, rolling back heavily. My pocket guidebook is still by the bed, and I open it so as to tuck the receipt next to the listing on Hemingway's café, where I felt his ghost snatching at my basket of baguette slices, eyeing me appreciatively, and I find it was not that café at all that I ate at, but quite another one with a similar name, several streets away, left and left again. My stomach lurches – had I gone to the correct café, navigated properly, met Hemingway's ghost, done things right, Tom would have felt it, felt our love. Tears slip down my cheeks and I take out my notebook and write *I'm sorry I'm sorry I'm sorry.* I look at the serene North African woman on the wall, and she smiles at me, unreadable.

22.

TO TELL YOU THE TRUTH, I CAN'T TELL YOU WHAT I did with my last evening in Paris. I remember white teeth in a beard, telling some German tourists about my job with no memory of a response; digging through my backpack for far too long, unzipping and rezipping minuscule pockets to find my lipstick, before discovering it in an inner compartment with a flourish and presenting it to someone who had lost interest by then. I remember trying to remember the name of absinthe, of purring *I'm the green fairy.* I remember laughing, great wracking gasps. I remember an apologetic waiter stacking chairs in an empty room, and saying, *I am sorry, mademoiselle ...* and shrugging in a gesture so comically French I cried with laughter before leaving and it taking me several walks up and down the street in the driving rain to find my bed for the night.

In essence, I got drunk. I woke to the detritus of late-night McDonald's wrappers from Croque McDos, a sharing box of McNuggets, and chips on chips on chips. The smell in the room animal and cardboard.

*

My knees are bruised, my palms smart with small, angry scratches and I lie on my bedroom floor at home, shavasana. I had skulked past my housemates who were having some sort of gathering, faux-intellectual conversations fluttering as they chortled together over spatchcocked chicken carcasses and a Pyrex jug of gravy; steamed tenderstem broccoli and pallid roast potatoes. An alert buzzes and I read that the Airbnb host has requested 150 euros for damage; I authorise it and let my phone slide from my fingers to rest on the carpet. I remember red wine dripping down the wall, pooling on the floor, just to the edge of the rug, and then contrition, scrubbing it to a smeared pink. I lie motionless and my lower back aches from the strain. *Listlessness does not become you*, my mother used to say, but I always had the feeling that nothing on earth would ever become me: listlessness, earnestness, short hair, fringes, dark nail varnish, stripes, bodycon, A-line, tomboyishness, girlishness, androgyny, bohemian carelessness, New York uptightness, smartness, sports kit, sports, sweating, civility, dresses, make-up, wistfulness, confidence, prudishness, sexuality, sexlessness, body hair, body weight, being overweight, that T-shirt of my sister's that I longed for – the one that I stole and wore and spoilt. *Your father's daughter*, my mother would say, turning away.

I just need to make it to Wednesday – the final push. How can I bring it back from the shock of red in the white toilet – yes, that word is the only one appropriate now – unwanted, animal, my flesh, my blood, the secret splashings and misery of my body. Perhaps He looked at it the way He looked at me yesterday – was it only yesterday – bared teeth, drawn brows, gorge rising, perhaps He worried for my safety. If I can apologise properly, if I can just explain, I can bring it back, bring Him back. Tom's box is on the floor with me; I ferret about in it, blindly, letting my fingers close over first one thing, then another. Paper, faded jottings, glossy features. Strands of hair twisted up in tissue paper. A sliver of a bar of soap that has slid over His body. I scrape my teeth over it and feel wafer-like shavings rest bitterly on my tongue. Every sensation Tom has had, I want it, craving that sensation of wanting to be someone, both to actually be that person, for each atom of your body to knit with theirs, disappearing entirely, and yet still able to hold them, caress them.

There is a tentative knock on my door and I am shaken from my reverie to Sasha poking her head around the frame, teeth first. *Hi, um, welcome back! You've got post* – she nods at my desk, where a thick envelope waits. *We borrowed your chair, I hope that's OK?* I roll my head to the right and look at the wobbly desk in the corner: no chair. I feel a flare of annoyance. *That's fine*, I say, rolling my head back so I am staring at the ceiling again. *Do you want to join us for dessert?* She asks. *Pudding*, my mother and Nancy Mitford say silently, knowingly. I think of my feeble attempts to join in, to be normal. *All right*, I say, and sit up. *Great, that's great, I'll just go and get the stool from—* she hurries away. I reach for and tear open the letter and a slippery stack of photos falls out with a note from my mother: *Sweetheart, was having a clear-out and saw these. Weren't you both sweet? Mummy xxx*

I steel myself then look at the photos – me and Cass, in identical Laura Ashley dresses, maybe three and four years old. It takes me a while to work out who is who; we really do look very similar. When did that change? Why did I bear the brunt of it, this cruel shift? Further photos show us as slightly older, maybe seven and eight, and then as pre-teens, eleven and twelve. I see the subtle changes, and can't bear to look, shuffling it to the back of the pile so the adorable sisters, so nearly twins, remain. I take a photo of the first shot and send it to the WhatsApp group with a heart emoji, then mute the thread and turn off my phone.

Pudding, I reluctantly admit, isn't bad. After an inordinately long time clearing the table, a bitter, dark chocolate tart is reverentially placed on the gravy-stained cloth. It has a thin, crisp crust that splits under the spoon, hand-made, hand-rolled, so for the first time, I look round the table for the person Sasha is trying to impress. I see him immediately, wearing a holey jumper that looks genuinely worn, rather than bought from a concept store in east London. The backs of his hands have a pinkish, eczema quality to them, as if he washes them too much, and when I find out he is a chef, it all makes sense. I look at him until he looks at me, and then I look away. They met at university. *This is great, Sash,* he says, as he shovels a forkful into his mouth and I do the same. Chocolate floods my palate – a bit one-dimensional, really, despite the crystals of salt scattered atop it – and I see Sash dimple at him with pleasure – *thanks, James, do you think so?* – making that coy gesture unique to women, tucking her chin in tightly to her neck to create a fleshy column of smiles and modesty, shoulders raised to the heavens, beaming, teeth everywhere. I swallow my smooth mouthful and feel hungover and disdainful and sad. *How was Paris, Al?* Sasha asks. Even though my mouth is empty, I work at it as if I have chewed paste to finish, swallow heavily, and smile. *Great, thanks, Sasha.* Heads nod around the table. *O, Paris, cool.* That's the end of that one then. *What did you get up to?* Someone I've probably never seen before asks. *O, you know. The usual,* I say. They nod sagely, and one says *I am, like, obsessed with the Musée d'Orsay? I literally got goosebumps when I saw Monet's Water Lilies?* I don't consider this comment worthy of a response so I eat another rich spoonful. *Les raboteurs de parquet,* which I'd seen when I was a child, made me gasp when I saw it again online recently; the lean, muscular arms, the turn of head of one of the carpenters reminded me so strongly of Tom I couldn't bear it; I looked and looked and hated that others could go and look at it too.

A couple down one end of the table are brushing their hands as they put their spoons down and pick up drinks; I can't tell if they're a couple or just dancing about the topic at this measly stage in their mutual life journey: Sunday lunch with friends. Someone says a thing and she (of the duo) laughs, hands flying to her face and he pulls her close with crushing disinhibition, planting an easy kiss on her unprotesting cheek. Why does it look so—

Actually, I say, loudly, and every head turns to look at me. *I went to a bar, La Meduse, you know it?* Everyone shakes their head apart from the chef, who gazes at me non-committally, presumably unwilling to appear as if he doesn't know of every dining establishment in Europe. *I had a few drinks, then, I was waiting for my friend, an old friend, but I couldn't remember what she looked like, so I had to ask everyone who arrived if they were her.* I laugh urgently and wrap my hand around my own wrist and press the precious bruises that mottle there. *I'm not even sure of her name: Léa or Chloé, maybe.* A few people round the table smile uncertainly and one chuckles quietly, politely. The couple look at each other, quickly, but I – I see it, see their grasp of the other's fingers tighten: *is she mad?*

Did you find her? Sasha asks. Her face shows a gentle, attentive expression; I'm not sure what it means and I hate her. *No,* I say. *I kept thinking I'd seen her, but it wasn't her.*

I'm sorry, Sasha says, and puts her hand on mine. *That must have been annoying.* I am being patronised, but I have to admit, it feels nice, warm skin on warm skin. James's hand gripping my fat body. I pull my hand from Sasha's and gesticulate. *Don't worry, it was fine, I just got battered and trashed my Airbnb.* Unsaid: I didn't sleep, I have not slept, I walked by the river and wondered whether I'd die if I let myself fall, if I would sink, dead weight that I am, to lie with the eels and catfish of the murky Seine, or if the cord, the connection in my heart to His, if it would pull me free, bursting through the surface, drenched, through the air, drawn to Him in His flat, in His bed, so I would crash into His arms and He would laugh in surprise at my wet clothes, wet hair, and stroke my face and hold me and say, *I'm sorry, I love you, I'm sorry.* I laugh and tears glitter the light. Relieved, everyone else laughs too and the strange tension I seem to conjure wherever I go breaks: thin ice. Conversation resumes and it transpires that the chef has an American girlfriend so I got that wrong too. Sasha is just eager to please, and tells him he must take a slice of dessert back for her.

196

I could hoover up this tart and have more, more, the whole thing, but I see the thinnest girl on the table has put her spoon down definitively, lolling in her chair, rosy-cheeked, as if stuffed and weary from this sensation, having eaten most, but not all of, her slice, the thin crescent of crust toppling. I, still hungry, halfway through mine, put my spoon down too, glaring. My eyes sting. I haven't even licked the spoon clean. I win.

I feel a spasm of regret as Sasha clears the plates later, less at her determined, neutral expression but at the remainder of my tart slice sliding into the bin, uneaten. I briefly consider slithering down the stairs later on, rifling about in the bin to salvage it, cutting through the thick chocolate, buttery pastry, loading it into my mouth, spoon after spoon after spoon until I drown, then end the thought. My weak offer to wash up Sasha smilingly declines, and I slope off upstairs, where I return to the floor, and replay the events of Paris in my bone-tired brain. Perhaps if I had been on the same train as Him, frowned as I passed Him in the aisle, a small double take, waited for the song of our hearts to richen, thicken, before tapping that shoulder, touching that arm. Worn the right outfit. Breathed in, been more beautiful, more charming, thinner, obviously, less – you know. Myself.

My phone is now full to the brim with missed calls from Cass and, I remember belatedly, a recording. Me and Tom. I play it, listen to the scuffles and buzzes from a breeze and my hand. *Sorry, you dropped* – what had I been thinking? My voice is too deep; I sound so peculiar and lonely. Strange. I talk and I talk and when it reaches the part where he responds I stop the recording in a panic. I play the alternative scenario in my head: *you're beautiful. I love you.* I press and press the bruises He has given me. At least He thinks of me. At least I have felt His touch. Perhaps this will allow our connection to germinate, at long last. It must.

In the late afternoon, I decide to go to Roseacres, despite Mr M's absence – his death. I wander around, lacklustre, unsure of whom to visit, pressing my pounding heart absently. Several of the staff stop and ask me if I am all right, if they can help me. Despite having met most of them twenty times, they don't seem to recognise me, although I appreciate the brief kind hand placed on my shoulder. I sigh and say *bad break-up* to the first, who tuts sympathetically, but change it to *my boyfriend is away* for the next, which warrants a distracted nod. I end up sitting with Dorothy, who listens to me play the recording, nodding deeply as I cry and patting my hand, gently running a dry finger over my bruises. *He sounds a wrong'un,* she says, her eyes very blue, *not worth your tears.*

   You don't understand, I explain slowly, pulling my hand from her weak grasp and pointing at my heart. *I'm the wrong one. Me. I was stupid to think He could love me, I don't deserve Him.* I look at my lap, pull a loose thread. *But you're ever so pretty,* she says. A flare of light in my breast, then I roll my eyes and say, *but you think I'm Elsie. She's dead.* Dorothy looks at me enigmatically so I stand up and walk out. *Alice,* she calls.

23.

I GO TO WORK ALTHOUGH I CAN'T TELL YOU WHAT I achieve. I pretend to Nina and the others that Paris was romantic and wonderful, that we spooned mousse au chocolat into each other's expectant mouths. They push for details and I smile shyly and shake my head. They blink and wink. All morning I worry at my nail beds, peeling fine strips of skin from my fingertips until they bleed and throb. I welcome sepsis and death. For the first time in my life I forget to eat lunch, leaving my desk to walk anxious circles in the hushed courtyards nearby. My face aches with unshed tears. I sit briefly on a bench, prepared to wallow, but leave when two gossipy young women join with salad-stuffed Tupperware lunches and a shared bag of lentil chips. I feel as if I am half a person. Back at my desk I openly write a lengthy review on Airbnb (in essence, *four stars, could have been cleaner*) and spend an hour trying to find that orange wine online. I can't quite remember its name, just that impish sun, just its bright taste. I close my eyes and when I open them I don't know if seconds or days have passed. Marta, passing my desk clutching an ostentatiously tall stack of files, looks at me askance and asks if she can help me with my list of priorities.

Tuesday is much the same except I go to the Vietnamese café and order a large, soft bánh mì for lunch, generously spread with garlicky pâté and packed with aromatic shredded pork and coriander, matchstick carrots, pickled daikon, with glassy summer rolls on the side, translucent white noodles and pink prawns coiled within, with a coffee, sweet with condensed milk, that makes my heart vibrate. When I have finished my meal, squashed into half of a bench with a suited man bellowing into his AirPods on the other, I feel sick. I buy a plastic-wrapped flapjack and a small chocolate bar from a corner shop right by the office and eat them both. If I were normal I would go and throw up now, but it sits heavily in my stomach and presses at my waistband. My heart feels chaotic and helpless, sore, as if the tie leading me to Him is being sawn away, thread by fibrous thread. I close my eyes and imagine the cord thickening again, strengthening, knitting together as it surely must.

Tuesday afternoon, my patience is tested when Marta keeps calling me into her office to tweak a letter I had drafted for her in the morning. The third time she does it, she seems exasperated even though I'm the one who has to pick up the phone when she calls, answer her, walk from my desk to her office, and open her stupid door, all to send a letter she could just write herself. I try to keep my face neutral. *Do it again*, she says tersely. I nod and leave, but misjudge the closing of the door behind me and it slams, shockingly loudly. One of the nearby secretaries gasps as if I've struck her. I wish I had. I look through the window into Marta's office and she is staring back at me unsmilingly. I return to my desk and make the changes to the letter. There is a frenzy of typing around me and I know my colleagues are messaging each other, struggling to contain their glee. I attach the letter to an email and send it to my boss: *Hope this is OK! :) :) :)*

I turn to the window and look at the strip of sky, absently pressing the bruises circling my wrist, now fading to yellow and green. The finger marks are indistinct; I wish I could see their lovely form more clearly. I try to reimagine the scene: we're holding hands, about to cross a Parisian street and o! a moped zips by, dangerously close, and Tom's warm hand wraps itself around my slender wrist – desperately, lovingly – pulls me back to safety, and His arms. The pain is soothed with many kisses, *you saved me*, I say. Tom's eyes roving my face, His features hardening into disapproval, disgust.

Nina touches my arm and I start so violently that the tears that have been sitting in my lash line drop down my cheeks and into my lap. Nina says, quietly, *are you all right? Do you want to go somewhere?* She swivels her chair to face the window and plucks a box of tissues from the sill, before spinning back and putting it on the desk in front of me. She looks uncertain and worried, and her hands dance by her hips hopefully as if she is thinking about giving me a hug. I want nothing more than to rest my cheek on a soft shoulder, to smell her expensive shampoo, to sigh and let my limbs loosen, let my eyes close, tears spill, to be held. I look at Nina, go through all the things I could say. I settle with: *I'm fine, just my grandfather died recently.* Marta calls my office line and I decline her call immediately. *Are you sure?* says

Nina. I lean back in my chair, pressing my hands to my eyes, then I summon all my strength and say, with an embarrassing wobble in my voice: *don't pretend you're not loving this.* She frowns, quizzical, and I stand up, turn to face the others, that row of faces, shocked, but surely about to explode into sneering laughter. *I know you all fucking love this,* I say very loudly, gesturing at them all and, as my chair rolls officiously away, I walk out, listening hard for a gleeful slap of sound that must follow, but it doesn't come.

I walk to Cass's office, even though it's absolutely miles away, and sit on a bench outside, heels throbbing, sweating and cold, watching the workers gust in and out of the revolving doors like autumn leaves, holding coffees, salads, laptops. Even these witless colleagues touch each other constantly, backslaps, handshakes, a jovial or flirtatious arm-touch at a well-rendered joke, a pointless nicety. My body hurts with longing, and every time I see a dark-haired woman my heart leaps with fear and misery. I feel like I might stay on this bench for ever, sitting and sitting, waiting and sitting, although just now I see a shining ribbon of hair, caught up in a ponytail but with just the right movement and sheen. Sickened, I get up and walk busily away, turning to look again from a safe distance, and I see that it isn't Cass. The way she walks is wrong, not Cass's delicate, measured pace, slender ankles. The coat is dark green, the colour of our school blazers and one we swore never to wear again. I feel dizzy, nauseous, so I take some deep breaths and put my hand to my chest to calm the beat of my heart. I close my eyes. When I open them, it feels so inevitable that I am unsurprised to see Cass standing outside the door of her office, getting out a vape and disappearing into a cloud of vapour before walking determinedly towards the Tube, towards me. I am rigid, unable to move from the spot, and so I hear Cass call through a billowing, fragrant exhalation: *Al? What are you doing here? Are you here to see me? I've been trying to call you.* I feel unexpected joy at seeing her lively face, eyes that match mine, and start to walk forwards, as if drawn to her. She is walking quickly, and then we are feet apart, closer than we've been for years. She holds her arms out and steps forwards to embrace me but I am suddenly afraid of the touch and step back.

I was nearby, I say, *and I had a question I wanted to ask you about buying art.* She stops and laughs. *This isn't about my calls? Listen, it's important—*

I have a horrible feeling she's going to bring up what happened at school so I take another step back and talk over her: *how much is a reasonable sum to spend on an unknown artist, oil on canvas, 200 cm by 100 cm?*

She looks at me with incredulity. *What the fuck?* she says. *Listen to me: you need to go to a doctor—*

I turn and I run from her, panting, heart fuller than ever, blood pumping wildly, animal fear. I reach the Tube and run down the escalator, into a carriage as the doors are closing, where I stand, chest heaving, lines of sweat running down my face, my sides, seeping into the waistband of my tights, my bra. I realise I am on the wrong branch of the District Line so I get off before the line splits, and start to walk instead, basking in the cool air drying my wet forehead.

*

Was it his cold, that caused it, I ask. O no, he'd quite recovered from that, says Jess. He unfortunately choked on a custard cream and we were unfortunately unable to resuscitate him. We broke several of his ribs in the process, punctured a lung, unfortunately. It was awful.

As I get off the Tube I scroll through the long list of beauty salons saved on my phone, calculatingly, and pick one, booking an appointment in ten minutes' time. The jet-setting, glitzy names of Brazilian and Hollywood are always depressingly at odds with the strip lighting and somehow stained ceiling tiles of the downmarket south London salon, the thin paper cover of the massage table tearing as I wriggle into position, the CD player in the corner piping out the mindful pan flute. I always switch salons, never going to the same one more than once in a year, giving the staff time to leave and get married and have babies and move elsewhere before I return. I never want to see the same beauty therapist twice. It seems counter-intuitive, I know, to expose my genitalia to more and more people but the anonymity of this revolving door of eyes, the knowledge that once they have removed every hair from my vulva, its monstrosity exposed, they won't see me again, I won't have to look at their faces and know they are thinking: *her again, I'd kill myself if I looked like that.*

I heel off my shoes, peel off my tights and skirt and recline on the rickety table, draping the tiny towel over my lap in some stupid nod to modesty, as if my legs aren't about to be manoeuvred into various degrading and exposing positions. As the therapist comes in, my stomach flips. I recognise her. I recognise her beautiful hands, her diminutive stature, her edges like crescent moons, the name on her badge: *Yassmina*. She shouldn't be here, that was a different salon, I'm sure of it. My heart beats and beats, and my breathing is shallow. I wonder if I'm going to pass out, then if I should sit up and bolt, but she is already smiling and moving about, stirring sweet-smelling hot wax, positioning my legs with cool hands, saying, *Hollywood, yeah? Everything off?* I nod mutely, tears swim. Then: *how's it going?* She says. *You were off to Paris, weren't you?* My body is stiff with terror. She laughs at me – or rather, she laughs, I think. *I recognise you*, she explains. *I remember* – your ugliness, your obscene genitals, your dull, fat body – *your lovely hair*, she says. *How on earth do you get it so shiny?* Even if I had a response to this inane question I wouldn't have been able to say it. Yassmina carries on chattering as she smooths scalding wax onto my upper thighs and wrenches it off again with surprising strength. It takes me five minutes of chanting: *am I normal?* in my head before I say it out loud. Yassmina stops what she is doing and is silent, and I wonder if she's heard me, and already know that I could not bear to repeat myself but she has, and she is still, her hands resting on my knee, and looks at me and says: *of course you're normal. Perfectly normal.* She smiles at me, and I scan her smooth face, high cheekbones, round eyes for guile, deception, mockery and there is none. *And I've seen all sorts*, she says. She squeezes my knee gently and that touch, that touch. Yassmina turns to stir the wax, pastes, rips and my throat is so tight with tears I think I will choke. When I leave, I tip Yassmina and smile tightly when she puts her hand on my arm and says, *see you next time?* I wonder.

*

That evening I slouch in bed in my knickers and a T-shirt, eating a slab of banana bread that Sasha had baked and left in the kitchen with a note: *help yourself!* I find Yassmina on Instagram and scroll through her grid, a combination of before/afters of eyebrow laminations at the salon and nights out with huns. Perfectly normal. I swipe away another message from Cass as it overlays the screen, return to Yassmina's world. Perhaps normal is what I've needed, like in a coming-of-age movie, the hands of James, the kind words of strangers, nudging me to the inevitable, cutesy conclusion: love thyself? I laugh aloud at this ridiculous notion. I, I could never do this but I am still sure, as my heart beats painfully, that Tom, Tom could. He does. It's clear now that it's not over yet, surely I can still make it right: perhaps He misunderstood the soaring hymn of my heart, perhaps He heard it at last in that street in Paris and was troubled by the answering call of His own heart, the accompanying rich pain. Perhaps He had meant to take my wrist gently, a caress, but did not know His own strength. Perhaps, fresh from His meaningless liaison with Tiggy, He was afraid of the profundity of our connection when our eyes met, the sheer promise of our love. It can be frightening, I know, my love, but I can guide you through it. One more go. Third time's a charm, I am told: there are always triples in stories of old: bears, billy goats, blind mice, benevolent fairies – three acts.

Hours pass and I try to sleep. I lie in bed and I scroll through the roster of childish, pathetic fantasies that usually guide me gratefully to oblivion. The Paris one, always a favourite, is ruined, but I try anyway: steam and strings and the crowd at the station, our gazes catching like lines thrown from boat to dock and made fast, fast forward to those first words: *it's you. I had always wondered if you would be beautiful.* I slow the dream down, think about the precise angle my head will have to tilt back to look into His eyes if we are centimetres apart. I imagine His face, His face that I have learned so diligently, framed by Haussmannian buildings, Eiffel Tower not entirely geographically accurately in the background, warming into a smile, kind words. His hand slides from the back of my head, fingers slipping through my hair, down my arm to grip my wrist, His smile fades and strengthens into a snarl: *fucking crazy bitch.* I hastily skip to weekends in the country: log fires, room service, champagne squashed into one little bath, lying on smooth white cotton, whispering. Unruly family suppers at His parents', Tom and me guessing each other's charade in seconds thanks to our love, the binding of our hearts, so unbeatable as to make others insist we are put on separate teams. Tom's mother kissing me goodbye after Christmas – *thank you for looking after Him, darling, we don't know what He'd do without you. He has never been so happy.* Farmers' markets on Sundays, heritage tomatoes and plump bundles of burrata in summer, watermelons, lemonade, or for inclement months, blocks of dark rye and walnut bread to toast and butter thickly, coffee meticulously ground for the week, our shared mugs, a slab of pork belly to bronze in the oven, gild under the grill. A basket in one hand, Tom's warm hand in the other, bumping into a university acquaintance while choosing a bag of sharp apples to crunch, a feathery bundle of carrots, natural wine: *Charlotte, it's been an age – sorry, this is my husband, Tom. Charlotte and I had a few modules together, Romanticism and Old English, was it?*

How have you been – o you and James broke up after eight years? Never mind, plenty more fish. You're only – thirty-one? There's still time. Tom's fingers squeezing mine, a gentle warning, bringing me back to kindness. *Charlotte – Tom has a rather dreamy friend who's a doctor . . .* Later, Tom will say *you're a little Cupid*, holding my face and showering it with kisses. Or rather *Venus, Aphrodite*. Hands running up and down my arms, squeezing my shoulders, caressing my back. It's the careless touches I want, the ordinary ones: a pulling of a thread from a sleeve, an absent-minded kiss, a tucking of a label, a squeeze of a socked foot as He passes me on the sofa, an arm slung around shoulders, a stroke of my hair, something light, thoughtless.

One blink and night passes; I am up before the sun has risen. I push Mr M's face from my memory. I shower, shave industriously and dry my hair, rolling the barrel brush vigorously until my wrists ache, even though I know it will wake the others, if the insistent clicking of the boiler hasn't already. I pat lotion into my limbs. I feel solemn, hieratic, as I put on make-up: toning and painting moisturiser over my round cheeks, cunningly smoothing my face with primer, foundation, concealer, coaxing in cheekbones with raw-looking blush, lining my wet eyes, brushing lashes to spindles slowly, reverently, as if taking part in a ritual or readying myself for a battle I am not sure I will survive. I feel like I should be praying, as if anyone, anything, were listening. The tarot deck I have pinned to my walls, and crystals litter my bedside table from which I take the two quartzes, rose and clear, and push them into a pocket. I miss the ancient gods, brutal and petty. I check the date again online: auspicious. I google the position of the planets: promising.

I smile and put on an embroidered jacket that my mother got me in Cambodia, one that Mr M once said was splendid, and my eyes sting. It is just under three and a half miles from my place to Tom's, and sometimes I walk it, counting the steps, but I want everything to be perfect, no burning heels or damp small of back. The bus I take is almost empty, and low London trails outside the window, so familiar to me, unchanging. That bus shelter with the men's shoe tossed on top, the tamely subversive graffiti under the railway arch by someone who is not Banksy, glowing Tesco Metros, chicken shops, black railings, the flat grey ribbon that is the river, the huddle of a sleeping bag in a doorway, blocky and serene churches that were once in the heart of villages, reflective armbands of runners huffing the dawn air.

I step off the bus near Tom's and walk slowly to His road. It is far too early, but I wait, wait while the sun paints fingers onto the pavement and up brick walls. The sky is red: shepherd's warning. My eyes are trained too fervently on His door, but I can't miss this moment.

Seconds, hours pass and the thin muscles of my back are protesting. I'm holding my phone in front of me, so it doesn't look too suspicious that I'm standing here; I repeatedly refresh His Instagram page as I wait, even though I can no longer access His profile. I had created a couple of fake accounts and followed Him on both but He seems to have culled them. I create a new profile, taking a photo from the internet, *Zara, 23*, and click *Follow*. I wish I could see His vision of Paris, intimate

Stories of His day there, perhaps a grid-worthy red and gold photo of His family in that bistrot, smiling and *cin cin*-ing to the fizz of champagne, perhaps a shaded figure beyond. His sister's profile is not private, but she posts so rarely there's never any point checking. I do anyway; refresh. Nothing. He leaves, carrying His bike lightly down the steps, and my heart feels wrung out. Even though I am across the road I can tell at once that He's had a haircut; it makes Him look younger, somehow, the white skin of His neck achingly vulnerable. I'm too far away to mark these details but I imagine, dreamily, the warmth of His just-shaven chin, His toothpaste and rosemary smell, the crispness of His shirt. I have been poised to hide behind my hair, turn, should He glance up but He does not, scrolling through His phone before pocketing it and cycling away. Perhaps, perhaps – I check my phone and see that He has not accepted Zara's request. More time unravels and then, this is it. A middle-aged woman approaches, checking her phone, capacious tote bag in one hand, buckling with awkwardly shaped bottles. She hesitates outside the apartment building and starts slowly up the steps, leaning heavily on the railing. It looks like walking pains her. I hurry after her and as she presses the Trade button for admission and laboriously enters, I am at the top of the stairs behind her, panting. As we traipse to the first floor, I discreetly fish Tom's key from my bra, indecently hot in my hand. We meet outside Tom's front door. She looks at me, warily, as I stare at her. I force my expression into one of innocent confusion. *Um, hi?* I say, holding up my key. *I'm here to clean Tom's flat?* His name in my mouth is delicious. She frowns and looks at her phone, and I see a glimpse of His face,

210

His words, on the screen. *That is strange,* she says. Her accent is unplaceable and I am momentarily distracted, disorientated. I open my app and wave the phone at her briefly, showing her the key with my other hand. *I've been cleaning His flat for over a year so I think there must be some mistake.* She shrugs and says, *well, that is what it say here,* and stoops heavily to find the key under the mat, as He has no doubt instructed her, the original from which my own keys were forged, nearly a year ago now. *I'll give you two hundred pounds if you leave and let me clean,* I say. She straightens and looks at me intently. *I like this job,* I finish, lamely. I smile in what I hope is an earnest, normal manner, although I am sweating. I think of Cambodian silk darkening to black. She pauses for a few seconds, running a pink tongue over her teeth, which are very small and even. Eventually she shrugs and nods. I give her the damp, rolled notes from my pocket, hurriedly withdrawn from the cash machine on the corner. She shrugs again, nods, and leaves, leaning hard on the banister.

A click and I am home. It's hard to believe that my breath last ricocheted off these walls only a week ago; it feels like a lifetime. The daffodils have gone from the table, a quick search of the kitchen bin finds them upended and shedding canary petals into the ends of spring onions, the cream jug returned to its place in the cupboard, looking like it hasn't even been rinsed. I wash it up, absently, drying it calmly with a tea towel that says *Tignes,* before returning it to the cupboard. There are two mugs in the sink, but I'm not worried; I know this must be because He has left a sign for me, that we will soon be to-gether. I look for shapes in the coffee grounds of each but they are resolutely unreadable. Automatically I move about the flat, cleaning, humming a shared favourite song. I fold trousers, cast off like snakeskins, pair and ball socks. I methodically spray and squeak clean every mirror and glass surface. Then I wait some more.

Was it his cold, that caused it, I ask. O no, he'd quite recovered from that, says Jess. Unfortunately, we found him severely weakened in the garden in just his pyjamas with a packed bag for what looked like quite a long trip – we brought him inside of course, but he died shortly afterwards of exposure, unfortunately.

24.

THE SUN MOVES AROUND THE ROOM AND THE HOURS
slide by. I read His emails: gym newsletter, an emailed receipt
for flowers delivered – by bike to Tiggy's address, Amazon dis-
patches, an effusive *thank you darling* from His mother. I realise
I am ravenous, so I rifle through His freezer, find squashed
boxes of fish fingers and potato waffles which I clatter onto
a baking tray, the whole lot, then cook and eat, sitting at the
table with my heaped plate, scooping and shovelling and barely
chewing. I wash up my plate and fork, dry them and return
them to their respective places. I am horribly full and tense all
over, primed to freeze once I hear His key in the lock. I wait for
hours. Six o'clock approaches and my heart can't sustain such
tension; adrenaline dribbles into my bloodstream and drains
from it over and over and I feel trembly and weak. I clean His
loo twice, obsessively. Finally, I just want to get it over with.
I quickly mop the floor, water a wash of brightness on the
tiles – take a wine glass from the cupboard – tap it lightly on
the metal sink. It shivers and sings. I tap harder and it breaks, a
clear half-bowl, smaller shards. I pick one up and in a detached,

experimental way press a point to the heel of my hand, veins green. The blood beads, rich in colour and shine. I arrange the shards on the work surface, then decide to move them to the floor, arranging the sharp shapes with a terrazzo flourish into a rectangle roughly the size of my two spread palms. My heart is painful, I can feel the twine tautening, bringing Him to me. O grant me strength, o muse Erato. I will lie serenely and wait for Him and He will be so moved by my frailty He will not be able to help but love me. I should have taken ibuprofen, to thin the blood, make it more dramatic – I am stalling – kneeling as if waiting for the nothingness of wafer, sweet wine – I take a breath and grit my teeth, let the great weight of my body carry the glass to my spread, open hands.

There is a cracking and, bizarrely, initially, no pain, although I was expecting a burst of it. Then it comes, as does the blood, hot. I lift my hands slowly from the floor and I am seeping, dripping, blotting the wet linoleum in little explosions, beautifully. Most of the glass remains on the floor, but some clings to my tender flesh, points pressing. I get to my feet. *What have I done?* I think. A clarity. The primary sensations, I note, are a bloody throbbing, a stinging, but no worse than pain I have felt before: not the fat slap of a palm to the cheek, the rough pinching of flesh, the searing path of a wax strip, a nipping, bitten tongue, the swift stripe of a paper cut, the insidious scraping of a razor blade on an ankle bone, discovered blooming only when stepping out of the shower, or the iron spasm of cramp. There is a lot of blood, but not, you know, too much. My phone vibrates and I start, as the only sound until now has been my heartbeat, thunderous, and my breath, rough and heavy. Of course it's Cass, and, I don't know why, perhaps it was the trembling in my fingers or the tears in my eyes or perhaps I want it but somehow I miss the right button and – my sister is on the line. I breathe and put her on speakerphone, put the phone on the work surface. My fingers seem small and pale against the raw slickness of my palms, which continue to issue slow sheets of blood. The threads of my childhood bracelet have turned black, the white letter tiles like bared teeth.

Hello? I say, and I am ashamed at the wavering, whispery nature of my voice. *For god's sake!* she says. *Are you OK?* I clear my throat and take a deep breath: *sorry, I've been busy.* She sighs. *I have been trying to get hold of you, properly, for weeks. Have you been getting my texts?* I am overcome with glowering adolescence, and clench my teeth and say nothing. *Never mind,* she continues, *I've been trying to get hold of you, you stupid twat, and I didn't want to say it over text, and I didn't have a chance yesterday, you lunatic, because you need to get checked out. I was in hospital for something else, and – to cut a long story short – basically I've got a heart condition and apparently you could have it too. Mummy's fine, so it must be from –* her voice drops, becomes sour, exasperated – *him.* My heart keens. *Brugada syndrome,* she is saying clearly down the phone: *b, r, u, g, a, d, a.*

Interesting, I think, Spanish, or Italian, perhaps. I imagine a swarthy, stubbly, Mediterranean dreamboat in a white coat tenderly examining my heart, pressing a stethoscope to my dun, fleshy breast, my pyknic form, *o si Dottore Brugada, cúrame por favor, per favore.*

Are you looking it up? she asks, after a suitable pause. *No,* I say, as blood runs and collects, tackily. She sighs. *It's inherited, it's serious. Have you noticed heart palpitations at all? Chest pain?* Silence. *Alice?* My hands have fallen to my sides and blood has made its measured way to my fingertips, and is tapping softly onto the floor. That wild rhythm in my heart, binding me to Him, that sure sign of our love and connection and affection – I, in a lifetime of unsurety, indecision, had never been so sure of anything and now – now – I pick up my phone, redly, and hang up, slipping it into my pocket. I need to leave; He can't find me here.

Do I clean up after myself? I don't know. I stand, panting, then start to pick glass from my hands. After running them – o, they smart – under the tap, I take two tea towels from the drawer in which I store them, weekly, folding and pressing and stroking and stacking, and wrap them tightly, one around each hand. From the brief glimpse of my freshly washed hands before they became glazed again with ruby, my left is the more badly hurt but I can barely feel it now. It must be at least seven o'clock, but I look at the time and it is only just quarter past six. I look at the kitchen, the glass-strewn floor, gleaming with water and spread with blood. Nothing to be done. There is absolutely nothing to be done. I close my eyes briefly, and they burn. It's over it's over it's over. As I walk down the entryway to the front door, so dear to me, I spread my wrapped hands, the towels already saturated with blood, my arms, wide, wide as wings, and trail them along the walls, as creamy and pale as the crook of His elbow, leaving brilliant smears that will darken, I know, from bright, thrilling life, to rust.

I feel a little light-headed but I must be quick. I step through the door, taking my bucket gingerly in my red, bound fists and as I start down the stairs I hear steps, light, pattering up, and I know it is Him. My heart quivers, longs to leap to Him, and I feel as if I might die. Brugada syndrome. I'd know if it were a mere condition, and not the ache of one soul longing for another. I tuck my chin in, and hurry down the stairs, face turned away. I wonder if this time His heart will hear mine, and hold my breath, half-hoping. He bounds past me, beautifully; He does not mark me, He never does.

It's over. I leave the building and run until I'm at the end of the road. When I turn the corner I slow to a walk. I walk all the way home, hands throbbing with each heartbeat. I imagine His shoulder finding the worn spot on the door, the weight of it. Will He notice the taste of metal first in the still air, the ferocious, ferrous stench of blood? Perhaps, head down, texting a friend, He'll stride past the tracing of my hands on the walls, intent on plucking a beer, or orange wine, from the fridge, only to stop, confused, at the broken glass, the blood, the blood, the blood. Will He worry about the wellbeing of His new cleaner? Crossly rate her one star, call the helpline to complain? Or will He think back to the small figure on the stairs with a bent head, wrapped hands, and wonder – think – perhaps – of me?

It is only once I have made it home to the thankfully empty house, unfurled the sodden tea towels, pressed cautiously down either side of each bloody slit on my smarting hands, tweezered out any remaining shards, rinsed my hands again, patted them dry with heaps of rose-tinted kitchen towel, wrapped dressings and bandages around the palms, applied plasters to the base of my thumbs, and sat down on my bed, that I allow the pressure that has been building up, hard, in my nose and throat to break, and I cry. Tears leak and I glimpse myself in my mirror across the room, a rictus splitting my wretched face, spit greasing my pleated chin, eyebrows drawn in anguish, hair stuck to my forehead. I clutch at the neckline of my shirt and tug. Buttons strain and slide open; my bra sags. I am monstrous. I think of the professional mourners of ancient times, baring their breasts, scratching their faces, tearing their hair, howling for someone they did not know. I dig my fingers into my cheeks and feel the sticky edges of the cuts on my hands pulling apart from each other. My heart beats and beats. I think of casting myself on the funeral pyre of my beloved.

I begin to feel ridiculous. I button my shirt up again.

25.

IT'S TWO IN THE MORNING WHEN I WAKE UP. I AM lying on my front, head resting on folded arms which are trapped under the weight of my grief and, turning onto my back, I discover my right hand is completely numb. Eager not to waste this happy accident, I gingerly use my left hand to press the lifeless right one on my face, like that of a lover. Its weight surprises me; gentle and alien. It is a dead weight though, bandaged and lifeless, if warm. Would that this was His hand – but no. I lie there, eyes closed, until pins and needles prick their way up my arm and I flex it tentatively to welcome the renewed flush of blood. My mutilated palms seethe. I stare at the enormous canvas that had been delivered from the gallery a few days ago, still partially covered by a nest of bubble wrap. I'd been intending to deface it, I wanted to laugh at Tiggy, to render her earnest patter about the artist meaningless, to see what it would feel like to destroy thousands of pounds (my grandmother's inheritance, supposedly to be put towards a house deposit) in one go, whether it would feel difficult, stressful, or shockingly sickeningly easy. It doesn't help that I like the art: a rough scene, chubby daubs of paint that must have taken a lifetime to dry, trees, a watchful shaded figure, a muted sun. I sit up, remove my shirt, unhook my bra, which has left tender red stripes on the padding of my ribs, and pull on Tom's T-shirt. I bring the neckline to my nose and try to identify warmth, lemon, rosemary, Him, but I only smell the doughy unclean scent of my own skin, the corrosive smell of dried blood. I turn my bedside lamp on, begin peeling off the bandages from my hands. They sting, the wounds raised and livid, but they've more or less stopped bleeding. I can't be bothered to seek out new bandages so I loosely rewrap them, skeins on a bobbin, then, hardly thinking about it at all, pick up my mobile and call my sister. She picks up immediately, sounding awake and very close, she must have been working – I almost expect to feel her breath in my ear, her head coming to rest on my shoulder, a soporific weight.

Tell me more about it, I say, and she sighs. *Go and see a fucking doctor*, she says, but I know she's smiling. God, she sounds posh. I wait. *It's fine*, she says, *I didn't want to worry you but I wanted to tell you properly. If you'd just read one fucking text. And the more you didn't reply, the more I wanted to get through to you – you're so bloody obstinate. I made Mummy promise not to mention it, we knew it might make things worse—* she breaks off. *I mean, I even emailed you, who does that?*

Sorry, I say in my head.

Look, I had to have an ECG test – my heart has these weird palpitations occasionally. Mummy's already been checked and seems fine. I've been told to keep an eye on it, really. Cut down on booze, basically – o god, I know, totally a nightmare – in response to my half-laugh – *and to make sure I don't get feverish.* I frown. *How are you supposed to do that?* I ask. *Don't know,* she says, *take medication I suppose. But it can be serious, apparently, you should really get checked out. I'll send you the name of my doctor, he's really good.* I contemplate the wringing, ringing pain in my heart, twitching at thoughts of Tom, and think of the tough nucleus of muscle contracting a fraction of a second early – or perhaps too late – a chaos of electrical activity interrupting and repairing and resetting the earnest beating of my heart. I think of my ridiculous performance last night and close my eyes. Cass breathes and I breathe too, the same. *Why did you rise to it?* she asks. I shake my head and see the school corridor and the uniform row of lockers, gum in mouths. I hear a feather-laden duvet-rustle as Cass tucks it more snugly underneath her neat chin, or turns over, or lets her head roll to one side, or sits up, frowning. She had been asleep, after all. *Sorry to wake you,* I say, voice thick. *It doesn't matter,* she says, and her duvet shushes its disagreement.

You were always the good one, I say, tendrils of apology leaking from my pores, eyebrows drawn tight. *People always used to think we were twins,* she says, wryly. *We're pretty bloody similar.* I feel the vessel of pitch in my soul threaten to spill. I think of her honey body and my shuddering dull corpulence, our forms once indistinguishable and now by some vicious alchemy, poles apart. That photo, pored over by everyone, my long-lasting and extraordinary ability to repel, revolt and sicken. *I'm so—* I cannot bring myself to say it out loud. *It was your fault,* I say finally. Her sigh hisses into my ear and I imagine her closing her eyes and pressing her spare hand to her temple. She breathes in. *I've said sorry before*, she says. The sickening flush of dread and shame makes its way hotly up my body and I am tired of feeling it, of feeling this way. *We were just children*, she says. *Children are stupid and cruel. Not just children*, I say, thinking of Tom's eyes, the disgust, disdain, dismissiveness, the slight crease in His straight nose, the drawing back of full lips from straight teeth, the tilt of His skull, hair caressing His brow, the leaning of His body back, away from me, feet poised for flight.

I don't know how this conversation should progress, and I think of the girls at work, their easy back and forth, and, briefly, of James and the candlelight touching the fine hair of his forearms, nodding at whatever it is I was saying, the next swift question tugging words from me. My hair rustles against the receiver. *I just don't know how to move on*, I say. *It's forgotten*, Cass interjects, earnestly, *a couple of weeks later everyone was talking about Caitlin and the locker room – you know they were.* I didn't: by that time I had isolated myself, cocooned and awaiting transformation. How do I tell her I have felt monstrous my whole life? I hang up and she calls me again, immediately. I answer without hesitation and I wonder if she can sense the tears running down my face, hear the tortured mechanism of my brain. *Sorry, we were cut off*, she says. *Al. It's been, like, eight years.* I am silent. *I know*, I say. *Cass—* Then, her voice both quieter and clearer than before: *can I come over?* I sit up, look at myself in the gloom, the sullen heft of my body. The beads on the bracelet from our youth, stiff with blood, gleam. *No, you can't*, I say, running my finger over the letters, and I can hear her clambering out of bed. *I'm coming,* she says, and I can hear the whisper of the duvet as she sits up, the click of a bedside lamp. *You'd better fucking let me in.*

26.

MID-MORNING THE NEXT DAY, I ATTEND A SURPRIS-
ingly prompt (private) hospital appointment where a neat,
cool-fingered Scottish doctor with a fine, even stubble on his
chin monitors me, listening, watching for the irregularities in
my frantic heart, drawing several little vials of blood – how
passionately it leaps from my body, how forcefully – which I
envision him pouring rapturously down his throat, down his
chest. The whole thing is a pleasant experience, and I could get
used to this standard of care, with a mini-fridge in the waiting
area fully stocked with Diet Coke and San Pellegrino, and
bowls of individually wrapped shortbread fingers and shiny
red apples dotted about the place. The loos have Aesop soap
in them.

The receptionist is a mid-sizer and is kind to me, sensing my
uncertainty and pointing out the amenities and where I can
charge my phone. I feel appealing, returning the curious or
flirtatious glances of a man in the waiting area at the hospital,
crossing my legs and flipping my hair. I have taken extra care
with it this morning, thinking shyly of Yassmina's comments,

asking my sister to help me. She had held my bound hands and looked at me with dark eyes; *I dropped some glasses*, I said, *slipped while clearing them up.* She had sighed – *O Alice* – but she had stayed. She'd stayed. She had washed my hair for me over the edge of the bath, to keep the dressings on my hands dry, kneading my tired skull with hard fingers, provoking goose-bumps at the deliciousness of her touch. She had rinsed my hair three times, smoothed conditioner through the lengths and rinsed again with cool water. *I wish I hadn't cut mine*, she said, absently, as she patted it dry with a towel and stroked on a palmful of coconut-scented serum. She had stayed, and we had talked in the dark and I cried at how bitterly I had missed her, at how lonely I had been. *I'm sorry*, we said, *I'm sorry*, we're sorry. She had listened to me and cried too. As I looked at her dark, shiny eyes in the half-light I felt for a moment it was like looking in a mirror, not a mocking funfair distortion but clear glass, flat and true. We'd said goodbye a few hours ago – she'd headed home to shower and dress for work – *and have five cof-fees*, she said, and we laughed. She hugged me and I was briefly stiff, unyielding, before slackening and sinking into her. The same height. My hair cloaked her shoulders, and I felt like I was being absorbed, Cass's tight arms impossibly strong and lovely, bending me into her, like twins in the womb. *I'll call my doctor today*, she'd promised, as she walked away from me, willowy and spirited. *I'll get you an appointment as soon as possible. See you soon?* The text had come forty-five minutes later: *got you an appointment in an hour. Go!*

As I sit in the waiting room eating biscuits and drinking sparkling water, waiting to book in a follow-up appointment,

I realise I have forgotten to tell anyone I will be late to work, truthfully for once. I open my work email and see at the top of my inbox a message from HR, copying in Marta, inviting me to a meeting tomorrow to discuss my performance. I reply with a brown thumbs-up emoji. I will decide tomorrow how to play it: contrite, tearful, having a difficult time at home, with my mental health – or queenly, coldly defiant: let me tell you what I think about this place and your managerial style, and the idiots you employ. I decide not to go in today at all, and instead to visit Roseacres on the way back from hospital.

Dot is sitting by the window, as usual, looking intently at the garden, her pale eyes following the birds as they wheel and settle and take wing. She looks restless, fingers first smoothing, then plucking at the blanket on her lap. *Would you like to go outside?* I ask her, for the first time, feeling stupid and selfish and sad for not having suggested it before. *O yes please, Elsie,* she says immediately, so I fetch her walking frame and we inch, agonisingly, along the corridor, me resting a hand on the hollow bird bones of her bent back, to the door leading to the garden. The lock and deadbolt spring open at my touch, as if waiting. Dot steps outside in her navy velcro shoes, and stoops to touch a leaf that mirrors the tremor in her fingers. I drop my cardigan onto her round shoulders as she dodders along to a bench, turning her bent head left and right to absorb the wet, the green, the living. Wick. The bench boasts a commemorative brass plaque reading *Grandad, Forever In Our Hearts.* I wonder if these grandchildren visited their grandfather here, whether this a true outpouring of grief, marking a spot he particularly liked, or whether it's an expression of guilt, of absence. Dot leans back and the message is obscured. The bird table is empty but as we sit in silence in the chill, a spherical robin perches upon it and looks at us, and I can feel that Dot is alert, thrilled. As I press the pinprick at the crook of my elbow from whence my blood had been drawn, I blandly parrot my mother: *when robins appear, a loved one is near.* Dot nods, and says, *yes, that's right.*

Do you believe in ghosts? I ask her. *O no*, she replies: *I believe in Heaven. And Elsie's in Heaven, I suppose?* I say, drolly. *Yes*, she says, *she is looking down on me, surrounded by angels.* I smile and look away, then think, shudderingly, of Mr M as I watch the robin's eyes, like bright black pearls, looking and looking. Might he be shuffling along the corridors of this drab place for all eternity, searching for grandchildren who care? I pull some crystals out of my pocket and clutch them so hard it hurts my palms. I have an urge to slip them in my mouth and swallow them all so that they might imbue me with their protection, radiating from my gut and permeating each cell. Dot turns her face to the sky and closes her eyes and is so still for so long I begin to fear she has died, so I touch her hand and she opens her eyes, looking at me beatifically. *It's ever so nice to sit in the sun with you*, she says, taking my fingers. *I've missed you.* I know she thinks I am Elsie but I sit there and let her chilly, dry fingers stroke mine, and I think about sisters. *Did you and Elsie ever fall out?* I ask. Dot turns to me and says: *o yes, she married a terrible man, just terrible, and they moved to Wales. I never saw her much after that, maybe once or twice … I never met her children, my nieces and nephews.*

I am discomfited by this information but before I can ask

about it, a carer squawks in alarm from the back door and shouts: *let's get you back inside, Dorothy, it's rather brisk!*, ostentatiously bringing a blanket for the short walk back inside. Dorothy smiles at me as she is set on her feet and bundled up, and says: *it was lovely to see you, Alice, will I see you soon?*

Yes, perhaps Saturday, I reply.

As I leave Roseacres, phone in hand, I set a reminder (*visit Dot*) for 9 o'clock on Saturday. My heart feels curiously still; I rest my hand on my chest and am relieved to feel its steady thud. I text Cass saying that her doctor is handsome and asking how her day is going, to which she immediately replies: *i know right* and *shit, u?*, and I even send a gif of a smiling cat to my mother, who responds after an hour or two: *How sweet. Thank you, sweetheart.* I wish I'd taken a photo of the robin to send them both.

I don't want my peaceful, kindly day to end – the hospital, the nice staff, Dorothy roused to wavering life in the garden – so, without thinking, I take the Tube to Cass's flat. I can show up with some wine, like a sister in a film might do. I turn my face from the column of orange wine in the independent wine shop at the end of Cass's road, pick a pale bottle from the fridge and watch with pleasure as it is twisted up in rustling paper like a present. *It's for my sister,* I tell the indifferent vendor, *we're having a girls' night.* As I walk the fifty metres up Cass's road, the gavel of my heart beats, and I feel free, light, optimistic. Cautiously, like probing a broken tooth with a tongue, I think about that day in school, that photo, the laughter. I feel anticipatory and shivery but its malignant power is miraculously gone. I slip into Cass's apartment block behind another person and knock on the door of her flat. I've never been here before, just been sent her address, unprompted, by my mother when she moved in a year ago. I wait and knock again; it's half five and when there is no response I realise, stupidly, Cass is still at work. I sit down on her doormat to text her, think about whimsically opening the wine and swigging, then pause. I lift a corner of her door-mat – nothing. Then I turn the mat over entirely and taped to the middle is her door key. I hesitate but it is only an act. I stand and let myself in. The key turns smoothly, the air inside is still and warm; the heating has been on all day. The smell is floral, the hallway is tidy, with beige walls and a little table upon which rests a small umbrella and a pair of gloves. I feel oddly like I've been here before, or even like I live here myself, as I toe off my shoes and walk further inside. I've been in so many people's houses, people's lives, I could plot what the layout of this flat must be in seconds – the kitchen through there, the sitting room this way, that room, door ajar, is the bathroom. I walk to the fridge and slip the wine inside. I look at the food on her shelves: fresh salady vegetables, protein yoghurts, miso paste, capers, a meal-prepped tower of chicken and broccoli, a single chocolate mousse. I sift through her post, rifle through her re-cycling, read the wedding invitations and postcards propped on a sill, stroke the clothes hanging in her wardrobe, holding them to my face, to my body. I open her bathroom cabinet and look at the organic tampons, the hair-removal paraphernalia, painkillers. Could this life, orderly, pleasant, have been mine?

As I move about her bedroom, touching the curtains, tap-ping the walls, I see a photo of the two of us in a gold-rimmed frame by her bed, neatly made and scattered with cushions. We are probably fifteen and sixteen and I don't think I've seen it before. I take a deep breath and look: our bare arms are hooked around each other's necks and our faces are splitting open with mirth – and it honestly takes me a few seconds to work out who is who. I look at our waists, and our thighs, and our arms. Cass is a touch shorter than me, her torso perhaps a little longer, but we look the same, we really do look the same. I look at my reflection in the mirror across the room and look quickly away, pinching my stomach, feeling a sear of pain as I have plucked at the blot of bruises there and a shallow, cracking scab. Perhaps we weren't so different after all.

I sit down on her bed, crisp ironed sheets, and text: *sorry for zero notice but am outside your flat! Wine?* [wine emoji]. Her response: *ah you should have told me earlier I would have skived! Twice in 1 day omg. Leaving office now. If you can get into the building have a key under mat let yourself in make yourself at home* [wine emoji].

I laugh a breath of relief, my uneasy trespass sanctified. I go back into the sitting room and sit on her sofa, looking around, at the unremarkable view outside, the pot plants with glossy, healthy-looking leaves and damp soil. I put on a record. I run my finger along the coffee table and examine the fine coating of dust on my fingertip. Her laptop sits gleaming on the sofa next to me, but I don't touch it and I feel proud of myself. I am still sitting there when she gets home, smelling of the outside and rain and expensive perfume and sweet, unidentified vape flavouring, gives me a hug, one I try to return, but some of our intimacy from last night has fluttered away, and needs to be caught, pinned down again.

Cass exclaims over the wine and pours us glasses, provides crisps. We talk about her day at work, she asks about mine and I try not to feel ashamed at the paralegal-level tasks I conjure from previous weeks, against her more worthy-sounding solicitor's role. As she talks about her head of department whom she dislikes, I consider telling her my boss loves me and thinks I'm great, is priming me for a training contract, then relent and tell her how difficult I find her, it, everyone. I am glad; it bonds us, and the warm look of recognition she gives me makes my heart, which until then had been calm, stutter and leap.

Are we friends or strangers? It's hard to tell. Beneath this woman is the memory of the child I thought I knew. I say I feel sad, lonely, no more than that. Perhaps the rest will come another time. She gives me a big hug and says: *I'm sorry, Al.*

She is dating a James, but it's not serious. How I wish I could summon her effortlessness. I feel little, and looked after, as I cry and she tucks a blanket around my knees and pours me more wine. My tears dry but I continue to dab my eyes and speak in a strangled whisper of emotion, to keep this intimacy alive, which makes her face taut with sympathy and she reaches out repeatedly and strokes my arm. We talk about our mother, not bitterly, but fondly, and I find myself rolling my eyes at and laughing at her foibles, which would ordinarily make me cry and scratch myself. I thought myself alone in this, my mother and Cass inscrutable, but now I have an ally.

I imagine life unspooling from this moment; perhaps fortnightly sisterly dinners, the odd lunch with our mother, weekends away to Vienna, Venice, Valencia. Home for

Christmas for the first time in years, twirling tinsel around a tree. One of two again: me, the sweet, churlish baby, she my protective, loving older sister. Does this measure up to the shining mirage of life with Tom, the hot, glowing centre of the hearth? Our hearts meeting, unifying into one tender, beautiful, bloody mass, pulsing with each other's quick circulation?

I feel quite drunk by nine o'clock – the wine and crisps are long gone and we'd started on gin and tonics – and as I rise to my feet and make a half-hearted attempt to find my shoes, I am unsurprised and gratified to find Cass struggling with the sofa, wrestling out a bed and laying pillows, a soft duvet upon it, saying: *please stay.* My hands throb and I am heavy-boned, lolling, unspeakably tired. *You've lost a lot of blood recently,* Cass reminds me, passing me a glass of water. I think of the blood that issued forth from my hands, my veins, with shattered glass, sterilised needles. I drink. I sleep.

I wake to the click of the front door closing gently, footsteps receding down the carpeted corridor and a clatter of stairs, then silence. It is morning; the air smells of shampoo and soap and coffee. I turn my head on the pillow, looking at the dim sitting room, and stretch. My hands prickle unpleasantly and I lift the bandage of one, wincing, and am shocked by the dark cuneiform lettering my palms – what mysteries does it describe? A thought begins to push itself to the forefront of my hangover, but I can't think about it now and focus instead on the chaotic composition of my wounds, the stitches, the beaded knots, the striking lines. I can't remember what the doctor told me to do for aftercare and, sitting up, I remember, too late, the pad of fresh dressings in my bag, which I should probably have used last night. My head thumps and my guts feel liquid: acidic and loose with wine. The empty flat, filled with Cass's things, and me. I lie down again, burrow. Is this happiness? I decide it might be, should be.

27.

I HAVE JUST GOT OFF THE PHONE TO THE HR ADVISOR
at work, explaining that I had not attended the scheduled,
mandatory meeting because I had been in hospital for a serious heart condition but I would probably be free at some point
next week, doctor's note pending, and am unloading a bag of
Whole Foods groceries in the kitchen (nori snacks, houmous,
olives, obscenely expensive cut fruit, kombucha) when there
is a knock on the door.

It's annoying because I'd been feeling pretty cheerful, and
had been looking forward to crafting a healthy little lunch to
eat while scrolling through Airbnb, LinkedIn, the first steps to
a new life. I had texted Cass a few times, giddy with this new
connectedness, friendship, but she'd been in meetings and had
not responded. I didn't mind though.

And now, I don't bother listening to the precise ins and
outs of what these uniforms are saying to me, the patter of
words so played out and tired on-screen I could recite them
by heart, with feeling; but know this: my initial emotion is
worry, swiftly turning to confusion as handcuffs are thrillingly

winched about my wrists: I think, dismayingly, of my father, then wonder if Cass has died, or been killed, or my mother has died, or been killed, or if I'd been an unknowing witness or passer-by to a crime, one of the crucial, seductive pieces of evidence in a knotty tale, caught on CCTV walking past minutes before or after some devastation or catastrophe, podcast on the matter yet to be recorded. This will all be cleared up and we'll laugh at it later, and it will be good icebreaker with new best friends: *did I ever tell you about the time I was arrested?!* And then, as I hear Sasha and the Canadian coming into the hallway from a bedroom where they have been cosily ensconced, and I realise that of course they're together, in love, amazed I hadn't noticed before, and then I think of Tom, and my heart feels hot and fuller than ever of blood. *I have a heart condition,* I tell the police officer talking to me, *Brugada syndrome,* even though my results haven't come back yet. They nod and steer me to the actual police car and van that are parked a little way down the road because of the ungenerous dimensions of this sad street. People are looking, mouths slack, absolutely agog, and it's almost exciting. Words flutter about my ears: breaking, entering, intent, grievous, harm. I see Tom lying on His bed, white, red ribboning His face, the linen, spread lovingly over His duvet by my hands.

You know, it's funny, I had genuinely forgotten until now, wiped it from my mind like a spillage: forgotten stripping the bed, forgotten picking up the wine-glass shards in my tea-towel-wadded hands, forgotten smashing more, furiously, all of those thin fishbowl curves, the shot glasses, Rzeczpospolita Polska, that took two throws to split into thick chunks, some sort of old-fashioned punch or trifle bowl, gilt coupes and crystal flutes; forgotten carrying armfuls of sharpness through to the bedroom, forgotten the delicate business of placing this sinister, lovely jigsaw in His bed, tucking them lovingly into His pillowcase, points pressing gently to the ceiling, waiting for a warm weighty body to be thrown gaily upon it, to pierce, forgotten the wish for Tom to hop into bed, rolling in eager anticipation of slumber before noticing the swift pricks perforating His sweet-smelling skin. Perhaps He would fling out a hand to steady Himself, scoring His hands as mine are, a mirroring. Most important would be the severing of the thick cord binding our hearts, the bind from which I wish to be free and fear I never shall. I'd forgotten breathing hard, clumsily mopping my own blood away, forgotten closing the cupboard doors to hide their emptiness, of the laughter threatening to spill over as I passed Him on the stairs. I am outside myself, amazed, at how easily these thoughts slipped from my mind. *Is He OK?* I ask, into the back of the police van. A police officer in the front glances at me (eyelashes as long as a deer's), a look I boldly return. Not a word is said.

I wonder what I am now, who it is possible for me to be, now that it's all over. My heart beats and beats and I listen for the echoing call of His, but there is nothing. My heart feels solitary, an unremarkable organ in the cage of my ribs, bones wrapped in muscle and fat and flesh. I have shed myself, sloughing all that it meant like a skin, and without it, I feel impossibly, devastatingly lonely. *Methought a serpent ate my heart away, and you sat smiling at his cruel prey.* How I long to feel that cord again, stretching tight to Tom. How deftly He has shaped me, and how willingly I have been moulded, for the books I read are Tom, similarly with the clothes I wear, the places I go, the things I do. He took me to Paris, behind James's hands was the promise of His. He is my silty unsweet coffee, my hunger pangs. The air in my lungs, the thoughts in my head, are His. I have been consumed by Him, this desire to be His, to be loved: our hearts were bound. I was nothing before. Am I nothing, now? A void, untouched? I think of my damaged heart and my body that was called beautiful, called normal. I think of Cass's blazing eyes in the dark, her loving arms, her quick smile, smoothing my pillow the way I have for so many others.

I discover that doing things slowly means they touch you more. Dawdling in the back of the van, dithering up the steps, dilly-dallying in the yellow-lit station corridors: more than once, a hand stern and gentle closing on my arm, pressing my back, and I burn at the touch, tears spilling from the corners of my eyes at this tenderness. Was this all I had to do? Doe-eyes regretfully passes me on to another officer, tall, and I feel little. I am patted down with swift strokes by an unsmiling, small woman. Everyone is frightfully severe and masculine, and I experimentally let my knees buckle. I am caught with hard fingers and set right. Someone brings me water when I'm sitting down, another offers me a cup of tea, to which I say *yes, please, with milk and lots of sugar.* Was this really all I had to do? *Is He hurt?* I ask, again and again, as I am questioned. I say, again, that I have a heart condition. I give my answers willingly and I am told His hands are injured and He needed stitches too. Like me. I think of a wedge of glass marking a pale palm, bright blood spurting forth, onto the bed sheets I had washed and folded and loved. He'll have to get those under cold water as soon as possible, really, apply bleach quick, bright lemon juice at a pinch: if He lets the red darken, soften, settle into the smooth fabric, well. It makes life harder. I know Him, though, seasons of *Line of Duty* watched, season one on DVD even, the odd police procedural novel flipped through by His bed – He'll have left everything just as it was, for evidence, this expression of my love. Because it was love, you do see that, don't you, true and pure: our hands, now twin hands, our pain doubled in the other – me, wishing He were dead, that He'd died and I'd killed Him, and wishing that I were dead too, that He had killed me too, that we had finally become each other and ceased to exist.

They are talking to me and I am pretending to listen, like a good student, but I am thinking of what they will find in my room, if or when they search it, Sasha and the Canadian hovering in the corridor, offering to help and aghast, titillated. I imagine these strangers' shoes on my Persian rug, their eyes trailing over my dishevelled bed, its single bedside table, smeared water glass, crumpled book. *She was a cleaner, you say?* The great canvas propped on the floor. I imagine their hands sifting through my underwear, my clothes, or pulling out the untouched boxes of meal replacement drinks from under my bed, along with the pristine yoga mat, resistance bands, hand weights, gym bag, running shoes, and wonder what they will make of me, my overstuffed, desperate make-up bags, the pocket dictionaries of Hebrew, Italian, Gujarati, Farsi; Snickers wrappers and bloody bandages, tissued mascara-wipings and nose-blottings in the bin. My search history. A multipack of rubber gloves, microfibre dusters, thick bleach, white vinegar, my faithful red bucket, the jar of keys to His flat. Crystals scattered about. Mirrors absolutely everywhere. The box of papers, photos, things, treasures of Tom, which I had meant to destroy, but couldn't. Perhaps it will help: prove that I didn't really mean to hurt Him, that I only want what's best for Him, that I really do love Him. I think of that box, and then the boxes behind it, older, the one full of programmes from student plays, a few small props stolen after a production was over, cast lists with his name on, faint from my finger running over the text. The letter from the faculty explaining he had been suspended, expulsion pending, and an investigation was under way; I had the university's full support in this matter but they did not condone violence of any sort, despite the unfortunate circumstances and so would have to suspend me too. I remember people's weak hugs after the news came out, the temptation to sink into their arms tangled with a desire to scorn their previous indifference. The thin laugh that threatened to bubble from my throat whenever anyone said, *he just doesn't seem the type,* or *I'm so sorry this happened to you.* Look, he probably wasn't the type, but the punishment matched the bloody welt he left on my heart. He was cruel to me and I hope his record is never scrubbed clean. Whenever I search him online, Facebook and LinkedIn, I am pleased, so thrilled, to see he never became a director, as he'd wished – apart from a self-written IMDb entry on a short film he had assisted on, those dreams died, along with a part of me.

Do I appear as lonely, and sad, and unlovely as I feel? *My mistress' eyes are nothing like the sun.* They can look and look at my things, turn them over and upend with rough fingers, pummel the pillow and lift the mattress, check behind the curtains and under the rug, comb through my notebooks and scroll through my phone but they won't find the secret I might have, the one in my thoughts: the second condom, kept warm on my body, the contents lovingly removed and pushed with fingers into my abhorrent, sickening vagina (or could it be, as Yassmina said – normal?) in the hope that something would stick, take root. Googling this suggests the likelihood of pregnancy is low, impossible, but I feel like luck should surely turn my way, now. It's too early to tell but I wonder if I feel the first stirrings of nausea, the lethargic beginnings of quickening?

I slouch in the hard chair, and look from under my eyelashes, spidery with moisture, at the two men in front of me, uniformed, and the dishevelled solicitor beside me, wondering for which one I could feel the blistering love I know I'm capable of. I think of easing myself into a lap, a steady hand slipping about my waist, fingers lodging between my ribs, painful in their devotion. *I'm cold,* I say, piteously. A blanket is brought. A solicitor, mine I suppose, shifts in the chair beside me, and I cautiously slouch until my knee touches his. He sits upright at once, knee snapping away from mine, and I shiver with the possibilities.

Was it his cold, that caused it, I ask. *O no, he'd quite recovered from that,* says Jess. *It was just old age. He was ninety-three. Good innings. Good innings,* I repeat. I hate cricket, but those were good innings. The memory is set.

*

As I sit, I think of Tom and wonder if we'd been so suited after all. I am rarely wrong but perhaps I mistook this arrhythmic pulse of my heart for something more, perhaps missed a trick. I think of Yassmina's cool hand on my knee. Perhaps I am beautiful. The police officers look at me expectantly, coffee cups arrayed before us, perhaps arranged in an auspicious way by a higher power. One has closely shorn hair, a hard chin, fine scars on his hands, the hint of a dimple in a cheek, a faint northern accent: brisk overcast walks up mountains, gloved hands touching, lolloping dogs, red noses and cheeks and sugary tea from a flask, oaty, spiced parkin, cobbled streets and flinty buildings, gossip in the village shop, walks home from the pub underneath the starriest skies. A farm, perhaps, a brood of bairns. But I want more: the other police officer has dark, fine brows curving together like wings, dark eyes beneath. A Casio watch embraces one wrist; simple, practical, classic. The white of his teeth against the black of his beard; the turban wrapped around what must be a knot of long, shining hair, and with it crowds into my head the life I could have: a small mother tutting and telling me I'm too thin, spooning gulab jamun into a bowl, spooning pale syrup, a sister, threading her arm around my waist, maybe my own sister could be there too – a tight press of a family gathering, an overheated room filled with shouting, gestures, laughter. I sit at the centre, the core. But no. I cast my net further, it spins from my spread, scarred hands. Sweet James James (Morrison Morrison) – jolly weekends at the rugby, a Labrador called Posy or Tilly, his broad pale back, his gentle, sleeping form – or, the Canadian – *we're sorry, Sasha, we're moving out* – to Canada, in fact – to the woods, just us two, knee deep in snow, tapping maple trees, keeping chickens, splitting wood for the fire, pancakes – or, someone at work – stolen stairwell kisses, smiling over cava or crémant at corporate networking events, meeting his parents who hated his previous girlfriend but will adore me – the carer at Roseacres who has shiny, kind eyes, holding me close in those firm arms, or, that fat man on the bus – feeling so small and sweet and loving and loved, loved, loved.

I have probably been in this room for hours. The police officers are saying words, dull words, and I say nothing, so the solicitor replies on my behalf, nodding and gesturing at me, and I feel very moved that he would do this. Finally. Chairs scrape and a hand helps me to stand. I can feel my gut and womb edging towards soreness, the very beginnings of a cramp, of spreading pain – perhaps my period is coming, red ribbons, after all. I'm sorry and glad and tired. Is this my last tie to Tom, dissolving? But no – that will be my loving, dangerous hands, the fresh wounds on my palm, smarting in their dressings, that will scab and harden to dark runes, the skin underneath pink with newness, then lightening over time, until what's left is barely perceptible, the palest, numb spiders' threads noticeable only in certain lights. I flex my hands and feel the cuts sting, loosen, as my womb aches. I think I've got a little time before I bleed into my underwear, but should probably let someone know – I'm not sure who to speak to. And as I am being led from this funny little room to another part of the building, a firm hand circling my upper arm deliciously, feeling delicate, feeling like a scrap of lace, I feel a thrilling in my breast, not painful, no, but powerful. It is hard to breathe.

Then, a lightning bolt. I say *o!* and bend double, my heart convulsing with love and joy. I clutch my breast and the officers grip me roughly, longingly. I crouch, and they bend, olive trees, to accommodate this. The balls of my feet balance my weight, my calves strong and tight, thick thighs aligned with my soft, sorrowful belly as I curve into myself, pressing the waistband of my jeans into my flesh still further, seams pinching, comforting the unruly ache of my womb, arms circling myself, embracing, consoling and loving, forehead on knees and hair streaming and rustling around my ears, in which my heart pounds and burns as I breathe and breathe. This body has done so much. Then, I find I can stand, and allow myself to be unfurled, straightened out, welcoming the rush of blood back to my legs which makes me feel dizzy and briefly, miraculously weightless. I am triumphant despite the tears falling and falling into my smile. It is still there, the cord is drawn tight, painfully so, a fishing line, a perfect catch, and I can feel Tom, feel and know that He is coming for me. Eyes closed, I envision Him staring at His bloody hands, feeling the resultant pain as I flex mine, thinking: how She must love me, and how She deserves my love. I know now that He reported me to the police so He could find me – how else would He do so? I laugh with delight and taste salt. I am in another quaint little room and the door opens and shuts, mindless people move. Each opening brings a gust of noise and I am primed, a string on a bow, an instrument, giddy, waiting for His step, true and sure. Even as I sit and hear a raised woman's voice, that of Cass, saying in the slow sarcastic tone she reserves for people she thinks are stupid: *I demand that you let me see her* – I am waiting and waiting for Him.

Cass's love is nothing compared to His. With the mirroring of our bodies, so He will finally hear my victorious heart, see its scarlet ensign bursting from my breast, He will take it in His hands, follow it like Theseus and come to me, His soul's joy. We will press palms, press our hearts together. O come, my love: I'm waiting for you, beautifully.

Acknowledgements

My eternal thanks to The Women's Prize Trust and the judges of the Discoveries Prize 2021 for seeing in my 10,000-word entry the novel it could become. To the powerhouse that is Claire Shanahan, thank you for your friendship. I am especially grateful to my prize, my stellar agent at Curtis Brown, Lucy Morris, whose serenity, good humour and absolute clarity of vision and the ability to express it helped me turn a shabby manuscript into something worthy of publication. Thank you as well to Rosie Pierce for picking up the baton during Lucy's maternity leave and guiding me with charm and kindness towards publication.

I am so grateful to my wonderful editor, Rhiannon Smith, for immediately loving Alice like I do, and for being endlessly enthusiastic and open. Thanks as well to the efficient Frances Rooney and everyone else at Little, Brown, who have come together to create this real, live, book.

I am grateful to my small but mighty team in New York, Lily Dolin at United Talent Agency and Edie Astley at Harper, for seeing a future for Alice across the Atlantic.

Rebecca Morgan-Sharp and Emma Yandle, you were my original readers; I will always be so grateful for your feedback and unbridled encouragement. Annie Caccimelio, thank you for always championing me, and for reading so swiftly. It is no coincidence that all three of you are godmothers to my girls.

Thank you to my friends and family who have shown such interest for the past six years, and listened to me when I needed it most, including but not limited to: Andrew Youngson, Arthur Billington, Caitlin Stubbs, Celia McKelvey, Claire Berliner, Claudia Goss, Dahlia Belloul, Ebony-Gale Ward, Evelyn Curtin, Julia Lammer, Julian von Nehammer, Kripa Gurung, Lucy Keeling, Max Foxall, Megan Brewer, Millie Basing, Miriam Longmore, Sam Baker, Sophie Bhutta and Will Basing.

A special thanks to the wonderful 2022 cohort of Discoveries talents who adopted me into their WhatsApp chat and have never failed to soothe, buoy and congratulate: Claire O'Connor, Claire Whatley, Jude Reid, Katy Oglethorpe, Nancy Crane, Niamh Ní Mhaoileoin, Nikki Logan, Rachel Brown, Rebecca Taylor McKay, Ruth Rosengarten, Sadbh Kellett, Sarah Williams, Sui Annukka, Tara O'Sullivan and Zoe Norridge.

Thank you to my wonderful in-laws, Kathy van Straaten and Chris van Straaten, who gave me a week of writing in a largely writing-free first maternity leave. The aforementioned Emma Yandle also gave up her afternoons off work to look after baby Coco while I wrote in the room next door, listening to them laugh at each other.

Thank you so much to my mother, Joanna Cooke, who gave

me and my sister Ellie everything she had when life was difficult, and always found a way to buy us books. I have enjoyed hours and hours of writing and editing over the past few years thanks to her willingness to entertain and enthral her granddaughters. I love you, Mama. Thank you to my father, Chris Cooke, who instilled a lifelong love of great literature at a young age with *Shakespeare: The Animated Tales*. I am so lucky that you are my parents. To my sister, Ellie Herda-Grimwood, and sister-in-law, Tracy Herda-Grimwood, thank you for the unconditional love and support and babysitting and snacks. I am also indebted to my Granny and Grampa, Mrs Elisabeth Grimwood and Captain John Grimwood, who always, always encouraged my writing, even when it was objectively quite bad.

To my gorgeous girlies, Coco and Goldie, aged three and one, your sunny natures and reliable naps have helped me more than I can say. I hope you won't read this for at least another thirteen years. I love you so much.

Finally – all the gratitude and devotion and love in the world to my darling husband, Patrick van Straaten. Your belief in me has never wavered. I am so thankful for the time and energy you have given to me and my writing, even when reserves were low. I truly could not have written this without you. I love you so much. Thank you for everything.